WITHDRAWN

Watch
Me

JODY GEHRMAN

Watch Me

ST. MARTIN'S GRIFFIN ☙ NEW YORK

WATCH ME. Copyright © 2018 by Jody Gehrman. All rights reserved. Printed in the United States of America. For information, address St. Martin's Press, 175 Fifth Avenue, New York, N.Y. 10010.

www.stmartins.com

Designed by Anna Gorovoy

The Library of Congress Cataloging-in-Publication Data is available upon request.

ISBN 978-1-250-14402-7 (trade paperback)
ISBN 978-1-250-17850-3 (hardcover run on)
ISBN 978-1-250-14403-4 (ebook)

Our books may be purchased in bulk for promotional, educational, or business use. Please contact your local bookseller or the Macmillan Corporate and Premium Sales Department at 1-800-221-7945, extension 5442, or by email at MacmillanSpecialMarkets@macmillan.com.

First Edition: January 2018

10 9 8 7 6 5 4 3 2 1

For David. Not only do you see me—you see through me, which is even better.

ACKNOWLEDGMENTS

As any writer will tell you, behind every book is a team of people who labor to bring it into the world. My team happens to be an especially stellar one. Thanks to my brilliant agent, Jill Marr, for seeing something in these pages that prompted the most exciting voicemail of my life. Alexandra Sehulster at St. Martin's Press has been my eagle-eyed editor; her insights mixed with generous praise made the process a dream. A big thanks to everyone at St. Martin's Press for your enthusiasm and energy. Major kudos to the team at Macmillan Audio: Robert Allen, Laura Wilson, Samantha Edelson, Danielle Prielipp, Brisa Robinson, and Mary Beth Roche.

Early readers provided me with much needed perspective: Matt and Kristin Hills, Bart Rawlinson, Rose Bell, David Wolf, Ginny Buccelli, Sherry Garner, and Ed Gehrman. You all helped me see exactly where this train went off the rails, and how to get her back on. Without you I'm a myopic mess.

Thanks to my collaborators and co-writers on other projects who indulged my obsession with this one: Wendy Goody, Kate Morein, Alexis Alex, and Naomi Wolf.

Most of all, thanks to my husband, David Wolf, who ordered me in no uncertain terms to drop everything and write this book. Your urgent faith is more precious to me than any words can express.

Watch
Me

SAM

After five years waiting for this moment, watching you for the first time still catches me off guard. I recognize you from your book jacket, but the reality of you—a three-dimensional object moving through space, flesh and blood and golden hair—makes my pulse race. You don't know me—not yet—but nothing spikes my pulse. I am ice. I ooze cool, unruffled detachment. It's the thing people find unnerving about me, the thing I try to hide. I know how to smile and raise my eyebrows and frown in all the right places, just to show I'm human, to communicate to the other hairless apes that I'm part of the tribe. If I don't control my face, it defaults to blank detachment, and that gives people the creeps. Watching you, though, I don't have to fake it. I can feel my lips stretching into an amazed smile of their own accord, the smile explorers must have worn when they first stumbled on the New World.

You're walking across campus framed by two rows of flamered maples. Your boots kick bright mounds of leaves strewn across your path. I can see from the slight bounce in your gait you're enjoying the flurry of each step. Though you're bundled against the cold, a bright green scarf wrapped around your throat, it takes no effort at all to imagine you in bed, the long sinewy lines of your body a feast of light and shadow as you stretch, catlike, back arching.

God, you're perfect.

I've never allowed myself to consider what I'd do if you turned out to be ordinary. If I started school at Blackwood, the place I've worked and schemed to enter, only to discover you're not the woman I thought you were. I didn't allow myself to consider the possibility because I knew, deep down, it would kill me. By the time I'd read the first page of your book, you were in my blood, in my bones. To live without you was unthinkable.

Of course, you write fiction, and you're private, so the number of facts I've managed to scrape together about your life could fit on a postcard. I love that about you—your mystery. In a world packed with blogs and Facebook updates and tweets and Instagrams, a world crowded with so much white noise from self-absorbed assholes who share every bowel movement in tedious detail, you are enigmatic. Like Shakespeare, it is much easier to find theory and speculation about your life than solid facts.

You are an onion I intend to peel, layer by layer. I will love every second of it. Your mystery will yield to me, your dark cocoon penetrated by my patient, steady hands.

Though I have little solid evidence about who you are and how you fill your hours, I still feel close to you. I watch your jaunty green scarf flutter in the breeze, your hair trailing behind you in a golden swirl. We are connected. It's undeniable. And it's not just the tie that binds a fan to his idol. Yes, it's impossible to read a great writer's work and not experience their essence. I don't see you the way I see Nabokov, though, or the Brontës, or Melville. I see you for what you are: the only person on earth who will ever understand me.

You stop to examine a woodpecker. From my position on a nearby bench, I have a perfect view of your motionless body. Your throat is white and exposed as you tilt your face to study the industrious little fucker. He pecks harder than ever at the trunk of a tall, elegant birch, as if urged on by his audience. I see you smile.

Without trying, I smile, too.

KATE

Sam Grist sits across from me, staring. His eyes are so piercing that for a moment I'm paralyzed.

I'm not oblivious. I've noticed him watching me in class. I've observed the way his gaze follows me, tracing the lines of my body like he's committing them to memory. Sometimes he wears a vaguely drunk expression, like someone two martinis into the evening watching you from across the bar—when you know you're caught in a glimmering vodka filter that makes everything luminous.

This is the first time I've been alone with him. The air in my small office feels thick, dense. His eyes lock on mine with such unapologetic intensity, for a second I can't remember how to breathe. When one of my students uses the term "piercing" to describe someone's bright blue eyes, I usually scribble "cliché" in the margin. Now, I'm forced to acknowledge just how apt the phrase can be. His stare pins me to my seat.

With effort, I look away. That's hardly better. My eyes sink as low as his throat. The skin there is that delicate peach color only youth can manage. So dewy. So tender. If I put my lips there—*goddamn it. Stop, Kate. Just stop.*

"Nabokov's my favorite. *Lolita.* What a fucking beautiful book—sorry." He blushes, his pale cheeks turning pink.

"It's okay." I adjust my glasses. "I'm a professor, not a preacher. I'm more offended by comma splices than 'fuck.'"

The word lingers in the air between us. It's there, like the traces a sparkler leaves behind, glimmering in the muted light of my office.

I glance at the floor lamp behind him. Its pale linen shade casts a soft glow. When I bought the lamp last week I told myself I needed it so I could kill the fluorescents in my tiny office; they were giving me a headache. I've never liked the cold, clinical mood they radiate. Now, though, I wonder if the vibe is too 'candlelit lounge.' It's something I do way too often, swing from one extreme to another—in this case, from morgue to topless bar.

His smile is slow and knowing as he watches me. Now his eyes dip to my cleavage, and I worry I've gone too far. Low lights, "fuck," *Lolita*. This is not the professorial persona my tenure team needs to see.

I clear my throat, and his smile vanishes.

"So, you have a question about class?"

He leans back. The glow from the lamp catches in his dark black hair. I try to look at him coolly. I try to channel all the bloodless, sexless professors I've ever had. The incredibly well-shaped muscles beneath his black T-shirt beckon from my peripheral vision, but I refuse to give in. *It's the divorce,* I tell myself. *You're hungry for distraction. Go easy on yourself.*

"I do." He nods. "Is it a good time?"

"Shoot." I glance quickly at my computer, then back at him. We don't have all day, but I can carve out some time from my frantic online shoe shopping to deal with his needs. It's important to prioritize.

"It's about the workshop." He rests his arms on my desk, waiting for me to meet his gaze directly before he goes on. "There's some really god-awful shit in there, you know?"

I watch him as he catches himself swearing again, see him decide against apologizing. He's young, but not as young as some of my students. Twenty, maybe? Twenty-one? It's nearly impossible to guess at age anymore. I've given up, especially during that breathless time between eighteen and twenty-five, seven years that feel like they'll last forever, when you wear the face and body of an adult but still have the blank, unmarked dewiness of a child.

"It's Sam, right?" I take off my glasses and clean them with the hem of my sweater.

"Yeah. Sam." There's a subtle reproach in his voice, like he's disappointed I had to ask.

I didn't have to. I just need him to know I don't think about him. I haven't singled him out. The fact that this is a lie makes it even more important.

"Are you asking if I think my students' work is shit?"

"I know you think it's shit." He tilts his head to the side. He's peering past my façade, into me. "I'm asking why you don't call them on it."

I pull my cardigan tighter and put my glasses back on. "'Shit' is a relative term."

"Either it sucks or it doesn't."

"Nabokov had a hell of a time getting published," I point out.

"Not because publishers thought his work was shit. Because he terrified them."

I nod, conceding his point, and change tack. "Workshop is all about getting better. New writers need to experiment."

"You and I both know those spoiled brats are never going to write a single word worth reading." His cynical smile makes me uneasy.

I've got no idea why Sam affects me the way he does. It's not like he's the first smug, talented student ever to sit in that seat lobbing overly confident truisms about workshop at me. And yet . . . and *yet* . . . there's something about this one. The way his eyes probe my face, the restless motion of his body. He keeps leaning back, like an actor trying to telegraph "relaxed." Within seconds, though, his sculpted torso tips forward again, his naked forearms on my desk, his body straining toward me.

"I don't know that." I can hear the crispness in my tone, the prim, professorial inflection. "Nobody knows what anyone else is capable of."

"Now *that* I believe." He points at me, like he's the teacher and I'm the student finally stumbling on the right answer.

I kind of hate him. I kind of want him.

His big, beautiful hands land on my desk again; for just a second, his palms lie faceup between us. I see the jagged scars carved into his wrists, red, angry lightning bolts zigzagging his blue veins. My gaze flies to his face. He knows I've noticed. His eyes hold mine. In that moment, I'm certain he wanted me to see. But then he pulls his hands back, presses them against his thighs, and stands.

"I won't take up any more of your valuable time." His gaze flicks to my computer screen. I must have accidentally jiggled the mouse because Zappos is now perfectly visible.

It's my turn to blush. Goddamn him.

"Don't be so harsh on your fellow writers." I try to sound sage, like someone who lives profoundly, someone who has actual wisdom to pass on. "If you're right, and they're all hacks, that's good news, right? Less competition."

He raises an eyebrow. I've always wanted to master that move but could never seem to manage it. When I try, it comes off strained and frightened. He pulls it off so naturally, like he came out of his mother's womb and fixed her with that sardonic stare.

"I'm not worried about competition." He twists the doorknob.

My eyes dart to his wrist, seeking out the pink, puckered wound. I force myself to dismiss him with a nod, like someone who knows what the hell she's doing.

SAM

I watch your gaze slide around the room. You've just asked us a question, no doubt something probing and insightful, but I haven't heard a word. I can't stop staring at the place where your delicate gold chain disappears into your white blouse. I see myself fishing it out, tugging you toward me with one firm yank. The look of surprise on your face just before our mouths collide. The way you'll taste—lipstick and cinnamon. The texture of your silk blouse under my fingers as I tear—

Your gaze lands on me, wrenching me back to the present. For two seconds, I am whole.

When you move on, I feel a chill.

"What do we know about first-person POV?"

This time I hear the question, loud and clear. In a desperate plea to feel your eyes on me again, I blurt out the first thing that comes to mind. "It's intimate."

Your gaze locks on me. "That's right. Tell us more."

"It's getting inside the mind of the character," I say, gaining volume as I speak. "You're in them, inhabiting their psyche. The advantage is the reader feels close to the narrator."

"And the disadvantage?" Your graceful neck tilts forward half an inch.

"The reader feels close to the narrator."

This gets a chuckle; I look around, surprised. I never try to make people laugh. As a result, they're amused by half of what I say. I've learned not to take offense. Making people laugh is a good thing, though I've never figured out why.

"That's right. It's a double-edged sword." You reward me with the faintest of grins. There it is again. That look. Shrewd. Knowing. It's not a toothy, game-show-hostess affirmation. It doesn't say, *You're good.* It says, *We'll see about you.* I passed the very first pop quiz, and I'm allowed to stick around until further notice.

You're mercurial. You've been known to drop a student for consulting a cell phone in class. Your standards are so high you're legendary. Some people hate you for it. Even those who call you names, though, want into your workshop. We had to submit a portfolio and be interviewed by your TAs just to be considered.

"Now," you say, letting your gaze slide around the room again, "what about omniscient POV? What are the advantages of seeing everything?"

Nothing, I think. Who wants to see into every mind? Because let's face it, most people's thoughts are limp and useless. God, if I could see into the brain of that anemic girl in the corner with the facial piercings and the Raggedy Ann hair, I'd kill myself. Or the twitchy guy across from me who seems to be fighting a bad case of Tourette's? The girl at the head of the table who keeps flipping her highlighted hair in my direction? I don't want inside those psyches.

A guy with Justin Bieber bangs launches into an explanation of omniscient POV. You cut him off after three sentences.

"Let me hear from someone else."

Bieber-head wilts like a deflated balloon.

The girl with the cleavage and the highlights gives it a try.

You listen with a bored expression. "Not exactly. Anyone else?"

God, I love you. I have never been as happy as I am right now, watching you shoot these pretentious fucktards down with your laser-like intelligence, your uncompromising standards. So far,

I'm the only one who's said anything of value. Of course I'm keeping score. How can I not?

"Omniscient POV is powerful when you want the big picture." I turn and notice, for the first time, the older guy with the shaved head sitting near the wall. He's in his thirties, looks like a vet. The tattoo peeking from the collar of his white T-shirt gives him an air of danger. It looks like an octopus, though it could be a squid or even a kraken. Hell, for all I know it's a clump of seaweed.

"Go on," you prompt.

"It's like film. You can move freely from one mind to another, unbound by time and space. It's the closest you can get to playing God."

Your smile is slow and sly. "Precisely why it's always freaked me out."

I hate Tattoo Man. He's lounging in your gaze, drinking in the smile you denied me, the look that says, *You're okay, kid.*

I scribble in my notebook, *PLAYING GOD.* Then I draw a line through it, pressing so hard my pen tears the page.

Here's the thing about Highlights and Cleavage: She has no idea how much I loathe her.

It's nothing personal. She probably has brothers and sisters, a prom anecdote, a story about her parents' divorce that will break your heart. She's struggled with bulimia, and once, in total despair, she carved an *S* into the tender flesh of her inner thigh just to make sure she could still feel something. She has a friend who died in a drunk-driving accident or overdosed on OxyContin. She has another who left everyone to become a model in Milan. She might even have an ex-boyfriend who got injured in Iraq.

Whatever. Looking at her, it's clear she's got a story.

I'm just not interested.

I know this isn't normal. She's wearing a push-up bra and low-slung skinny jeans that reveal the neon-pink of her thong. The blond highlights in her caramel hair are expensive and under-stated. She is money and sex, all the things I'm supposed to want. Yet, looking at her, I feel nothing except an arctic wind blowing through my chest cavity.

She sidles over, pushing a strand of hair behind her ear. "I'm Jess. In case you didn't catch that."

It's the second week of class. She is marking her turf. Her blinding smile makes me wince.

"Nice to meet you." I'm polite, distant.

"So formal." She laughs, her cleavage jiggling. How does her mother sleep at night, knowing her eighteen-year-old daughter's wearing a push-up bra and a visible thong, spending the family's hard-earned money getting an "education"? They must know she's reading more pregnancy tests than books, consuming more alcohol than ideas. I shudder. I'm only a few years older, but I feel a paternal concern for old Cleavage.

"You an English major?" I ask.

"Communications." She nods. "I want to go into PR."

"So why take a fiction workshop?"

"I might write a book." She shrugs, like writing a book is some-thing you may or may not squeeze into your spare time, akin to yoga or French cooking.

"Nice to meet you." I turn away and head for the door.

"Hold on!" She says it with an air of authority that surprises me, her tone going from sugar to steel. "Come have a drink with us."

I look around. "Who's us?"

"I'm meeting a couple friends at McCallahan's."

McCallahan's is a pub a block from campus, a stale, seedy place where the smell of vomit's always at war with the sharp perfume of bleach. Its chief attraction is their willingness to take fake IDs without a second glance. I went there once. They won't welcome me back. Anyway, I'd rather carve my own eyeballs out with a rusty spoon than drink tepid beer with Cleavage and her circle of thong-flashing friends.

"Can't," I say. "Maybe next time."

"Who knows if I'll ask you next time?"

"I'll try to live with the suspense," I deadpan.

Across the room, you gather a stack of manuscripts and shove them into your oversized leather tote. Jess follows my gaze. When she swivels toward me again, there's a new expression there. Her jaw's tight, and her eyes glint with suspicion.

"Sad, really." She dangles the words before me.

I take the bait. "What's sad?"

She leans toward me and whispers, "Everyone knows she's extra harsh on hot girls. Wonder why?"

I don't say anything. The gall of the stupid bitch.

"I'm, like, *So sorry you're old, but don't shit on my work just because you're having a hot flash.*"

Still, I say nothing. I just stare, my hands twisting at my sides, aching to slap her. She takes my silence for agreement.

"Can't wait to read your stuff!" She grins, holding up the pages of my story. As she walks away, she assumes I'm watching her ass. She's about as subtle as a baboon in heat, the low-slung skinny jeans, the over-the-knee boots, the pink thong. Her hips sway from side to side. She casts a quick glance over her shoulder, just to be sure.

I look away.

KATE

Zoe's holding up a pair of sneakers that look like they're made for a doll. Her pregnant belly fills the space between us, a swollen reminder of everything that's about to change.

"Don't these just break your heart?" She gazes at the tiny shoes, eyes shining.

I swallow around the lump in my throat. Zoe's my best friend. Until now, we shared all the same passions: chocolate cupcakes at Miette's, lemon drops at Le Chat Noir, talking all night and smoking weed and watching the sunrise from her rooftop garden. Last year, she met a baker who looks like a low-rent Brad Pitt. He's got a gap between his front teeth and his hairline's receding, but otherwise he's a dead ringer. She got pregnant on their third date. They moved in together a month later. I've had six months to get used to the idea, but I still do a double take whenever her belly swims into view, an interloper at a private party who just won't take the hint.

Of course I'm happy for her. The Brad-alike is named Bo. He's dumb but harmless. We went to *MacBeth* last weekend for Zoe's thirty-sixth birthday. Afterward, while Zoe and I were going on about the nuanced performances, the timeless resonance of the quest for power, Bo scowled at his phone, his fingers working furiously. I thought he was texting, but then I caught a glimpse of his screen and realized he was playing "Angry Birds."

Not a Mensa member, Bo. But he makes amazing bread.

Zoe illustrates children's books. She paints these wild pictures that make you want to crawl inside them. In Zoe's world, everything is lush and jewel-toned, vivid and hazy as a Chinese opium den. I'm afraid she's wasted on Bo, who probably thinks her work is pretty.

Can I just say? *Fuck babies.* I can't wait to get through this slice of life when everything is all about procreation. Call me cold and inhuman, but I hate the little fuckers. They shit and piss their way into the center of sane people's hearts, turning them into brainwashed automatons. The thought of losing Zoe to all that makes my stomach twist into a pretzel.

"They're adorable." I nod too emphatically at the tiny sneakers. "You should definitely get them."

Her eyes find mine. "Kate? You okay?"

I nod again, not trusting myself to speak.

"It's fine if you're not." She reaches out and squeezes my hand. Her voice is so gentle it makes everything harder.

I push my hair back from my face and force a smile. When I'm sure I can get a few words out safely, I say, "Don't worry. I'm good."

"It's okay to want things, you know." Her thick, dark bangs form a curtain above her eyes. She looks so sincere, but I can't stand the pity seeping through the empathy. It's not my fault every woman rounding the corner of thirty goes crazy and gives up everything for a tiny shit factory. Being the only sane one might make me lonely, but it shouldn't earn me pity from the bitches who lose their minds.

Not that Zoe's a bitch. Far from it. She's got the biggest, warmest heart of anyone I know. Back in grad school, I had my hands full protecting her from the vampiric bloodsuckers who flocked to her in droves. Something about those big, blue, innocent eyes and the china-doll hair. She's a magnet for deranged psychopaths. Even if Bo is bland as unsalted oatmeal, he's a total catch compared to Zoe's usual boyfriends. She once dated a pill popper who sold her first-edition James Joyce for some Oxy and a hand job. I had to hire two bouncers from Le Chat Noir to scare the shit out of him. At least Bo's addictions are limited to domestic beer, Instagram, and reality TV.

Out of the corner of my eye, a flutter of movement catches my attention. I turn. Across the aisle, in the bedding section, I half-recognize the shadowy figure fingering gold sheets. Sam Grist. The name lights up inside my brain before I even have time to search for it.

Zoe follows my gaze. "Someone you know?"

"Sort of." I turn away.

"What's that mean?" She tosses the shoes into her basket and pushes forward to examine a miniature pair of overalls.

"Student."

"Well, don't look now," her eyebrows shoot up, "but he's coming this way."

"Professor Youngblood."

I turn and find his icy blue eyes scanning my face. There's cockiness there, and also naked curiosity. I can't decide which is more unnerving.

"Sam." I nod. "How are you?"

"Good. Yeah." His eyes dart to Zoe.

"This is my friend, Zoe. She's having a baby," I add unnecessarily.

His eyes drop to Zoe's bump. "So I see."

"You an MFA student?" Zoe's gaze moves quickly over his body and up to his face.

"Undergrad." He shrugs, self-deprecating. The cockiness has faded to an ember. "Started a little late."

"How old are you?" Zoe's uncensored question makes me bump

my foot against hers. She gives me a look like *Shut up, I'm just asking.*

"Twenty-two." He looks at me as if he expects me to challenge this.

"English major?"

He nods with a rueful smile. "Not the most practical choice, but I've never been practical." His eyes drop to her bump again. "Boy or girl?"

"Boy." She sighs. "Limits the shopping options, sadly."

"Anyway, we have to run." I look at my phone. "We're supposed to meet Zoe's husband."

Zoe widens her eyes at my lie but says nothing.

"Didn't mean to interrupt." He looks at the tiny yellow overalls Zoe's holding. "I'd get the faded denim. More manly."

"Oh. Okay. Thanks?" Zoe looks doubtfully from her hanger to the faded-denim version on the rack.

"See you in class." I smile in dismissal.

He must see something else in my expression, because he leans close and whispers, "Hang in there."

"I'll try," I squeak.

Just like that he's gone. Zoe's holding the faded-denim overalls, staring at me with the strangest expression on her face.

"What?" It comes out defensive. I glance over my shoulder to make sure he's gone.

"You like him," she says, way too loudly for my taste.

"Shut up."

"You do." She strokes the denim overalls, but her eyes never leave my face. "Kate's hot for a student. God, I knew it was only a matter of time."

"Don't read more into this than—"

"I know you. That's the look you get when you're wildly attracted to someone but are trying not to be."

"Stop!" I shove her gently. "You're just stirring the shit."

"I call it like I see it." She puts the denim overalls in her cart.

"You really think 'manly' is something your infant son should strive for?"

She shrugs. "He's a guy. They know about these things."

"Whatever. I liked the yellow ones."

"Shows what you know." She tosses a green micro fleece blanket into her cart. "Must be nice, being worshiped all day by guys like that."

"I'm not worshiped."

"Shut up. You totally are."

I change the subject. "I need a drink. We haven't been day-drunk together in ages."

"Hello!" She gestures at her belly. "Fetal alcohol syndrome?"

"Right." I can feel myself blushing. It's a bit of a sore spot. I always bring a bottle of wine to dinner at her place, though by now I should know I'll drink the whole thing. In solidarity, Bo's given up alcohol for nine months. I'm a fuckwad. A fuckwad who can't adjust to this new reality. Pretty soon—who am I kidding? already—Zoe's going to put someone else first, always and forever. After a decade spent looking to her as my true north, my emergency contact, my person, the habit dies hard. It leaves a sour taste in my mouth, thinking about how much of her I'm losing to the force gaining weight daily inside her.

"Maybe you can drink a martini and I can just . . . watch," she says, the slightest apology in her voice.

"Stupid idea. Let's go get a cookie and coffee."

She runs a hand over her belly. "Decaf for me. I already had my daily allowance."

"Excellent. We can sip herbal tea by the play area and contemplate the miracle of life." It comes out snarkier than it sounded in my head.

She grabs my hand. "Kate. It's okay. You're upset. I get it."

"What? No, I—"

"You're getting divorced, and I'm having a baby." She waits

until I meet her eye. "It's a shitty situation. Let's not make it worse by pretending it's not happening."

I relax under the weight of her steady gaze. "It is kind of shitty."

"Totally." She nods. "But pretty soon, I'll be buried in diapers, and you'll be holding office hours with Gregory Pecs."

"Don't even start with—ugh!"

"Tell me you didn't notice that perfectly sculpted torso, and I'll know you're a liar."

I giggle. "He is pretty hot, huh?"

"Beyond hot." She strides toward the register.

Only then do I notice Sam Grist hovering near the escalator, grinning like he's heard every word.

SAM

You live on Cherry Street.

It's a poem. It's a haiku. I want to tattoo the words on my forehead.

You stand in the slit between the opaque ivory curtains. Your hand snakes up to rub the back of your white, slender neck. The light pools in your hair, gathers along the sharp lines of your collarbones. You wear a wifebeater, yoga pants. I train my binoculars on the tight peaks of your nipples, erect beneath the thin, white cotton.

You are even better than I imagined.

I move the binoculars up to your face. I'm not a pervert, a Peeping Tom.

I am Romeo, gazing up at Juliet by moonlight.

And yes, okay, so I'm crouched in a urine-scented alley. That doesn't make my mission any less noble.

To study you. Understand you. Observe you in your natural habitat.

You lean over and grab something from the table beside the couch. A glass of wine. It's the color of blood. I bet you drink brooding, inky Malbecs, Kate. I bet you deliberate for long minutes before stretching out your long, white fingers and seizing the right bottle. Your taste is impeccable. Now your plush, pink lips fasten around the glass. You take a long sip. That wine sat in some barrel in southwestern France for years, just waiting in darkness for your tongue; now it unfolds on your taste buds, smooth as butter.

You put the glass down and stare out the window.

Even from here, I feel the weight of your stare. The sadness you keep in those eyes, shadows stored behind the light. Your eyes have seen things. They know things. I feel my throat closing; my binoculars tremble.

"Hey! What are you doing back there?" A sharp nasal voice cuts through my vigil.

I turn and see a hooded figure looming just beyond the alley. His glasses glimmer in the streetlight. Not a thug, then, just a hipster looking to do the right thing. Neighborhood security.

"Thinking about buying." It's an automatic response. When questioned, behave like a spoiled prick. You'd be surprised at the number of people who leave you alone if they think your dad's lawyers can make their life hell.

"Yeah?" As predicted, the man before me deflates. He thought he was being a hero, stopping a pervert. If I'm just a venture capitalist, my value as an interesting anecdote plummets. "Which one?"

"House across the street."

He looks puzzled. "Didn't know she was selling. I mean yeah, they split, but I figured she'd hold on to the place."

"Insider tip." My pompous voice makes me shiver. I smirk like an asshole.

"Well, good luck, I guess." He looks around. "Not a bad neighborhood. Quiet."

"Thanks, man."

He chuckles. "Thought you were, you know, stalking someone."

We both laugh. *As if.*

He leaves.

I'm not a threat to you, Kate. I'm watching over you. Biding my time. Waiting for the right moment.

You appear in the window again, a worried frown creasing your forehead. I travel down your body with my binoculars. You're everything I've waited for and more.

KATE

He hammers out sentences like a blacksmith. Each one is dirty-black but also red-ember hot.

I've never seen writing this good in workshop. It's unheard of.

This is Harper Lee and Hunter S. Thompson's sticky, malformed love child. His work is raw, sloppy, quick. It's slow where it should be fast and fast where it should be slow. And yet . . . and *yet*. There's something there, the X factor, the mark of genius.

As I read his clumsy short story about a girl who slaughters her pet bunny so her family can survive, I discover I'm sweating. The punctuation is all over the place, the timing haphazard. Still, it's good. Really good.

I've never discovered anyone. Before my first novel sold, I taught at the local community college. The students' writing there was mostly abysmal. I stumbled on a few original voices I tried to nurture, but wading through the sea of barely literate fan fiction to find a few gems proved exhausting. Even when I did stumble on someone whose work showed promise, half the time their life was too turbulent to sustain a writing practice. I recall a single mom with three kids who had a knack for lush, darkly imagined historical fiction. Right after I offered to help her whip her manuscript into shape, she disappeared. I later noticed an article about

her in the local paper. She had been shot in the face by her dis-
gruntled ex.

The kids who come to Blackwood College are mostly insur-
ance brokers and housewives waiting to happen. They may strut
into class harboring fantasies about a writing career, but I am not
merciful when it comes to dreamers. If they haven't got the talent,
the drive, the vision, I find a way to tell them. No, I'm not a prophet,
and God knows many appalling books mysteriously become
bestsellers, but I recognize shit when I read it. I consider it a service to my students and to the English language to gently steer
them away from their delusions. They can edit blogs, or write
press releases, or design apps. They cannot and should not write
novels. Not if they can help themselves.

But this one. This one's different.

He must write novels. If he doesn't, then nothing I'm doing
means anything.

The girl in his story is holding the buck knife to the struggling
bunny's throat. He writes violence with restraint, all the more
horrible for the details missing. He choreographs the scene with
an understated insouciance.

His unflinching honesty is sexy. Usually, a writer dithers at
the edge of something, never diving into the heart of the story. Sam
dives in headfirst and keeps going. His words trace a sharp, clear
trajectory. It's not the bunny or the girl that has my cheeks flushed,
my heart pounding; it's the way he dives deep, never doubting himself, plunging into the depths of his characters' psyches. To be that
young and fearless on the page. . . .

Beautiful sentences. Finely wrought images. This stuff is rare,
precious.

There's nothing self-conscious about his prose. It is naked
observation, unfiltered. He's there in the woodshed with his nine-
year-old protagonist, her greasy hair bunching up on one side of
her head. She holds the struggling rabbit, fighting against its pan-
icked thrusts, soothing it with one hand even as she readies the

blade with the other. The room steams with angst. He is there, and because of that I am there, seeing what his words force me to see.

Feeling what his words force me to feel.

He's a fucking genius.

And I have the misfortune of mentoring him.

I take a long drink of wine and tap the manuscript pages into a tidy stack beside the couch. A hint of movement flits past my half-closed curtains, drawing my eye. The phantom shape melts away before I can make it out. I look around the living room. Probably just Emily out there, sniffing the garden for adventure, weaving in and out of the shadows, her paws wet with dew. Charlotte's curled into a tabby-colored ball beside me, purring with steady, monotonous pleasure. I drink more wine, staring into the glow of my gas fireplace.

In spite of having hoped for this—a blinding, half-formed star that will drift into my workshop—I'm flustered now that it's happened. More than flustered. Just this side of terrified. Yes, in some secret room deep inside the haphazardly constructed building of my teaching career, I've been saving space for The One. The Voice. The Talent. A writer with so much unrefined potential I'll instantly abandon all my stinginess and cynicism. A writer who can bring out the best in me—as a teacher, an editor, a person. Show me an English professor who doesn't secretly long for that student, and I'll show you someone even more self-centered, jealous, and fucked up than me.

Yet, now that I'm holding the pages that prove it's happened at last, I'm scared I'll make a mess of it. I'm an archeologist who, after happily digging away for decades, has found only crumpled Coke cans and candy wrappers; now my shovel's hit Tutankhamun's sarcophagus, and I've no idea what to do. Should I use a toothbrush to unearth the treasure slowly, train myself to exhibit a painstaking patience I never cultivated? Do I hand my find over to more experienced hands?

Everyone knows genius is mercurial. What if I say the wrong thing, and he shuts down? I might make an editorial suggestion that sends him spiraling down some dark rabbit hole, obscuring his original vision. We all long to discover the next Melville, some acne-riddled Nabokov just learning to wield his power. But what do we do when fate hands us just that? There's no instruction manual for cultivating artistic brilliance. I've never shown any special talent in the classroom before. Nobody has ever accused me of nurturing an emerging talent, let alone inspiring greatness.

I go to pour more wine, but the bottle's empty.

SAM

It's Sunday, crisp and bursting with golden October light. I'm walking through the streets of Blackwood, past the quaint plaza and the shops selling useless objets d'art and five-hundred-dollar cashmere wraps and chairs nobody wants to sit on. The mother-fucking trust-funders push their babies around in strollers. They cradle unbleached coffee cups full of organic, free-trade soy lattes, and they order their toddlers to "use their words." They are miserable, lumpy people. All the money in the world, and still they can't manage the thinnest sheen of sex appeal.

I cradle my 7–11 coffee and stare straight ahead, walking fast. The trust-fund toddlers career toward me, but I keep going. They almost crash into my shins on their unstable rolls of baby fat. I sidestep each one, not slowing my pace, slicing like a shark through a school of herring. Kids find me compelling. Their chubby hands reach for me in grocery stores, in parks. They sense life in me. Surrounded all day by their parents' rotting husks, their nannies' dead eyes, they see me and grasp for the living.

Sorry, kids. I've got somewhere to be.

At the edge of campus, I pause to breathe it in. Blackwood smells of apples, dead leaves, and woodsmoke. Fresh new life rubbing elbows with decay. The perfume hits me hard as I inhale. I take in the soaring spires and ivy-covered towers. It's the quintessential small, beautiful college. They've filmed seven movies here, and I've seen every one. My whole *idea* of college revolves around this setting—the rows of flame-red trees, the brick lecture halls, the white-domed planetarium. It's a sacred place, in spite of all the fucktards here. It's sacred because it's where I met you.

I head straight for your office. I've studied the janitors. I know now, at three in the afternoon, Janet's cleaning your office. I've been cultivating her friendship. She's heavy through the hips, a craggy-faced smoker with a smile full of tobacco-brown teeth. She never made it past the sixth grade, but she's not stupid. Not by a long shot. No, Janet has the street smarts of a Compton thug and the instincts of a jungle cat. She suffers no fools.

"Hey, Janet!" I feign surprise as I swing around the corner, my backpack dangling over one shoulder in the jaunty affect students seem to favor. "Fancy meeting you here."

She starts to smile, then stops herself, self-conscious about her teeth.

"I'm so glad you're working."

Her age-spotted fingers pluck at her baggy, striped shirt. "Oh, yeah? Why?"

"Because I'm doing some work for Professor Youngblood." I study her face. "Only she forgot to make me a key."

"I can't let you into—"

"If you want to know the truth," I put a hand on her arm and lean toward her, my voice dropping, "I lost it. She made it for me and I got wasted last night. God knows where it is now. At the bottom of Josh Bloom's pool. Or worse."

She narrows her eyes at me. "Scared of getting caught?"

I nod. My face blends the right mixture of sheepish, contrite, and pathetic. I've practiced this look many times in a mirror. You'd be amazed how often it comes in handy.

I know Janet. She's the underdog. She feels for someone who fucked up and might get caught. I noticed the tat on her forearm the first time I spotted her—the clock with no hands. She's done some serious time. I'm nothing if not observant.

"You'll be sure to lock up when you leave?"

I let my face flood with gratitude. "Would you really? Oh, Janet, you're the best!"

"Just this once." She winks, and I follow in her wake, which reeks of stale cigarette smoke. I smile.

It smells like you in here.

I stand in the center of the small, cramped space and inhale. Something musky and electric. Warm and red.

I sit in your chair and power up your computer. My fingers touch where yours have touched a thousand, ten thousand times before. I caress the keyboard, fondle your expensive mélange of pens poking out of a *Blackwood College* cup.

The sunlight streaming through the one window has a rich, buttery quality. Just beyond the glass, there's a Japanese maple so red and vibrant it's obscene.

I remember a line from your first novel, *Pay Dirt*. "She turned to the Japanese maple outside her window and tried to lose herself in its layers." I whisper the line to myself. Maybe you sat right here when you wrote that. I whisper it again as I run my fingers over the titles lining your shelves. Nabokov, Joyce, Dickens, the Brontës. You do love your classics. There's something so intimate about touching your books.

But I should hurry. Janet might have second thoughts; she might worry about her job, about getting caught. I need to focus.

I dig through your drawers until I find it: a tiny Moleskine notebook, midnight blue. I open it, and there they are on the first page: your passwords.

I try them on your computer, just to be sure. I won't be greedy. What do I care about your Zappos account, your Netflix? I realize you only have two passwords for everything, though, so greedy or not, learning those grants me access to your entire online kingdom. Two passwords, and both of them so simple—too simple, Kate. I worry about you. Don't you know about identity theft? Don't you realize there are bad people out there who will use your innocence against you? I commit both passwords to memory and feel better. I'll notice if anyone tries to hack you. I'm your protector, Kate. Your invisible knight.

There's a page filled with your doodles and random words. Unable to resist, I tear it out and put it in my pocket. The passwords you might miss. This? Never.

I'm assailed with a vision of us at a party in SoHo. You have one hand on my arm; you're laughing, a little tipsy, telling Donna Tartt about how we met. "Can you believe he broke into my office and memorized my passwords?" At Donna's horrified expression, you'll laugh even harder, then press two fingers over your mouth like a naughty schoolgirl. "I realize that sounds bad, but you have to know Sam to get it—he's protective. He knew me." You'll turn and kiss me on the mouth, your plush, pink lips crushing against mine, off target because of that third glass of wine. "He knows me better than I know myself."

And fuck Donna Tartt if she doesn't get it. Because it will be you and me against the world by then, Kate. It already is; you just don't realize it. By the time we're living in New York, you will know that everything I do now, I do for us. That's all that matters.

I can hear Janet in the office next door, vacuuming. Just another quick look around for anything useful, then I'm out of here.

In one of your desk drawers, I spot it: a golden key sitting in a coffee cup. It's stuffed all the way into the back, behind a pretty carved box containing a letter opener, a deck of playing cards, and an owner's manual for a DVD player written entirely in Chinese. I pull it out and study it. If I know you—and I do—it's an extra house key.

Thank god you are not methodical and careful, Kate. You are

never suspicious or paranoid. You float through life like a dancer doing pirouettes straight through an army; you are the prima ballerina, so they have to part for you, they have to give way. You think that's how it works for everyone, that the world is one great performance of *Swan Lake* and obstacles melt away so long as you keep dancing. It makes you vulnerable to sinister, crazy people. I'm here to guard against that now. With my street smarts and your innocence, together we have everything we need.

I pocket the key and head into the bright October day. My heart flames like the Japanese maple outside your office. I walk under it, and lose myself in its scarlet layers.

I hear a giggle and jerk around in surprise. It's Cleavage. She's standing there in leggings and running shoes, one hip popped out to the side. Her sweatshirt hangs askew, exposing one shiny shoulder. Does this girl ever cover up? It's disconcerting how much she craves eyes on her tits and her perky, miniature ass.

"What are you doing?" Her voice, girlish and bright, feels like an ice pick driving into my brain.

I return to my contemplation of the Japanese maple. It occurs to me that the light has shifted inside this living kaleidoscope of reds. Maybe I've been staring at it for an hour. My high starts to fade. I have your sweet, golden key in my pocket, your passwords committed to memory, the musky smell of your office still thick and warm inside me. These things matter, and if I concentrate on them, the October Sunday twilight that threatens to fall any second cannot touch me.

And yet, here's Cleavage, poised to rob me of happiness. She watches me in her stretched-out sweatshirt, her spandex leggings that might as well be painted on. Her presence pierces the taut balloon inside my heart. You can't patch that shit. My joy leaks out, leaving me vulnerable to the heartbreaking nectarine hues of the messy autumn sunset.

"You okay?" She inches closer, watching me, her effervescent tone evaporating.

"Yeah. Fine."

"Are you waiting for someone?" She looks around.

I start walking, fast, and she hurries to catch up. "No. Just checking out that tree."

"That's weird." When I look at her she grins. "But cool."

Her flirty eyes make me want to hit her in the face. She's so young, so clueless and mixed up. You'd point out I'm only four years older, max, but let's face it, Kate, you and I are old souls, and this creature, this slender Barbie doll bobbing at my side, she is young—it will take lifetimes before she's even progressed past infancy. I can already see the lawyer she'll marry, the babies they'll have, the hours she'll spend shopping at Bed Bath & Beyond, the craft room filled with row after row of colored ribbon, the tame sex she'll have with her litigator in their tasteful, Danish modern bed. I can see the depression she'll fall into when she realizes her children are boring and her husband's fucking some waitress at Applebee's, a girl not unlike the perky little thing walking beside me right now. She puts her hands into the sweatshirt's kangaroo pouch and pulls down, exposing her tanned flesh, the deep cleft, the edge of a lacy push-up bra. She is subtle as a neon sign, and I miss you so much I ache deep in my bones.

"I read your story," she says.

"Oh, yeah?" I hate how much I care about what she'll say next. Even this fluffy little cum-dumpster has power over me when it comes to my writing. "And?"

"It's amazing. Reminded me of Stephen King."

She might as well have pulled a butcher knife from her back pocket and plunged it into my eye. I keep my expression neutral as I stare straight ahead.

"I could so go for a bowl of soup right now." She shoots me a sideways glance. "There's a cute little café by the plaza that makes an amazing roasted red pepper bisque. Want to come with? I hate eating alone. We could talk about your story. Maybe you can help me with mine."

"Don't you eat in the dining hall?" I'm stalling. I can only turn her down so many times before she'll get ugly. I know girls like her. I've known them all my life. They're drawn to me, just like babies.

She nods. "Yeah, I've got a meal plan, but some nights I can't face it, you know? The greasy pizza and the vats of lasagna. The iceberg lettuce. One thing the Midwest does not do well is food, especially if you're a vegetarian."

"Where you from?"

"California."

"What part?" I'm still stalling, but she seems happy enough to make small talk.

"Orange County." She's proud of this, I can tell. There's a little bounce in her step when she says it.

I loathe her more than ever.

"What about you?" she asks.

"New York." The lie is out before I can stop it. I have stood here beneath the canopy of your Japanese maple for at least an hour, seeing our future in its shifting red leaves—the mornings we'll spend eating French pastries in bed, the afternoons in Central Park, the nights spinning through a series of parties, each one more packed with literary rock stars than the last.

"Really? That's cool. New York City?"

I nod. She's impressed, I can see it in her wide, brown eyes.

Fuck, I don't need to impress her, don't *want* her cheap, un-earned awe. But I also don't need to tell her the truth. The grimy suburb outside Albuquerque where I lived until I was ten with my grandparents. The series of nowhere towns Vivienne dragged me to after they died, when she could no longer fob me off, when she had to take me with her like a bag of dirty laundry you can't wash and you can't bring yourself to shove into a Dumpster. Someday, when we are lying in bed, sweat glazed and sated and tangled in sheets, I will tell this story to you, Kate. I can already see the tiny quotation mark creases that will appear between your brows. You will smooth my hair back, listening with that intense silence of yours, empathy and compassion shining from your blue-gray eyes. Cleavage doesn't need to know any of this, though. She doesn't need to know about my sordid, underprivileged childhood, even though it would get her wet. Rich girls like her always love bad boys with whorish junkie mothers and dead grandparents. She can go fuck herself.

"So? How about that soup? They also make a BLT that's supposed to be awesome, if you're into meat." She's relentless. Cloying. Pathetic. The way she says "meat," it sounds like a dirty word.

I try very hard to force my expression into apologetic regret. "I'd love to. Really. But I have a huge test tomorrow."

"Second time you've blown me off." She looks down, then back up again. Her brown eyes search mine, dig for some scrap of approval. Behind her, the sunset is all tangerine and cotton candy.

I fondle the key in my pocket, wondering if I can make it to the hardware store before it closes. Probably not even open on Sundays. This little college town is nothing if not god-fearing.

We reach a fork in the path, and I shoot off to the right, picking up my pace. "See you in workshop."

"Fine. Be that way." She's trying to smile, but it looks forced, tight, the way she'll smile twenty years from now, when she knows her husband's going off to meet his stripper girlfriend. "Just remember one thing."

"What's that?" I'm walking backward now, already ten feet away.

"You can run, but you can't hide." And now her smile loses its fake edge, and I can see she enjoys this. The chase. The game of cat and mouse.

The more I tell her no, the more she thinks I'm worth having.

KATE

After workshop on Tuesday, I pop a breath mint and try to figure out how to get Sam alone. I've read his story five times over the weekend, scribbled so many notes in the margins it looks like a crime scene. The class, predictably, glossed over its genius. Most of them probably read it while watching TV. The vet with the tats was the only one who indicated he appreciated its potential. No wonder *Fifty Shades of Shit* charged to the top of the bestseller lists. Young American sensibilities are as refined as raw sewage.

I need to tell him he's not crazy. He's the most talented student I've ever worked with; I'll be damned if I'll let him leave this room thinking his classmates' lackluster response says anything about his work. Ever since I read his first sentence, I've agonized over how to convey the story's brilliance. In workshop I held back. If the others think I favor him, they'll just lash out with jealousy. Besides, I don't want my praise going to his head. Conceit can be as dangerous to a writer as despair. Maybe more so.

It feels important to do this right. So much hangs in the balance.

I could call his name, ask him to stay after. Somehow, though, my self-consciousness won't allow me to utter a word. I dither, organizing the workshop manuscripts, not meeting anyone's eye. The class files out, laughing, joking, making plans. Those not caught up in the river of conversation pull out their phones and text furiously, as if to prove they are wanted elsewhere, they are loved.

Sam, I see, does none of these things. He hovers at the back of the room, watching me. Looks like I won't have to seek him out after all. He's doing the hard part for me.

I see the girl—what's her name? Tess? No, Jess. A gender-ambiguous name for the girliest girl in class. She wears a tight, short skirt over sheer, black tights, a leather jacket that nips in at the waist. The outfit reminds me of the "slutty cop" costumes so popular every Halloween here at Blackwood. She lingers near the door, glancing back at Sam. When he refuses to notice her, she flounces out the door, hips swinging.

I'm still shuffling papers when he crosses the room. He stands there a long moment, just a chair between us, and I can feel his eyes on the side of my face, burning into me.

I turn to look at him. Those wolf-blue eyes lock on to mine. He's so intense. Standing this close to him, I can feel my nostrils flaring, trying to pick up his scent. Animal instinct. He smells of crisp leaves and rain.

"You have a minute?" he asks softly.

"Yes. I want to talk to you, actually."

"Really?" He is sweetly surprised, almost bashful. "About what?"

"Your story." I hand him my marked-up pages.

He takes the manuscript from me. Scanning through my notes, his face falls. "That's a lot of red ink."

"I know." I shoulder my leather tote and glance toward the hall to make sure we're alone. "Which probably seems like a bad thing. I know today's workshop wasn't easy."

He just shrugs, like he can handle it. I know better. I can see the pain behind his cool exterior. I know every word of criticism feels like a jagged shard of glass raked over tender flesh. I remember my own painful workshops. When I was working on *Hidden Depths,* I got a revision letter from my editor that felt like a rusty razor blade carving through my sternum, searching for my heart. Sometimes I read Amazon reviews so scathing and casually cruel I want to hurl my computer across the room. I know. It never goes away, that sense that you have turned yourself inside out for the world, that you have slaved to expose every muscle, tendon, and vein; in response, the world casually throws acid at your steaming innards. It's the flippancy that always gets to me. The offhand savagery of it, like they've no idea it hurts.

His eyes finally meet mine. Something passes between us, a flicker of understanding. He knows I get it. The tightness in his jaw softens.

"Listen," I lean toward him, lowering my voice. "I don't want this to go to your head, but your work is incredible."

"Incredible?" he echoes.

"I've been teaching more than ten years, and I've never seen anything like it."

He lets this sink in. The ice blue eyes darken slightly; his pupils dilate. Then, ever so slowly, he grins. "You wouldn't lie to me, would you?"

"Not about this."

One eyebrow jerks up. That look again. The sardonic, amused teasing. "You'd lie about other things?"

"My agent's coming to town tomorrow," I blurt. Jesus, what's wrong with me? That eyebrow got me flustered. I didn't mean to mention Maxine. Not yet. He should develop his voice more, clean up his punctuation. He's still raw. He doesn't need an agent hovering, exerting pressure. She'll want him to consider what's commercially viable. She'll want to push him in a specific direction. Here I get a chance to mentor someone with legitimate talent, and I stumble on my first move.

"From New York?" His face is a pot about to boil over, but he clamps a lid on it. His self-control is really something. I could learn a thing or two from this kid.

"Yeah. She's speaking at a conference in Cincinnati." I swallow.

There's no avoiding it now. I've introduced the topic; I have to follow through. "You should meet her."

"That would be amazing." As overused as that word is, I can tell he really means it.

"You have a novel?"

"In progress. Yeah." He shoves his hands deep into his pockets, like he doesn't trust himself to let them loose. "I'm a couple hundred pages in."

I sigh. "It can be hard, having pressure on you at this stage."

"How do you mean?"

"Trying to please others before you know what you want to say."

He doesn't hesitate. "I know what I want to say."

I offer a wan smile. The overconfidence of youth. What can you do? They have to make their own mistakes. "I'm meeting her at Oliver's tomorrow for lunch. We'll need the first hour to catch up, talk shop, but maybe you can join us for coffee and dessert? Say, around one-thirty?"

"I'll be there." His smile is radiant—a sunrise, a meteor.

He turns and hurries out of the classroom, leaving me to stare after him, wondering what in God's name I've done.

SAM

You're getting it at last. The force that pulled me through two interminable years at community college, the dream that seethed inside me when I didn't get into Blackwood the first time, the nights I spent poring over sentences, dissecting them like fetal pigs. I spent years with your books, staring at your photo on the back, you in your leather chair, feet curled beneath you, looking sideways at the camera like you were daring me to see you.

And I did.

I've always seen you. Even before I met you.

The first time I stumbled on a copy of *Pay Dirt*, something woke up inside me. I was seventeen, clearing out this trailer for Tony. Motherfucker Number Twenty-two. Vivienne tore through men in a way that was both casual and desperate, like a bulimic gorging on junk food she'll soon puke up. Since she'd picked me up from my grandparents' apartment in New Mexico, we'd lived in a dozen different towns, each of them more forgettable than the last. She had a job on occasion, at a casino or a mini-mart, once at a truck-stop diner. She sought out the scummiest lowlife in a ten-mile radius and shacked up with him. I had a pocket notebook where I kept a catalog of the men in her life, a list I labeled "Motherfuckers." It pleased me to use the word in such a literal way.

Tony was a real piece of work. He liked to find houses or trailers that had gone unoccupied long enough to ensure a little privacy. He'd go in and ransack the place, steal anything worth stealing, even if it was just the copper wiring. He tore it from the walls, leaving behind deep, angry gouges like stab wounds. Tony wasn't my favorite Motherfucker, but he was okay. He had a little style, which is more than I can say for most of the dickwads on that list. His clothes were always pressed—he had a kind of phobia about wrinkles. He'd give me thirty bucks to help him gut a place. I found grim satisfaction in the mindless violence of the work, using a sledgehammer to pound Sheetrock to dust, ripping the wiring out like tearing the veins from a living creature.

That's where I found your first book, in a trailer outside New Orleans. The place reeked of mold. The walls were peeling, and there were rats nesting in the tiny bathroom. A fetid perfume of sour meat and fungus wafted from the bedroom. I wanted nothing more than to destroy the place, swing Tony's sledgehammer and bring it down. But Motherfucker Number Twenty-two was looking for something this time—a stash of heroin rumored to exist in a Folgers can.

As we rummaged through the owner's sad belongings, I spotted *Pay Dirt*. It was lying amid a tangle of winter clothes and eight-track tapes.

Your face stared up at me from the back of the book jacket.

Plucking it from the wreckage, my fingers started to tingle. I took my bandanna from my pocket and wiped the dust from your soulful face. Will you think I'm being dramatic if I say it was love at first sight? I turned to the first page. Your words ripped through me like arrows.

I'm still high on your praise when I strut into the Happiness Club. Whoever names college bars should be shot—the Happiness Club?

Really?—but I find a booth toward the back and order a Jameson on the rocks anyway. This place is new, which is good because I don't want any memories right now. I want to sit here in this dingy new dive, sip my whiskey, and think about us.

On my phone, I google your agent. It seems ridiculous I haven't done this before. Maxine Katz looks the way Cher might look if she hadn't gone crazy with the face-lifts. Deep lines around her mouth, a little jowly, with a wild mane of gray and black hair that shoots in every direction. Very witchy. Arty with a twist of the mystic. I like her.

This is where it starts, Kate. Tomorrow, you and I will drink coffee and eat crème brûlée with this woman. You will have inside jokes with her, references that predate my existence, and I will be the outsider, the acolyte, the upstart gazing wide-eyed into the Wonderland you call The Business. I will listen and laugh in all the right places. My fingers will graze yours once by accident as we both reach for the cream. I don't take cream, I drink my coffee black, but I will reach for the silver pitcher so I can feel the electricity of your skin against mine.

Maxine will tell great stories about growing up in New York, and it won't seem pretentious when she mentions her famous clients, living and dead. You and I will glance at each other in a private, knowing way. Your eyes will say, *Isn't she great? Don't you just love her?* And mine will say, *Yes, yes, yes.*

Soon we will share the same agent. You will read and re-read my novel, which will be brilliant, frightening, profound. You'll help make it even better, with your red pen and your ruthless insights. Sometimes you'll suffer a pang of jealousy because my sentences will carve out places in your mind you didn't know existed. My work will make you feel things you didn't know you could feel. In those moments, you'll pout, or lash out with a nasty comment, and I'll know you're not trying to be unkind; you're just jealous. That's okay. It's natural.

Flash forward to the documentary about us. An Ira Glass–alike sits with me in our Meatpacking District loft, studying me from behind horn-rimmed glasses.

"But wasn't it difficult?" He tries to balance curiosity and tact. "I mean, come on. Two prize-winning, bestselling authors, one in his twenties, the other in her forties, both of you possessive, competitive. How did you make it work?"

I will stare at him with wisdom beyond my years. "We have our demons. Always. Sure. Did I sometimes feel like bludgeoning her and dumping her in the Hudson?" I'll chuckle. "Of course. But it's that spark, that hunger, that makes us who we are. Together and apart. It's that savagery that binds us."

"You want anything?" A flat voice jerks me out of my reverie. A redhead wearing jeans and a T-shirt bearing the idiotic name of the bar stares at me, a tray of Coors balanced on one palm.

I'm so deep into my vision of us it takes me a second to understand her question. "Sure." I swig the last of my whiskey and hand her the empty glass. "Jameson on the rocks."

"You bet, honey."

That's when I see her. Vivienne. Entering in that stealthy way of hers. Like a thief. Like a junkie. She is both, of course. Her ravaged face races across the room at top speed, and all at once she's sitting across from me. One eye is puffy and the skin on her nose is peeling, as if from a bad sunburn. It's got nothing to do with a lack of sunscreen. Whatever's causing her skin to flake like that, I'm positive it's not anything as wholesome as a sunburn.

"Vivienne." The whiskey's taken the edge off; her name comes out sounding hoarse and empty. If I hadn't downed my drink too fast on an empty stomach, her face would look even uglier, even more deserving of my contempt. As it is, she's more comical than sinister, her head swiveling from side to side like that of a cartoon robber searching for cops.

"I hate it when you call me that."

"It's your name." I am calm. My breathing stays even. I count to five for each inhale, five for each exhale. She cannot touch me. I am in your world now, your narrative, and she belongs in a darker story.

Her brown eyes fill with tears. I notice she's tried doing something with her hair—dyed it black, from the looks of it. Either she didn't get it all or it's grown out, because the gray of her real hair shows at the roots. The effect is skunk-like.

I try not to remember what she looked like ten years ago. She had jet-black hair that moved around her shoulders like liquid smoke. Her Cherokee cheekbones were sharp as knives back then. Now her face has gone sallow, pitted. The proud, warrior features of her girlhood have eroded beneath bloat and decay.

Before she can say what I know she's about to, I speak again. "How'd you find me?"

"I've got ways." Her expression turns hard. Determined. "I need that money you owe me."

I bark out a laugh. It comes out too loud, too angry, and a couple people at nearby tables turn to look. I inhale even slower this time, counting to seven.

"I don't owe you shit."

"Come on, Waya."

"My name is not Waya, it's Sam," I hiss.

She rolls her eyes. This, more than anything, makes me want to pick up a chair and beat her until she's a pulpy mess, witnesses be damned. She sees this but doesn't back down.

"You're my son." It sounds like an accusation. "I think I know what your real name is."

Waya is Cherokee for "wolf." I left that shit behind me a long time ago.

I pick up a saltshaker and study it. This ghoul cannot get to me. She is from my past, and soon I will bury everything that happened Before You and I Became One. I've lived twenty-two years before our story begins, and I'll live twenty-two years after. By then you'll be sixty and I'll be forty-four. It'll be a good year for us to get blind drunk and put matching bullets through our brains. Because who wants to live past sixty? I'll check out a little early because I won't want to breathe a single breath without you.

Vivienne knows nothing of this. The closest she ever came to love was a needle.

I try not to remember the mother I saw in glimpses. Tender. Devoted. Trying to make things better. She'd drag us to a new nowhere town full of promises, brimming with hope. This time, she'd get a good job, and we'd rent a nice house near a big, leafy park. I'd go to school, and she'd help me with my homework. Once, in Barstow, she managed to hold down a restaurant job for almost three months. I was proud of her. I went to school and even joined the drama club. She started talking about selling her art, these crazy, beaded dream catchers she made. I helped her build a website. Everything looked good, like we'd finally settle down and be normal.

I came home from school one day, found her passed out with a needle in her arm. Everything we had was stolen. We moved to Las Vegas the next day.

I study her face now, searching for signs of that woman. The one who made dream catchers. The one who tried.

She's gone. Buried under track marks and regret.

"Can't you help me out? Just this once?"

"I'm a starving college student." I shake my head. "I don't have anything to give you."

"You're drinking in a college bar. Bet this place don't come cheap."

Only Vivienne would walk into this dive and imply it's the Ritz.

"You stalk me, you accost me, and now you expect me to reward your behavior with charity?" Loathing drips from my voice, but I don't care. I want her to know just how much I hurt every time she shows up like this, feral and hunting for funds.

"Sweetie, I know I've done wrong." She bites her lip like a child. "I know I should of done better."

"Should *have* done better."

She looks baffled. "That's what I said."

"Just out of curiosity, how much will it take for you to walk out of here right now and not show your face for at least six months?"

"A mother wants to know her son's—"

"How much?" Again, I'm too loud, and more people pivot toward me, frowning.

She won't meet my eye. "Fifty bucks."

"Fine." I reach for my wallet, yank out two twenties and a ten. I'll have to eat Top Ramen for a month, walk everywhere, but fuck it. If this gets her out of my way while I seal the deal with you, it's worth it.

Besides, it won't be long until I'm cooking you an elaborate meal in the deluxe kitchen you never cook in, the one that's waiting just for me.

Vivienne shoots me one last tearful look. The money's in her pocket, though. Her urge to score, as always, outweighs any latent maternal instincts. She jumps up, pecks me on the cheek, and shoots out the door.

I pick up my cocktail napkin and wipe at the place where her lips fell.

KATE

The waiter takes our plates away. Maxine's barely touched her salad. Women of her sort rarely eat, I've noticed. They're too busy flitting from city to city, calculating, arranging. Her eyes briefly follow the tall, dark waiter's retreating backside with a predator's casual fascination. She clasps her hands under her chin, plants her elbows on the table, and leans toward me; her wild corkscrew curls wobble in the air like antennae.

"So, about this boy. Quick, fill me in before he gets here."

I smile. "His work's extraordinary."

"Of what ilk?"

"Hunter S. Thompson meets Harper Lee?" It comes out like a question.

She refreshes her lipstick, throws me an impatient look. Maxine hates hesitation. "You sound like you're not sure."

"Here's the thing . . . I may have rushed the introduction."

"He's not that good?"

"He's extraordinary," I repeat. Since when do I use that word so much? Sometimes I hate how I act around Maxine, like a needy little girl. She's made some money off me. Sold two of my novels to big houses, several translations. I'm no bestseller, we're both painfully aware of that. I do have talent, though. If she didn't think so, she never would have signed me. So why do I feel so insecure around her, always pulling myself back from the edge? She's got the connections, the insider's eye, but shouldn't the impulse and ability to tell a good story trump that? Somehow, I can never escape the sense that I'm her student, fishing around for the right answer, trying to find the magic words that will earn me a gold star.

"So? What's the problem?" She examines her lipstick in a silver compact, blots it with a napkin. She looks older than when I saw her last. Her hands are veiny and gnarled, in spite of the flawless manicure.

I choose my words carefully. "He needs time to develop. He's going to be a wonderful writer, but right now his voice is so young, so new."

"Young is good. As long as he delivers."

"You know what I mean. Commercial pressure at this point could be . . . problematic."

She rolls her eyes. "You academics!"

I can't help bristling slightly. I'm not an "academic." I'm a writer who happens to teach. There's a difference.

She laughs, her cherry red mouth opening wide and letting out an enormous sound that startles me.

"Don't look so offended, Kate. I'm just saying, don't overthink it. You professors spend so much time in your ivory tower talking about great literature, you start believing every book is the Sistine Chapel."

"I see your point, but—"

She cuts me off. "I hate to sound crass, but I don't make a living off the Sistine Chapel. Good, solid commercial fiction. That's my bread and butter. If this kid can swing that, fantastic. If not, c'est la vie, you know?"

"I'm not sure he's ready," I say.

Maxine's eyes bounce up and land on something behind me.

When I hear his voice, so close and quiet, the little hairs on the back of my neck stand up.

SAM

You say it without conviction. I'm standing behind you, wearing my only good pair of black pants and a shirt I ironed five times this morning.

"I'm ready." I don't raise my voice.

But you should know, Kate, this is a betrayal. I've never been so pissed off in all my life. How could you undermine me? Right here, in front of the very person we need on our side? Are you really this fickle? Yesterday, I'm your rising star; now, I'm "not ready"? Is that jealousy rearing its ugly head already? What the ever-loving fuck, Kate?

I've known—always known—you would have to wrestle with your demons. I've been prepared for those moments in our relationship when your envy of my rise to stardom will interfere with our tranquility. You will get drunk some nights. You'll throw things. That's how artists live. My books will sell more copies than yours; my awards will pile up. After the Coen Brothers' adaptation, my fame will be off the charts. You'll start seeing your name in the press as an afterthought. *Sam Grist pictured here with his lover, Kate Youngblood, also an author.*

And let's face it, Kate, there will be other challenges. You'll feel old sometimes. The girls who throw themselves at me will be half your age, and you'll wonder why I stay with you when every model in Manhattan yearns for me.

But your worries will be misguided. Because you are more beautiful, more enchanting, than any woman, no matter what her age. That's forever. Though my books will sell better, they will not *be* better, because you write with such style and grace, such razor-sharp clarity, that the masses cannot and will not see your genius.

Just like that, my anger vanishes. I get it. You're protective of me.

The agent, Maxine, stands. Her bony hand shoots out to grasp mine. "You must be Sam."

"Sam I am."

She laughs. It's an eruption of sound. Everyone in the restaurant turns to look. She shakes her crazy Cher hair out of her eyes. I can see by the way she holds her rail-thin body, the hyper-erect posture, the tilt of her hips, this woman likes to be fucked. She's old enough to be my mother, but it's easy enough to see the sensual greed in her sparkling eyes. I doubt it's aimed at me in particular. It's just the way she moves, out of habit or sheer, stubborn will. Twenty years ago I bet she had a different man in her bed every week. Maybe every night. She's fierce and obstinate and fuckable. I like this woman. She's the agent for me.

I wasn't sure until now.

We sit down, and the waiter hurries over. He looks at me with a polite, neutral expression, but I can tell he's trying to figure out how I fit in here. I flash him a cryptic grin—*wouldn't you like to know?*—and order coffee, black.

"Kate tells me you're an 'extraordinary' writer." She doesn't do that thing with her fingers, the dreaded air quotes, but it's not hard to hear the quotation marks in her voice.

"Though she obviously thinks I'm too green." I shoot you a scolding look, though I've already forgiven you. "Green can be good though, right? Salinger was twenty-two when he published his first story in *The New Yorker*."

"Green's my favorite color." Maxine's smile is slow and sly. "Why don't you tell me a little about your book?"

I nod. Under the linen tablecloth, my fingers grasp each other and start to go numb. Of course I knew she'd ask. I rehearsed my response to this exact question all morning. I even cut class to practice in front of the mirror about five thousand times. It's all about brevity, confidence, and intrigue.

I will myself to exude bulletproof charisma. I like Maxine, but it's easy to see she has no time for weakness. Even you, with your ethereal beauty and your crisp academic diction, you try her patience. That's not your fault. Maxine is a New York native, through and through. Manhattan traffic was her lullaby; her first martini was at the Algonquin. Just look at her. She's not an easy woman to please.

I clear my throat and launch into my memorized pitch.

When I'm done, she smiles. We study one another for a long moment. I refuse to plunk disclaimers into the pit of silence that follows. We're two panthers circling, sizing each other up.

"Uplifting." She's sarcastic, but I can see the greed lighting her eyes. Sure, it's all in the execution, but she knows and I know it's a fucking great premise. High-concept. Marketable. Money in the bank.

I risk a sideways glance at you. Your face is a closed flower, unreadable.

"Have you got a title?" Maxine asks.

"*Red-Blooded American Male.*" I know the trick with titles. Say it like you mean it. I sell every syllable. Then I lean back in my chair, spent. The waiter brings our coffee. Maxine never moves her eyes from mine.

Again with the smile, the panther sizing up her dinner. "How very bold."

"That's me." I return the smile, not as a clueless gazelle about to be clawed into ribbons, but a bigger, stronger panther ready to take over the whole fucking jungle.

When Maxine turns her attention to loading her coffee with artificial sweetener, our eyes meet at last. You're proud of me, I can tell. I want to dive under the table and go down on you right now, make you pant and scream. Instead, I bump one knee against yours and fix you with a humble, grateful look.

From: Kate Youngblood
To: Zoe Tait
Subject: Wedding Apocalypse!

The invitation to Pablo's wedding came today. Felt like a bomb going off in my belly. I don't know what it's like to have someone kicking the shit out of you down there, but this sure as hell seemed like a close approximation, especially if the baby was actually an explosive device.

I can't believe I'm still upset by this. The asshole left me nine months ago.

I'm not going. Of course not. Right? Or would getting dressed up in something drop dead gorgeous and eating their overpriced canapés bring the necessary closure?

I just want to move on.

Why won't my heart get the fucking memo?

xo
Kate

From: Zoe Tait
To: Kate Youngblood
Subject: RE: Wedding Apocalypse!

Darling, you are totally allowed to be thrown by this. Who wouldn't be? The dick left you for a fat, pubescent hairdresser. It's disgusting. You have every right to be repulsed by this insensitive reminder. Who does he think he is?!! Of course you shouldn't go!!! That's not a step in the right direction.

I'm a human beach ball. I have no way to look directly at my toes. I have acid reflux so bad, my mouth continually tastes like vomit.

Just so you know.

Kisses,
Zoe

Your ex-husband is getting married. I stare at my phone, re-reading your email. You're depressed about it. He's marrying someone half your age with a quarter of your education.

I google *Kate Youngblood Pablo,* and a picture comes up. This must be his Facebook page. Pablo Morrera. I study you with your suave ex, both of you radiant on some exotic beach. Behind you, the turquoise sea sparkles. Did he filter it? Must have; the colors are unreal. You're pale and glorious in an old-fashioned, emerald green bikini. He's dark, broad-shouldered, naked from the waist, with the biggest, whitest teeth I've ever seen.

I zoom in on his swim trunks, which are clingy and wet. He could never satisfy you, Kate. You deserve so much more.

Though I know he had to leave you so we could be together, I'm still pissed at him for making you feel unwanted. His stupid-ity amazes me. The thought of some guy chucking you for a brain-less nobody makes me want to find him and teach him a lesson.

I feel my phone vibrate and open another email. It's Zoe again with a P.S.

From: Zoe Tait
To: Kate Youngblood
Subject: RE: Wedding Apocalypse!

P.S. I have someone I want to fix you up with. Don't groan and hide your eyes, Kate. You need, and I emphasize *need,* to get on with life. Pablo was a mere tangent. Okay, so you spent ten formative years of your life with him, but that doesn't mean you can't move on. You can, and you will. That's an order.

From: Kate Youngblood
To: Zoe Tait
Subject: RE: Wedding Apocalypse!

Who is he?

From: Zoe Tait
To: Kate Youngblood
Subject: RE: Wedding Apocalypse!

His name's Raul Torres. He owns a string of high-end Italian restaurants across the Midwest. Just moved here, owns that place with the cannoli to die for. He's handsome, he's got hair, and he's comfortable. Plus he's unspeakably hot. No, really, if I didn't have Bo, I'd totally fuck this guy. Something about his aura is very sexual.

I'm not trying to pimp him out (well, a little), but honestly, if you don't snatch this one up, you're missing out.

From: Kate Youngblood
To: Zoe Tait
Subject: RE: Wedding Apocalypse!

Okay.

From: Zoe Tait
To: Kate Youngblood
Subject: RE: Wedding Apocalypse!

Okay?

From: Kate Youngblood
To: Zoe Tait
Subject: RE: Wedding Apocalypse!

You said it yourself. It's time to move on.

From: Zoe Tait
To: Kate Youngblood
Subject: RE: Wedding Apocalypse!

Hallelujah! You are not going to regret this, Kate!!! I'll tell this story at your wedding!!!

I can't help feeling a little peeved at your easy enthusiasm for Raul Torres. Sounds like a hero from a telenovela. What is it with you and these Latin Lovers? Is that your type? Do I seem pale and thin next to your hulking Mayan warriors?

I saw the beach photo, though. I know Pablo's got nothing on me.

Zoe, I both hate and adore. She wants you to move on. Good. Perfect. But she's trying to facilitate that by setting you up with a dickhead restaurant owner? Not even the chef, for god's sake, the owner! Does she honestly think you'll be satisfied making polite conversation with someone so far beneath you? At least chefs have some passion, some visceral connection to the senses. They're artists, poets. But the owner? Not going to cut it. You deserve and require a genius. Geniuses do not open a string of high-end Italian restaurants known for their cannoli.

Does. Not. Happen.

KATE

I'm so not in the mood for this.

Zoe scrolls through her phone, looking for a photo of the man she wants me to fuck.

It's hard not to read into this.

We're in her living room. Zoe's such an artist. Her home is a visual mashup of Frida Kahlo and Dr. Seuss. The red sofa we're sitting on is all curves, like a beautiful velvet comma. Colored Moroccan lanterns dangle from every corner. It's bohemian, but not random. Stylish, but never fussy.

"Okay, okay, here he is." She holds the phone up to my face. A photo of a dark-eyed, broad-shouldered man swims before my eyes.

I take the phone from her. "Wow."

"Right?!" She sounds excited. There's something else in her voice, though, too. Wistfulness?

"He looks like a model."

"I know!" She snatches her phone back and stares long and hard at him. "He's delicious."

"What's the catch?"

"No catch." Zoe studies her phone, then thrusts it back at me. "Totally your type, yeah?"

I'm not sure how to break it to Zoe that just because I was married to a guy from Argentina, that doesn't make Latino men my "type." But she seems so happy. I haven't seen her this excited about anything in ages. I want to please her.

"Hard to tell from a photo." I'm trying not to get her hopes up, but I also don't want to dash them cruelly. I need to meet this guy without big expectations. Those inevitably lead to disappointment. It's like seeing a movie after it's already won an Oscar. Nothing can live up to the hype.

"He owns, like, seven restaurants. Totally loaded. Has a house in Santa Fe, another in Tahoe. The man's a genius when it comes to money. He came from nothing, worked his way up."

"Classic 'rags to riches,' huh?"

She frowns. "Don't be bitchy."

"I'm not," I protest. "What did I say?"

"I can tell you've decided not to like him."

"That's not fair. All I said was 'rags to riches.'"

"What do you have to lose if you fall for him?"

I consider. "My pride. My self-esteem. My heart."

"Small price to pay." She grins. "Did you see his abs?"

"Like a corrugated roof."

"Mmm . . ." She stares off in dreamy contemplation.

"You sure you don't want this one yourself?" I'm sorry, but it has to be asked.

Faint worry lines appear between her brows. "Of course not."

"I'm just saying . . ."

"Just because I see his appeal doesn't mean I want him for my-self." She gives me a prim look. "I'm married, with a bun in the oven."

"True. Kind of skanky to be cattin' around in that state."

"Completely."

"You really think I'll like him?"

"You're going to love him." She pockets her phone and gives a theatrical shiver. "There's a party this Saturday. He should be there. You could come with Bo and me. Low stakes, not a date."

"What sort of party?"

"At Abby's."

I give her a blank look.

"Abby Lacy? Owns the bakery? Bo's boss?" She shrugs and moves on. "You met her once, I'm pretty sure. She started the mommy group I'm in."

"You're in a mommy group?" I try not to sound bitchy.

"Yep." She doesn't elaborate.

This is new. Her eyes move around the room, not meeting mine. Normally, Zoe and I avoid women's groups with dogged determination. This one chick in grad school tried to recruit us for her book group. She got so aggressive about it, Zoe and I showed up drunk and offered everyone fake tabs of acid. We were not invited again.

Finally, I break the silence. "Isn't that a little premature?"

She arches one eyebrow at me.

"Like, shouldn't you be mommies first?"

"I know, right?" She laughs. "That's what I said. We mostly just get together and bitch about acid reflux."

Still my Zoe, then. The tension in my shoulders relaxes a millimeter.

"Anyway, it's a harvest party." She sips her tea.

"Oh. Okay." The term conjures vague images of pumpkins and pilgrims. Corn husks? Jesus, I don't know. "What does that mean, exactly?"

"I think her husband brews his own beer—hard cider, that kind of thing."

"So, like, Oktoberfest?"

"Something like that." She's noncommittal. "The point is, Abs Lincoln will be there."

I almost choke on my tea. "Jesus, you're too much."

She smiles, pleased with herself. "Also, it's the same day as Pablo's wedding. You'll need a distraction. Raul Torres can be very diverting. I'll email you the invite."

I make a face. "Don't be disappointed if sparks don't fly."

"They'll fly," she says, all confidence. "Believe me, they'll fly."

SAM

The huge brass sign at the entrance off the highway features ornate Edwardian script. *Aspen Heights.* I love how subdivisions take their names from whatever they bulldozed.

A quarter mile of look-alike McMansions later, I'm standing on the porch of Abby and Greg Lacy, trying not to gag. It's a faux Colonial. Its hulk fills most of the lot, putting their ornate dormer windows spitting distance from their neighbors'. The garage could double as an airplane hangar. No fewer than six Doric columns flank the front door. The yard is littered with festive symbols of autumn. It looks like somebody—Abby, I'm guessing—inhaled everything in Walmart's seasonal aisle and puked it all over the fake grass.

I ring the doorbell, wiping my hands on my charcoal wool pants. It took me three hours at the Goodwill to put together this ensemble. Wool pants, button-down cream shirt, classic tweed vest. Nobody fears a guy in a tweed vest.

I pray I don't reek of mothballs and somebody else's sweat.

"Hello!" The woman who swings open the door has one of those "Can I Speak to Your Manager?" haircuts—longish in the front, short in the back, with chunky, gold highlights so unsubtle she's striped. Her belly is the size of a watermelon. She cups it with one hand like she's guarding it. I can tell by the high, bright circles of color staining her cheeks she's been hitting the merlot.

"Abby!" Before she can stop me, I pull her into a hug.

I'm an expert hugger. I used to avoid them—full-body contact made me queasy as a kid, especially with strangers—but once I figured out their function, I put my mind to perfecting the art. Turns out I'm something of a hugging savant. The pregnant version takes some slight adjustments, but the basic principles remain the same. Women love it when you clasp them full-on, no sideways, bullshit half-hugs or squeamish pelvis-tilting. They long to be contained.

"Thanks so much for inviting me," I say into her hair.

"Welcome!" By the time she disentangles herself from the hug, it's too late to ask my name. Her smile's so muscular the tendons pop in her neck. "Glad you could make it."

"Wouldn't miss it." I gesture at the yarn-haired pilgrims, light-up pumpkins, and glittery cornucopias. "Amazing job on the décor."

She guffaws. "Any excuse to get crafty!"

A gnome pops out of the doorway, one hand swathed in a pumpkin-colored oven mitt. He's at least fifteen years older than Abby and half as attractive. I know from Facebook (thank you, Mark Zuckerberg!) this is Gary Lacy, the man Abby chose to produce children with. His asset portfolio must be his prime attraction. God knows Abby's bakery, Stud Muffin, isn't bankrolling this Ode to Conspicuous Consumption. Gary was a chemist for Procter & Gamble. Now he's a day trader and a remote-control-airplane enthusiast.

I feel profound sadness for their progeny.

"Who do we have here?" Gary doesn't share his wife's allergy to direct questions. No problem. I've done my homework.

I shove a hand at him. "Great to see you. Gary, right?"

"Yes." He pulls the oven mitt off and shakes. His smile says, *Welcome,* but his eyes say, *Who the fuck are you?*

"Sorry! I'm Sam." When this produces deer-in-the-headlight

stares from both of them, I push it one step further. "I went to school with Troy—at St. Andrews? Just moved to town. I'm a freshman at Blackwood. Troy forwarded me your Evite, said I should stop by."

Relief floods their faces.

Abby nods like she knew this all along. "So sweet of you to come."

When Gary traded in Wife Number One for Abby, Wife Number Two, he paid off Wife Number One with expensive boarding-school educations for the first set of kids, Troy and Amber. Wife Number One has a bitter, confessional blog that narrates all this in mind-numbing detail, interspersed with recipes that feature various kinds of canned soup. Troy's two years younger than me, but I figure that won't matter.

"We met at Parents' Day." I aim an injured expression at Abby. "Sorry, thought you'd remember."

"Of course we do!" Abby gushes, putting a hand on my back and guiding me through the threshold.

Just like that, I'm in.

KATE

I'm standing in a sea of people, adrift. My hand grips my glass of wine like a lifeline. The tides of conversation push and ebb around me, swirls of laughter rising toward the vaulted ceiling. A child's cry pierces the other sounds. She keens, her pink face contorting into ghoulish shapes. The mother swings her onto one hip, drops a kiss on the crenellated forehead absently, resuming her conversation without a pause.

I want to throttle Zoe. Why didn't she tell me this was a family thing? Okay, maybe I should grow up, but I can't ignore the sting of betrayal. She used to share my dread of child-friendly social engagements. Back in grad school, we got together with a bunch of girls from the English department one night, intent on getting smashed and neglecting our stacks of student papers for at least twenty-four hours. This one chick, Joni, had a kid. We were all at Zoe's apartment pre-gaming to vintage Madonna and putting on too much makeup when Joni shows up with her six-year-old, no advance warning, just—bam!—there they are. Nothing spells buzzkill like a boundaries-free six-year-old playing with your lip gloss when all you want is a shot of tequila or seven and an all-night dance party.

Joni didn't even give us a chance to flee. We ended up watching Disney and eating mountains of Doritos. Zoe and I bitched for days about our aborted mission.

Now Zoe's done the same thing to me—trapped me in a family-friendly nightmare I never signed up for. I recall her evasive gaze when I asked for details about this party. That scheming little con.

Now I get it. She knew I'd never come.

We arrived half an hour ago. Abs Lincoln, aka Raul Torres, is a no-show, at least so far. I'm wearing a short dress over gray tights. Back home in front of my mirror, I thought I looked just tarted up enough—not too slutty, not too dour. Now that I'm here, I realize my folly. Everyone here walked straight out of an Eddie Bauer catalog, so wholesome and pragmatic they look ready to run a 5K or build a school for needy children.

Zoe's been swallowed by a cult of pregnant women. They shrieked her name and circled her the second she walked through the door. She made valiant attempts to include me in the conversation, introducing me as Her Friend the Mystery Writer. Her efforts were wasted. One of them asked how old my kids are. She blinked in confusion when I said I don't have any. That's when I made a beeline for the bar.

I almost spill my wine when I spot him. He's watching me hard from across the room. In the churning sea of festive sweaters and active gear, he's still as stone. An island. A beacon.

What the hell is he doing here? Why didn't I wear higher heels and redder lipstick?

He crosses the room with his hands shoved into the pockets of his wool slacks. He's wearing a ridiculous tweed vest that looks anachronistic and dapper on him. I feel an alarming blush creeping up my arms toward my neck. The closer he gets, the more my skin burns with it. He takes his time, sidestepping a knot of soccer moms and their preteen daughters, all of them casting furtive looks. He weaves past fresh-faced caterers bearing trays of canapés. They notice him, too. Not once does he shift his gaze from my face.

"You look amazing." He says it in such a matter-of-fact way I'm not sure I heard him correctly.

"What are you doing here?" I avoid the compliment. The vast, ghastly house throbs with noise. Children run past, sticky hands outstretched like supplicants'.

His mouth twists into a knowing grin. "You saying I don't fit in?"

I snort with laughter.

A woman near us bellows, "Gwen, honey! Don't eat those! You know you can't have gluten!"

A swarm of sugared-up kids races past, nearly knocking me over.

He leans close, his lips grazing my ear. "You don't fit in either. I mean that in the best possible way."

I've never stood this close to him. His proximity is terrifying, but also familiar, like I've dreamed this moment many times. He smells good—walnut, lemons, cypress.

"I was hoping I'd see you here." His voice holds a note of urgency I've never heard before. Usually he's laconic, his opinions tossed out lazily, like someone throwing a Frisbee on a Sunday afternoon.

The chaotic noise levels—children screaming, classical music blaring, women laughing—forces us to tilt our heads very close. "Why did you think I might be?" I get a whiff of his shampoo; maybe that's the lemon.

"I just hoped." He shrugs. "It's a pretty small town."

"I don't know anyone here." I frown as a girl no older than two dithers toward me on chubby legs. She stretches her hands out, fat fingers opening and closing like sea anemones. A part of me recoils. Another part of me wants to sweep her into my arms and sniff her head, drink in that deep, sweet baby smell.

"You want to go outside?" He puts one hand on my waist, blocks my vision of the toddler.

My throat tightens with gratitude. "Yes, please."

Outside, the cool air is sweet and pure enough to drink. We pause on the back patio, under the brilliant twilight. He looks around before leading me to a small alcove at the far end of the deck with a stone bench and a fountain. The latticework enclosure drips with jasmine; the flowers give off a heady perfume, their dying gasp before winter. We huddle in the refuge, surveying the yard. Ghastly decorations crowd together like refugees. There are scarecrows with puzzled button eyes, fake pumpkins, light-up cornucopias. For a moment, I'm struck dumb by the spectacular ugliness of it.

We burst into giggles at the same time.

"It's so hideous!" His eyes shine with glee.

"What the fuck?" I hear footsteps, press a finger to my lips until they pass. "So damn tacky."

"I'm not a snob, but holy Jesus," he whispers.

"I know, right?"

When we've stopped giggling enough to breathe normally, he gives me a quizzical look. "So, you really don't know anyone here? You crashing the party?"

"My friend Zoe tricked me into coming."

"Right, Zoe. The pregnant one?"

I'm surprised he remembers. I nod. "She knows I hate this kind of thing."

'What kind of thing is that, exactly?"

I shrug, self-conscious. "Suburban neighborhood parties where everyone's kids play soccer together."

"Got it." His expression shifts, a silvery shadow moving beneath the surface.

"Don't get me wrong, families are great." I can hear a shard of defensiveness in my voice. "Community is—you know . . ." I trail off.

He laughs.

"What?"

"Breeders, man. Who needs 'em?"

I'm not sure what it says about me when my twenty-two-year-old student understands me better than the full-fledged adults inside that house, including my best friend. Or I do know what it says, and I just don't want to admit it. I'm an adolescent girl two years shy of forty, still so selfish and stubbornly ambitious that babies fill me with dread rather than longing.

He studies me with keen interest. "You don't think these people have something you want, do you?"

I'm thrown by this. Most of my students see everyone over thirty as background characters, their voices little more than white noise. Sam really wants to know what's bothering me; either that or he's doing a damn fine job faking it.

"I don't want what they have." I tilt my head. "But I'm supposed to, so I guess that makes me odd."

"Damn right, you're odd." He quirks an eyebrow. "Thank fucking God."

I hide my smile in my wineglass. He digs in his pocket and produces a pack of American Spirits. I watch him tap out two, hand one to me.

"How did you guess my secret weakness?" I take it from him with a bashful glance.

One shoulder barely lifts in a noncommittal shrug. He fishes a Zippo from the other pocket, flips it open. His thumb jerks, and the flame flares to life.

I put the cigarette between my lips and lean closer. He holds the lighter out, one hand cupped around my cigarette to guard against the jasmine-scented breeze.

The first lungful feels like heaven. "Do I strike you as a smoker?"

"Not at all." He lights his own and takes a long, slow drag.

"What then?"

"It's your hands." His eyes meet mine. Once again I'm struck by how blue they are. They have an eerie intensity. He doesn't just train his eyes in your direction, like most people. His gaze hooks into you like a cat's claws, slowly contracting, razor-sharp.

I glance down. "That can't be good, having smoker hands."

"It's the way they move." There's a soft note of rebuke in his voice. "Your fingers are very expressive. They're never still. You're always touching something—your hair, your clothing, your skin."

"Oh." It comes out startled, prim. I have to laugh at myself.

"Restless hands will never say no to a smoke."

I hold his gaze. Time seems to lose its meaning. The moment becomes elastic, a strand of taffy, stretching gossamer-thin.

With a start, I feel a small starburst of pain. I look down, my body already jerking away before I have time to register what's happened. My cigarette, left unattended, has dropped a clump of hot ash onto my thigh. I brush it away, embarrassed.

When I look at him again, his gaze lingers on the tiny black fleck. He looks at me, his face full of amusement. "Don't set your tights on fire."

"No." My voice sounds thick. "That wouldn't do."

He takes another drag off his cigarette and lets the smoke out slowly. It curls toward the brilliant blue sky, sinuous and ghostly in the cold.

I look at my hands. Nobody has ever offered observations about them—not that I can remember.

It takes me a moment to realize why I feel so light-headed. I can't remember the last time someone paid this much attention to me. His awareness of every detail—my face, my hair, my hands—rips through me, concentrated and intoxicating as heroin. He brings back wispy memories of boys from my youth, the concentration they put into earning that first kiss. The world's started depriving me, year by year, of this particular pleasure: the hungry way boys watch from across classrooms, parties, nightclubs. I'd forgotten how delicious it feels, the way your skin prickles under the heat of their gaze. God knows it wasn't always fun; the wrong stare can feel like a greasy hand probing, groping. But basking in the light of Sam's eyes feels like coming home.

"Oh, God, *there* you are!" Zoe appears suddenly, her dark head poking around the alcove. "I've been looking for—" She stops short when she sees Sam.

The cigarette between my fingers is little more than a smoldering butt. I let it fall to the deck, grind it under my kitten heel. Zoe looks at it with raised eyebrows, then at me, then at Sam.

"Hey! How's it going?" My voice sounds too perky.

"Just thought I'd let you know, that friend I mentioned? He's here." She casts a sideways glance at Sam. "But I hate to interrupt."

"Sam Grist." Sam transfers his cigarette to his left hand and offers Zoe his right. He's unfazed, his expression bland as he squints through a cloud of smoke. "We met a few weeks ago. I suggested the denim overalls."

"I remember. Kate's student." Her gaze slides to me. Anyone else would see only polite interest there, but I read the question like it's stamped on her forehead: *What the fuck are you doing?*

"Thanks for the cigarette." I put a hand on Sam's arm. I hope it looks teacherly, but who do I think I'm fooling? It's Zoe. "I should probably mingle."

"You do that." He flicks the cherry from his cigarette, tosses it into the bushes and takes a step away from me, then another. Without the heat of him near me, the air feels like icy mist against my skin.

"See you later, Sam," Zoe calls to his back.

He doesn't turn around.

Zoe gives me a long look. She produces a tin of breath mints from her coat pocket. I take one obediently. Neither of us says anything.

Finally, I break the silence. "What? Just say it."

"Nothing!" Her face expresses it all too clearly, though. The quirk of her lips. The tilted eyebrows. *I hope you know what you're doing.*

SAM

You're listening to the guy across from you, but you're bored. It's clear from the way you cup your chin in your hand. It's not an engaged chin-cupping. It's more a *Christ, when can we pay the bill and flee?* chin-cupping.

Raul. I can only imagine the tales of restaurant-ownership he's regaling you with. You're trying to be polite. You're attempting to maintain a receptive, interested grin, however thin. I see the way you're sucking down your wine, though. I see the tired strain at the corner of your eyes, the nervous way you tap your finger against the edge of your glass, as if counting the seconds.

This guy is king-douche-bag-level self-absorbed. I've clocked his mouth moving through my binoculars for a solid seven minutes.

You deserve so much more, Kate. I abhor Zoe for thinking you'd settle for this guy, even for a night. I mean, yes, he has thick black hair that sweeps up from his forehead in a stylish, offhand way. His suit looks expensive, and he wears it well. I haven't gotten a good look at his feet, but I'm guessing pricy Italian loafers are involved. Still, this is all textbook Lover Boy stuff. You can't take him seriously.

I shift my position, trying to ease the pins and needles in my feet. Surveillance isn't comfortable. Thank god you two sat at the window. I'm crouched in a damp alley again, this time between a bookstore and a coffee shop. The Dumpster I'm leaning against smells of coffee grounds and rotting meat.

The man is still talking. God, how do women do it? I realized long ago the key to winning any girl's heart is listening to her. Most guys suck at it. That's even more appalling when you think about how sex-starved most men are, and how they could have three times as much pussy if they'd just shut their mouths. Best-kept secret.

In my boredom, watching you watch him, my mind drifts back to Eva. She's the one who taught me to listen. It was valuable training to get at fifteen. I remember her small, pale face, her wild hair. The feral look in her eyes.

Vivienne and I were passing through Wyoming that winter, crashing one night at a KOA near Jackson Hole. At the campground, Vivienne started flirting with a hairy Rasta dude who called himself Phoenix; we moved into his yurt on this big hippie commune the next day. It's not like we were headed anywhere, anyway. We were drifting, like we always did, wandering from town to town like dandelion fluff caught in a light breeze.

That's where I met Eva. Her parents were hippie freaks, back-to-the-land types. They grew all their own food; she was raised in a tepee. I'm not making this up. The commune was a hundred-acre parcel they called The Mercury Ranch. You'd have to see the place to understand Eva's peculiar brand of unselfconscious innocence. The people there lived as they liked, without regard for social customs or taboos. They wore clothes or didn't, depending on the weather and their leanings. The land pulsed with anarchist moodiness—the sense that anything could happen at any time, and probably would. In the sleepy, quiet peace there lurked the constant possibility of danger. Mercurial.

Eva and I met on a frozen lake just down the hill from the yurts and tepees my first day there. Her hair was crazy curly. She always had her hands in it, trying to direct it out of her face, but it was hopeless—untamable. It was snowing. We were the only two people for miles, so it would have been weird not even saying hi. After we exchanged names, we wandered the frozen lake together. Right away, I started talking too much. I was nervous under her watchful gaze. Her wide-set eyes, so devoid of pretense, unleashed in me an unexpected panic.

"You shouldn't talk unless you have something to say," she said, interrupting my lengthy monologue.

I stared at her. She was five feet tall. Her long, dark curls trailed behind her in the breeze.

"That's rude," I said. "Take it back."

"I'm trying to help you." She stared at me, her brown eyes devoid of malice. Her voice sounded husky for someone so young. The few girls I had encountered before then all seemed giggly and frivolous. Eva was the opposite. She had no time for fakery.

"I don't need help."

She shrugged. We walked in silence for a few minutes.

"You're in Phoenix's yurt, right?" she asked after a while.

I barked out a cynical laugh. "Yeah. Total dump. Smells like bong and ass."

We walked in silence again. We stopped to look at a tricycle that lay beneath the frozen surface of the lake. We stared at it for a long moment. There was something sad and also beautiful about it.

As we walked on, I started telling her about the Donner Party. I'd just read a book called *Desperate Passage*. I explained how they got stuck in the snow and ate each other to survive. I made sure to include lots of gruesome details.

"People think they have to know stuff." She stopped walking and turned to me. "That's not important. All anyone wants in this world is to be seen, to be heard."

I'm not kidding you. She actually talked like that. Her childhood in the wilderness among hippies had preserved her childlike absence of bullshit.

"Are you always this blunt?" I asked her.

She nodded. There was nothing but blank honesty in her eyes.

"That's cool." I started walking again. "This place is pretty fucking weird."

She grinned. "Welcome to paradise."

"What do you do around here?"

Her gaze swept over the snow-dusted landscape. "We do this."

It was hard not to notice her perfect, tiny body—the breasts that swelled beneath her thick wool sweater. Her slender, twig-like legs sprouted from black combat boots and striped, mismatched socks. Most of all, though, I noticed her eyes, so big and full of wonder. I started to think The Mercury Ranch looked promising.

Everything I know about girls I learned from Eva. She was my first love. My first tragedy.

The sight of you laughing brings me back to the present. Raul must have said something funny. I long to brain him with his dinner plate. I train my binoculars more tightly on his mouth, but I'm not good at reading lips.

Whatever he's saying, you're entertained.

Surely, you're not considering sleeping with him. He's not your equal, Kate. I don't care how expensive his suits are, how black his hair. One look tells me he's a douche.

But maybe you're the sort of woman who sleeps with douches.

I've known such women. Vivienne, for example, routinely chooses the stupidest man she can find. It's baffling. In spite of her drug-addled decrepitude, Vivienne has a decent mind. Sometimes she read to me from the books of her favorite author, Roald Dahl. Those are my first memories of words—my mother reading about a giant peach. How I loved those nights, curled up in her lap, listening to her smoky voice make each word come alive. She painted beautiful pictures in my brain. I assumed for years that she created the stories. She only looked at the pages to remind herself of what she'd written. Back then, Vivienne was omnipotent; she had the power of a deity.

I feared and loved her with equal savagery.

You and Raul continue with your meal. He makes you laugh once more, but overall you look glazed. I'm good at all the things he's bad at, Kate. When I have you in a candlelit restaurant, a glass of wine before you, I'll ask you all the right questions. I'll find your tender spot, that thing you want to talk about but never do. I'll be patient. When your voice cracks, and you reveal the secret you've never told anyone, I'll nod encouragement. I won't say anything, won't try to fix it. I'll just bear witness to your pain.

You don't need the Rauls of this world, Kate. You've got me.

KATE

I've got to hand it to Zoe; Raul is sexy. His voice is pure velvet. His subtle accent turns every sentence into a spicy mélange of rolling r's and quirky phrasing. He tells stories of his childhood in Oaxaca, and his words form a steady lullaby, a seductive lilt to every syllable. There's something soulful about his eyes. When he looks at me, *You fascinate me* and *I want to fuck you* chase one another across his face. His thick, luxuriant, blue-black hair is artfully mussed. His smile radiates boyish, dimpled charm.

"I love the steaks here." He stabs a hunk of bloody meat with his fork. Everything about him is decisive, confident. "They cook them just right. Of course, I like all kinds of food—Asian fusion, tapas, dim sum—but sometimes an old-fashioned filet mignon just—how do you say? Hits my spot."

"Hits the spot," I correct him, smiling. "But I know what you mean."

He dominates the conversation. I don't mind. I'm tired. I spent all day trying to lead discussions, struggling to say things worth listening to. He makes it easy to sip my wine and drink him in. He talks about his restaurants like treasured children. What I know about the hospitality industry wouldn't fill a postcard, but it doesn't matter. He makes it sound fascinating. All the intrigues, the liaisons, the backstabbing. I sip my Bordeaux and listen.

"Forgive me," he says after a while. "I talk too much. You must tell me about you."

I shake my head. "Not much to tell."

"You are a *profesora*, yes?"

"Yes." I nod. "I teach English at Blackwood."

He considers me. "You are very good at it, I imagine."

"Not especially." I'm not being modest. My student evals are consistently gruesome.

"I know you are." His dark eyes go serious, penetrating. "I can see that."

"How can you see that?" I don't bother to hide my incredulity. A strand of hair falls into my eyes, and I tuck it behind my ear.

"Because you are beautiful to look at, and beautiful to listen to. If they do not appreciate that, they are fools."

"That's nice of you."

"What I mean is, they can see how intelligent you are. In spite of your beauty." He grins.

I wait to feel something. A flutter in the pit of my stomach. My heart perking up like a dog catching a scent. Heat between my thighs. Nothing.

"Zoe tells me you are a *novelista*." His eyebrows slant upward.

I sip my wine. "Yeah, that's my other job."

"What sort of stories do you write?"

A chasm opens between us, the one I always face when trying to explain my work. How do I express my war with words, my torrid affair with verbiage, my love-hate relationship with my characters? How do I squeeze any of that into the one-minute summary expected? It's daunting, impossible.

"I write crime fiction." I pull out my tired, trite old line. "I kill people for a living and get away with it."

He laughs loudly. For a second, I do feel something—the tiniest flame in my belly. It settles into powdery ash almost immediately, though, a brushfire quickly extinguished.

"It is quite sexy." He leans forward, his dark eyes scanning my face. "I love a woman with danger."

I bite my lip and will myself to flirt. Nothing comes to me. No witty rejoinder. I can't even bat my eyelashes. I wish to God I could.

He goes on, undeterred, "Have you ever had a book turned into a movie?"

"No. Not yet."

"I must confess I consume more movies than books."

"You and most of America." As soon as it's out of my mouth, I know it sounds judgmental. I backpedal. "Not that there's anything wrong with that. I love movies."

"Would you like to see your story on the big screen?" He shows no sign of being offended.

"Sure, I guess."

"You guess?"

"Well, I've known writers who had their work adapted for film—"

"Who?" He looks intrigued.

I name a friend from grad school who had his short story optioned by an indie filmmaker. Predictably, Raul's face remains blank.

"Anyway, he had a terrible experience," I say. "The director wanted to change just about everything. In the end, he felt no connection with the project."

He shakes his head. "That must be very difficult. Once my restaurant in Athens was featured in a TV show."

"How interesting!" My voice sounds overly bright, even to my own ears. "What was that like?"

This prompts a long diatribe on the joys and sorrows of his brush with fame. He's not a bad storyteller—funny, self-deprecating. In spite of my obsession with dramatic structure, I can't even convey a simple anecdote on a date. All the words that spring easily from my fingertips get stuck in my throat. It's easier to let him pontificate, to half-listen while leaving my other half burrowed in my own private thoughts.

Keeping a fascinated expression frozen on my face, I pick over my day, feeling more and more depressed. Workshop today was miserable. I tried to facilitate an honest discussion about the rape scene Kayla submitted, but the conversation quickly devolved into emotionally loaded barbs and college-girl pseudo-feminist slogans ("Rape isn't about sex, it's about power."). I like to think the open forum is my strong suit—my ability to draw people out and guide the conversation—but today proved even that power's failing me. I can't write. I can't teach. What can I do?

"Kate?" Raul shifts slightly in his seat to catch my eye. "I fear I am boring you."

"No. Not at all." I put one hand on his. "I just had a shitty day."

His smile's a little sad. "I talk too much."

"Seriously, you're fine." I let go of his hand and swig the rest of my wine. I put the glass down with a definitive thunk. "You're wonderful."

"Zoe said you were moody."

"She knows me well."

He lowers his voice. "Moody is okay with me."

"You sure about that?"

Are we flirting? Is that what we're doing? There's nothing wrong with him. He's warm, attentive, charismatic. My nerves should be wide awake by now, alive with anticipation. Instead, my body remains stubbornly inert. Nothing's stirring. I can't understand it.

My mind keeps slipping back to Sam; there's a strong river current pulling me toward him. Today he wore a black hoodie to class, kept the hood on throughout workshop. Sometimes he descends into dark, solitary funks. On those days, no amount of bait will draw him out. Today, I kept waiting for him to join the discussion. He always has something to say about violence and how it's handled in fiction. No luck. His eyes were opaque, unreadable.

"You are thinking about your 'shitty day'?" I can tell by the gentle reprimand in his question I must have drifted again.

"Occupational hazard." I offer a wan smile. "Hard not to take your work home."

"Your writing or your teaching?"

"Teaching. If I obsessed over my writing as much as I do my students, I'd probably have another book worth reading."

He pours more wine into my glass. "Perhaps I can help you forget about your shitty day."

As we slip out the door of the restaurant, the cool night greets us with a gentle slap. It's October thirteenth, and though the temperatures have been unseasonably warm, tonight I can feel the cold coming. Blackwood's winter is harsher than any place I've ever lived—frigid, snowy, blistering. I love it. Growing up in California, I never imagined how dramatically the Midwestern seasons turn, one cartwheeling into the next, transforming the landscape completely. Now, the smell of coming snow and the perfume of rotting leaves stirs a swirl of delight in me. I look up at the blanket of stars, the crescent moon, and beam idiotically.

"You have a beautiful smile," Raul says, eyes glued to my profile.

"Thank you."

"Are you parked on this block?"

"Oh, I walked." I pull my coat tighter as a cold wind lifts my hair, tickling my neck.

He looks surprised. "You live very close, then?"

"About a mile from here."

His eyebrows shoot toward his hairline. "What a healthy girl you are." His smile is teasing, but there's also a thread of insinuation there, a gleam in his eye that implies he's picturing me naked. Possibly sweaty. I don't mind. It's been so long since anybody looked at me like that. Okay, yes, there's Sam, who watches me with an intensity that makes Raul's gaze look cursory, but I've promised myself I won't think about him tonight.

"That's me!" I shove my hands into my coat pockets. It comes off way more *aw, shucks* than I intended.

"May I drive you home?"

"Sure."

We've reached an enormous black Range Rover by now. He clicks the key fob, and the car lights up inside. With a flourish, he opens the passenger's side. As I climb in, a wave of smells washes over me. Aftershave. A whiff of ancient cigar smoke. Leather. I wait for my body to respond to this manly potpourri. Nothing. I'm flatlining here. My sexual dashboard is awash in darkness.

I keep flashing back to Sam. His ethereal blue eyes. His eerie way of watching me—so intense, like I'm the first woman he's ever seen.

"You are okay?" Raul asks, settling into the driver's seat.

"Sure. Fine."

"In my experience, when a woman says she is fine, she is not so fine." He fastens his seatbelt, then turns his searching gaze on me.

"Yeah, well, I am." I can't keep the irritation from my voice.

He starts the car, and warm air blasts from the heaters. I ask myself what's going on here. He's lighting up all the old pleasure centers: exotic accent, boyish dimples, strong jaw. Yet somehow, watching his profile, I can't muster a single erotic impulse. It's like the part of me that responded to these signals is now dead and buried.

Did Pablo kill my receptors? Am I doomed to walk the earth a numb, dead-eyed spinster?

Pablo and I argued—God, we argued. That man could turn a paper bag into a knock-down, drag-out fight. His temper would flare at the slightest provocation, his muscles coiling, the tendons popping in his neck. He never hit me, but he always looked ready to give it a try. He did punch things—walls, doors, the dash of my car. There's still a gentle indent in the glove compartment of my Saab, a fist-sized reminder of the good times.

What a bastard.

But the sex was phenomenal.

"I've kept you out too late. Can you forgive me?" Raul's accent caresses each syllable. He ducks his head slightly.

"No problem." I manage a thin smile.

As we're driving away, a quick, darting movement catches my eye. A blur of dark blue in the alley across the street. Someone in a hoodie? I crane my neck, peering into the shadows. For half a second, I'm certain there's someone looking back at me. Eyes on mine, staring from the darkness. Then nothing.

Raul parks in front of my house. He doesn't turn off the car; the heaters go on shooting hot air at my face. At first it felt wonderful. Now it's claustrophobic. The cold night air beckons. I shift in my heated leather seat, trying to avoid the furnace-like blast.

"Your house is very charming," he says.

"Oh. Thanks." I look at my darkened windows, the glow of my porch light illuminating a couple of pumpkins. Zoe gave them to me. She's obsessed with holiday decorations. Unlike her new friend Abby, she pulls them off with admirable élan. I doubt I'll get around to carving the pumpkins, sadly. I always mean to and never do.

"It is a nice neighborhood, yes?" Raul takes in the rows of orderly houses and matching tidy lawns. "Very quiet."

"It is."

Nervousness makes my pulse quicken. Should I ask him inside for a drink? The fluttery indecision in my belly feels foreign. The whole situation is like a bad dream, the kind where I find myself trapped back in high school. It feels so wrong to be dating at this age. Repulsive, really, like trying to squeeze myself into the low-slung jeans I wore as a teenager.

I try to picture Raul curled up next to me on the couch in front of the fireplace, highballs in our hands, ice tinkling. Will he smell like his car when he leans in for a kiss? Sam smelled like lemon aftershave and leather, the ghost of old cigar smoke? The fantasy does nothing for me. I long to pull on my stretched-out yoga pants and my ancient sweatshirt, the one that's so old it's disintegrating. The last thing I want to do is play seductress, pouring drinks and enduring soulful gazes.

What's wrong with you? He's hot and age-appropriate. He's got a full head of hair, a steady income, and his stomach doesn't dwarf the rest of him. You really think you can do better?

Glancing at the side mirror, a car parked down the street catches my eye. It's a battered silver Honda. It looks a little rust-eaten for this side of town. The dark interior reveals nothing. Something about it tugs at me, though I can't say why. I tell myself I'm just being neurotic, looking for distractions.

"I had a great time." Raul's voice is low and intimate. He runs a finger over his brow, glances at me sideways. "You are an intriguing woman."

I smile. I've always wanted to be intriguing. I think "distracted" would be more accurate, but I don't correct him.

"You say little, but I can tell your mind is very active." His eyebrows arch suggestively.

"Sorry to be so laconic. I'm not trying to be difficult."

"Difficult is okay! It's good." He laughs. "Where's the fun in easy?"

I reach out and subtly turn the vents so the hot air stops blasting my face. He notices and turns the heat down a couple notches. I know this is the moment when I should ask him in. I just can't bring myself to do it.

"Well, thanks for dinner. It was lovely." I grope for the door handle, can't find it, have to turn away from him to locate the cool metal at last. I'm inept, adolescent, clumsy. The thought of enduring night after night of this tedious social ritual makes me so tired I want to fling myself under a bus.

"May I walk you to the door?"

"Oh, that's okay," I mumble. "I'm fine."

"Don't be a stranger," he says as I open the door.

"Yeah. Okay."

"Perhaps next time we can go to a movie. Something exciting, where the characters kill each other and get away with it."

I'm out on the sidewalk now. The cold air fills my lungs. It tastes fresh, searing. "Sure. That sounds right up my alley."

While Raul lingers in his SUV, I hurry toward my front door, hands stuffed into my coat pockets for warmth. I turn and wave when I get my key into the lock. The Range Rover eases away from the curb slowly, regretfully.

Just before I shut my door, I glance back down the street, looking for the silver Honda. It's gone.

SAM

After dropping you at your place in that tank of his, Raul goes to The Woods. It's a fitting destination for this douche. A college bar at the edge of town with half-price drinks and wet T-shirt contests—just the place for a man with his hair. I'm sure you've heard of it, but I'm willing to bet you've never darkened their doorway.

Tonight, the rickety marquee reads APOCALIPSTICKS LIVE! TWO DOLLAR SHOTS! LADIES HALF PRICE!!! As if all those exclamation points will make up for the '70s brick exterior and the vomit-scented, cracking-vinyl booths.

I pull up in my Honda and park two cars down from Raul. As I pass his Range Rover, I can't help marveling at how much some guys will spend to overcompensate. Nothing screams "tiny dick" like a 340-horsepower engine wrapped in glossy, never-been-dirty black.

He didn't even get a good-night kiss. Thank god. Tonight I know you're making progress. You refused to be seduced by his heated leather seats, the torque of his engine, the boy-band, messed-up hair. You're over that shit. Already I can sense you preparing a place in your heart—a hot, moist place—just for me.

There's a short line at the door. Raul's right in front of me. He stands behind a gaggle of girls all digging through their purses for their IDs. They reek of cloying, sweet perfume and wear so much eye makeup they look like drag queens. I watch as Raul's gaze bounces from one pair of tits to the next.

It catches me off guard when I hear my name singsonged at top volume. "Sam Grist! Oh my god, what are you doing here?"

It's Cleavage. As usual, she's working the push-up bra, putting the girls on display in a tight, pink tank beneath a black leather jacket. Her heels are so stacked she's almost eye-level with me. Her friends check me out. They wear identical supercilious expressions, their mouths tight as puckered assholes. Their gazes sweep over me as if they are a quartet of imperious queens. Fuck them and their Victoria's Secret body glitter. Jesus, like I'd bother to ride them if they paid me.

"What's up, Jess?"

"I didn't even think you went to bars." Her glossy lips spread into a candy-colored smile.

I give her a dismissive look. Just because I prefer my own company over anyone but yours, that doesn't make me a misanthrope. I almost feel sorry for this girl; she infuriates me every time she opens her mouth, and she has no idea.

Raul's staring at me. He's wondering why this hot little chica's salivating over me when he's the one with all the horsepower. I can't help shooting him a sideways glance. *When you've got it, you've got it, buddy.* The stupid motherfucker just had dinner with you, the most glorious creature on the planet, and he wasted every minute of it talking about himself. He deserves so much more loathing than I can spare right now.

The bouncer's got his stamp out, waiting for Cleavage's crew to get on with it already and produce some fake ID. They do. The guy's too tired and cynical to study their pictures for more than a second beneath the glare of his flashlight. He's built like a bar of soap—a nose that's been broken in a couple places, a receding hairline he remedies by buzzing the whole thing military-short. I try to imagine what it must be like standing at this door, watching an endless parade of tarted-up jailbait and drunk frat boys stream past year after year. When he stamps my hand, I try to catch his eye.

"Thanks, man." I want to tell him I'm not the usual brand of asshole he ushers through these doors. That he and I are on the same team—the one that would love to throw a Molotov cocktail through these blacked-out windows and rid the planet of these bubbly clubbers for good.

His dead-eyed stare goes right through me.

Inside, the air is thick with sweet perfume. Why do girls want to smell like fruit and flowers? The last thing I want to fuck is a strawberry. Guess the half-price ladies' night is working, because the place is packed with chicks. Could be the band, too. Apocalipsticks seems to be one of those girl bands modeled after The Bangles or The Go-Go's. The lead singer's tall, with knee socks under her short, pleated skirt. Very Catholic-schoolgirl, though the facial piercings and the tats add a layer of irony to the look. Behind her is an overweight, sour-faced bass player, a lead guitarist who looks like Courtney Love, and a tiny drummer from the Manic Pixie Dream Girl mold. They're in the middle of a Led Zeppelin cover, "The Rain Song." Their sound's a little too sugary, even when they're doing Zeppelin, and the drummer must be snorting Adderall—she keeps rushing it—but they're not bad for Blackwood on a Thursday night.

I watch as Raul orders a pint of beer and sips it, his back against the bar. The fifty bucks I gave Vivienne means I don't have money for overpriced whiskey, so I grab an abandoned glass from one of the counters lining the walls and hold it in my hand, trying to fit in.

As soon as Cleavage has done a round of shots with her girls, she comes bouncing over, bright-eyed and half-naked. She's shed her leather jacket, and now her tanned, gym-toned shoulders reflect the red of the neon Coors sign. She smells of tequila and spearmint.

"Big night on the town, huh?" She grins.

"Not really." I shrug and watch the band. There it is again, the implication that I'm some kind of mouth-breathing psycho who never leaves his mother's basement. "Just felt like having a drink."

She wrinkles her nose at my glass. "What's that?"

I look down and notice, too late, what she's staring at. The half-empty glass I grabbed has a perfect semi-circle of bright red lip-stick on the rim.

Cleavage gets in my face. "Are you wearing makeup?"

"Fuck off." I push her away without thinking. I can't tolerate people invading my space.

She almost topples over backward in her fuck-me stilettos. I grab her arm and pull her upright before she crashes to the floor. The last thing I want is a scene.

"Asshole," she huffs, pushing a strand of hair out of her eyes. "What's your problem? Did I hit a nerve?"

"Sorry. Instinct."

She tilts her head to the side, the caramel hair swinging off her shoulder. Everything about her is smooth and shiny—her hair, her skin, her glossy, pink mouth.

"What's the deal with you, anyway?" she demands.

"The deal?"

She shrugs, impatient. "I can't figure you out."

"Why would you need to?"

"I don't *need* to." She licks her lips. "I want to."

I catch sight of Raul asking a girl to dance. She's a total BAG. Big And Grateful. Easy prey. Perfect for a blow job in the parking lot. Her wide ass swings side to side like a pendulum as she leads him onto the dance floor. He watches it with total concentration.

Jess, who's not stupid even though she tries to be, follows my gaze. "You know that guy?"

"No. You?"

She looks at her phone, shoves it back in her pocket. "Friend of mine went out with him. He comes here a lot."

"Yeah? How often?"

"Dunno. Most the times I've come here he's hanging around."
A look of understanding lights up her face. "Wait, are you gay?"

I fix her with a tired frown. She laughs.

"I'm sorry, you're just mysterious."

"Man of Mystery," I say. "That's me."

I turn my attention back to Raul. He's not worthy of you, Kate.
Not even close. One way or another, I'm going to make sure you
realize that.

KATE

It's the weekend before Halloween, I haven't carved my pumpkins, and Zoe's nagging me to go out with Raul again. He's texted
me three times. He's more eager than I expected, given our limp
chemistry. Probably my standoffish attitude only fuels his enthusiasm. I'm playing hard-to-get without trying. The crazy thing is,
indifference only really works when it's authentic. I've played this
game in the past when I really did care, and it always backfired.
Now that I'm truly uninterested, he can't wait to see me.

It's a mystery, my immunity to his charms. Our first date
wasn't disastrous. So why can't I whip up any desire for a repeat
performance?

I would probably just ignore his texts and let it fade into nothing, but Zoe's fixated on her fantasy that we belong together—no,
not fixated, *obsessed*. She talks about him so much I'm pretty sure
she's harboring her own secret crush.

She stands at her kitchen counter, spooning lemon custard
into tiny pastry shells. She's making lemon tarts. Like everything
Zoe touches, they're tiny works of art. The custard gleams a
rich, glossy yellow, and the pastry shells look light enough to float
away.

"I don't get what's wrong with him," she says, licking filling
from her fingers.

"Nothing's wrong with him," I repeat for what feels like the hundredth time.

"Then why won't you give him a chance?"

I sigh. "There's no spark."

"Hmm . . ." She hands me a spoon coated in custard.

I lick obediently. Lemon-sugar creaminess explodes on my tongue. I cup my hand over my mouth and moan.

She grins wickedly. "I know, right?"

"Unbelievable." I put the whole spoon in my mouth and suck.

"Here's the thing, though." I can tell by her stern tone she's about to unleash a Zoe-ism—some proclamation about my life I definitely don't want to hear. "Maybe all those years with Pablo warped your idea of 'normal.'"

"What's that supposed to mean?" I can't help sounding a little hurt.

"Don't take it the wrong way. You guys fought all the time, though. I know the sex was good, but maybe now you confuse turbulent with sexual."

"Good sex *is* turbulent."

She waves a hand dismissively. "Sure, okay, but you don't have to be at each other's throats to have chemistry. In the long run, that's not sustainable."

"We were together for ten years," I remind her.

"Before he started banging his child-bride."

"Ouch."

She slides the tray into the oven and sits beside me in the breakfast nook, taking my hand. "I'm not trying to diminish what you had—"

"Sure sounds like it."

"I just want you to be *contento*." Zoe and I spent a summer in Madrid together. Ever since, when we want to say we're sorry, we drag out our clumsy Spanish. She waits until I meet her eye. "Give Raul one more chance. If there's still no attraction, I'll never mention him again."

I hold her gaze. "Feels like you're trying to pack me off into domestic bliss."

"Not at all."

"I don't want kids. There's no big rush to find someone."

"I know." She squeezes my fingers. "I get that. Raul has two kids. He doesn't want more."

"What?" I can't believe he never mentioned that.

"Not kids, really. They're in college. Twin girls."

"Weird he never said anything about them."

"Maybe he thought you'd find it repugnant." She releases my hand and strokes her belly. "Do you?"

"No." I think about it a moment. "Not at all. College-age girls are perfect. Out of the house. Old enough to have brains, though judging by some of my students you wouldn't think so. Raul must have had them when he was twelve."

"Pretty young. Twenty?"

"How do you know so much about him?" I ask.

She twirls a strand of her dark hair. "Jealous?"

"Shut up!"

My phone buzzes on the kitchen table. She grabs it and sees the caller: Raul.

"Answer," she orders, thrusting my phone at me.

"I'll call him back."

"Do it now. I know you!" She gives me a pleading look. "One more date, then I'll never ever say 'Raul' again."

"Promise?"

"Promise!"

I answer my phone.

"Would you like a program?" The girl at the door to the Blackwood Center for Performing Arts beams at us like she's auditioning for a toothpaste commercial. Theater majors. They wander into class bursting with big dreams, blinding smiles, and abysmal punctuation. You'd think learning to say lines with the proper pauses embedded would teach you about commas and periods, if nothing else. I already know this one would pile on the exclamation marks, layer them in exuberant, random splashes like cheap perfume over body odor.

"Sure. Thanks." I take a program and step into the auditorium, silently cursing Zoe. Why did she have to insist on this second date? I was ready to let my acquaintance with Raul simmer quietly into nothing. My resolve to end the night as soon as possible throbs in time with my headache.

I chose the opening night of *Oleanna* because I hoped to kill two birds with one stone. Finn Hobbs, the director, happens to be on my tenure committee. I want to believe showing my face here will ease the constipated frown he always wears in my presence, as if the very sight of me interferes with his digestion.

It's an optimistic (read: hopeless) plan, but I can dream.

My irritation ratchets up another notch when I glance over my shoulder and catch Raul ogling the usher. As he takes his program, his eyes cast down a moment, landing on the place where her rhinestone necklace disappears into her blouse. He must sense my disapproving gaze because he pockets the program and meets my eye like a scolded child.

Great. Now I'm the jealous shrew. Not a role I savor.

I had way too much of that during my decade with Pablo.

As I turn back around and search for our seats, fury rises inside me like a geyser. My anger is totally out of proportion to the crime—he just glanced at the girl. Jesus, I haven't even kissed him. Knowing my reaction's irrational only makes it worse. Rage you have a right to can be cleansing. Rage you have no claim to is just cheap and crazy.

Suddenly the black Eileen Fisher dress I chose for its understated elegance seems menopausal. The boots I always wear because they're both comfortable and chic strike me as orthopedic. God, I want to go home. Now. Not in two hours, certainly not in three—this minute.

I feel Raul's hand on my elbow. "Kate. You are okay, yes?"

"Yes, of course." It comes out prim. I'm a wretched liar.

He puts his hand on the small of my back. "You look very beautiful tonight."

"Ah, here we are. Good seats, right?" I fold myself into the velvet chair, avoiding his eye. If he thinks he can objectify girls his daughters' age and then buy me off with a generic compliment, he can go fuck himself. Seriously. I may be a hair's breadth away from forty, but I'm not desperate. Not yet.

He turns his attention to the program. "So, do you like this David Mamet?" He mispronounces the name, rhymes it with ballet.

A mean sliver of satisfaction slices through me. I may not have tits that defy gravity, but I know the iconic American playwrights. Jesus, is this what it's come to? Dredging up feelings of superiority to combat girls with beautiful skin and shiny hair? It's like fighting off feral beasts with a limp dishrag. I remember how much I pitied women like me ten years ago, tenured professors who interviewed me with pinched, sour expressions, like I gave off an offensive odor.

"Mamet's a little on the misogynist side of the spectrum, but I appreciate his humor. You?" I gaze at him expectantly. I'm being mean, asking him to expose his ignorance. So what? Let him feel inadequate, see if he likes it.

He widens his eyes. One thing about Raul, he's got no pretensions. "I do not know his work. I am not accustomed to seeing live theater."

"No? What do you prefer?" I still sound bitchy as fuck. I don't care.

"Music." He says it with such warmth and sincerity, I melt a little around the edges. "I love the live music. Blues, classical, jazz, flamenco, rock—I don't care. Musicians are my gods."

I chuckle, the clenched fist in my belly releasing a little. "Everyone needs a passion."

"Yes." His dark eyes hold mine. "What is yours?"

"Writing. Reading. The magic of books. Though, lately, my passion feels more like a pathology."

"How so?"

I shrug. "My agent's not happy with my latest manuscript. I don't blame her. I hate it, even if I did write it. The muses can be cruel and fickle."

"Do you know Pedro Calderón de la Barca?"

I shake my head.

"He was a great Spanish dramatist and poet. According to him, 'If love is not madness, it is not love.'"

"Nice." I can't help smiling at that.

A face in the crowd catches my eye. It's Sam Grist. He's heading up the aisle straight toward us. Jess, the girl from workshop whose stories always end with someone giving someone else a blow job, trails in his wake. I'm not surprised Sam's asked her out. She flirts with him so boldly in class. At times I feel embarrassed for her, but I suppose that brand of naked aggression is normal these days, not cheap and dirty the way it would have looked when I was in school. Everything about her is so sexual, a walking candy store of glimmering, moist promises. Sam has every right to date her. For some reason, though, I feel another pang of irrational jealousy. God, I'm a mess tonight.

Sam's eyes lock on mine as he takes the seat next to me. Heat spirals through me.

"Professor Youngblood," he says quietly.

"Hi, Sam." My mouth feels dry.

"Ah, is this one of your lucky students?" Raul's voice sounds too loud.

I nod and try for crisp, detached. "Raul, this is Sam. And beside him, that's Jess."

Jess leans forward until she can see around Sam. Her face is so fresh and young, yet she cakes it with makeup. Why do girls do that? Don't they know it's their naked, peachy complexions the rest of us try to imitate when we slather on foundation and blush?

"Nice to meet you," she says with a little wave.

We make small talk for a few minutes, commenting on the size of the audience, plans for the coming weekend. Every word tastes sugary sweet in my mouth—fake and saccharine. All the while, I can feel Sam's eyes on me, his silent intensity like a force of gravity. He says nothing. As soon as possible, I murmur a polite conversation closer and pivot in my seat to focus on my date.

My overwhelming awareness of Sam persists. I can feel his heat caressing my back.

I try very hard to concentrate on Raul. He tells me about re-modeling one of his new restaurants. I nod repeatedly and smile, hearing nothing. My concentration's shot. Sam's low voice behind me pulses like a bass beat. I long to turn around and yank him from his conversation with young, peachy Jess. I want to monopo-lize his attention, make him talk only to me.

Look only at me.

The lights go out, and the red velvet curtains sweep open. When Raul takes my hand, I don't resist.

That's when I start to notice the oddest sensation.

My body's slanted toward Raul. Our knees rest against one an-other. His forearm wraps with mine, and our palms lay pressed together, our fingers interlocked.

Yet it's the tiny spot where my elbow touches Sam's that's on fire.

The right side of my body's cold and lifeless.

The left side of my body's in flames.

God, I'm hopeless. How can I be so perverse? Raul's an age-appropriate, attentive, attractive man. He owns restaurants. He drives a Range Rover. He's got a stock portfolio. Most of all, he's a bona fide adult, and fucking him—even irresponsibly, once, with-out feeling—runs zero risk of getting me fired.

Sam's still a child. From where I sit, I can see one loose tube sock bunching around his ankle. It's heartbreaking. He's way too young and way too impulsive. I have to be out of my mind to want him.

Yet the evidence is there—the heat rushing through my elbow straight to my core. The heightened, prickly readiness. It's almost like fear, when every nerve in your body goes taut, ready to fight or fly. Except this isn't fear. It's longing.

It's sick and wrong, but it's there.

About twenty minutes into the first act, Sam leans over and whispers, "You like Mamet?"

His hot breath in my ear sends shivers up my spine.

"He's an asshole," I murmur. "But also kind of brilliant."

Sam chuckles softly.

Raul looks over sharply, a flicker of annoyance in his eyes. Chastened, I lean toward him again.

My traitorous elbow goes on basking in Sam's heat, though. The electric current is so palpable; it's a wonder there isn't a blue spark glowing in the dark between us.

"I had a nice time tonight." I can hear the question in his voice. His eyes compel me to ask him in.

I can tell by the awkward silence filling the car I've been sitting here wordlessly for too long. For lack of a better way to break it, I blurt, "Do you want to come in?"

He smiles, and I instantly regret the offer. My craving for solitude pulses like a toothache. I just want to be alone with a joint and a drink. I want to think about Sam.

Raul's white teeth gleam in the dark. "I thought you'd never ask."

Inside, I become instantly clumsy. I drop the bottle opener, trip over a pair of shoes I left in the kitchen. It's a bad habit of mine—leaving shoes everywhere. Pablo used to berate me for it.

My hands feel like puppets I can't quite control. I even crack one of the wineglasses, a clean spiderweb break that appears when I tip the bottle too forcefully against its rim. I shove it quickly into the garbage, hoping he didn't notice.

At last, I manage to pour us a couple of glasses of pinot. He sees my hand shaking as I hand him his.

"Do I make you nervous, Kate?" He holds the wine beneath his nose and inhales.

"No. I'm just tired."

"So I make you sleepy?" He takes a step closer.

"Not at all." I raise my glass, taking half a step back. "Salud."

"Salud." He keeps his eyes on my face as he sips his wine.

I sit on a stool at the breakfast bar, not wanting to lead him into the living room. The couch in front of the gas fireplace seems way too intimate. I don't want to send the wrong message. A glass of wine is one thing, but I'm not ready to sleep with this guy. We're adults, right? We don't make out without intending to have sex. Or maybe that's wrong. Maybe I'm putting too much pressure on myself.

He raises his eyebrows a little as I perch on the stool.

"Everything okay?" I ask, trying to sound light and clueless.

"I'm not trying to be forward, but maybe we would be more comfortable . . ." His gaze moves past me to the living room.

"It's a bit of a mess in there." I'm not lying. That's how determined I was not to ask him in—I didn't even tidy up. I still don't know what made me extend the invitation. Politeness? I don't think so. I'm not in the habit of doing things to save face, or to save other people's feelings.

"Very well." He leans against the stool and drinks more wine. "Your house is cozy. I like it very much."

"Thanks. It's old and cranky, but it's coming together."

"You own it?"

"It owns me, more like."

"That is impressive."

I shrug. "It's the only adult thing I've ever done."

"I'm sure that's not true."

"Anyway, what did you think of the play?"

"It was . . ." He searches the air for the right word. His jaw clenches. "Disturbing."

"I know. Mamet's like that."

He shakes his head. "By the end, I really hated her—Oleanna. She was such a *puta loco.*"

"I don't know about 'crazy bitch.'" I force myself not to lecture. "They were both feeding into the dynamic."

"What about you?" His eyes rove my face, resting on my lips.

"I liked it. The actors were decent, the set disappointing, but—"

"That's not what I meant."

I tilt my head sideways. "What?"

"Have you ever faced a situation like the professor in the play?"

I laugh in surprise. "Oh."

"Forgive me. I could not help but notice how your attractive male student looked at you."

"Who, Sam?" It comes out defensive. "I doubt that."

"I assure you. A man knows."

I open my mouth to reply, but nothing comes out.

His hand cups my knee. "And anyway, you didn't answer the question."

"Which was . . . ?"

"Do your students often try to sleep with you?"

"No." I say it too quickly, though.

His skeptical look makes me blush.

"Not openly." I swirl my wine around in my glass. "But sometimes I get the feeling . . ."

"Yes?" His voice catches. He looks at me with avid interest. It occurs to me that the possibility turns him on.

"Crushes happen. It's no big deal."

"Maybe not for you." He leans close and inhales, smelling me. "For them, it must be torture."

I lean back, clear my throat. "I'm, ah, not really—"

"Of course." He backs off reluctantly.

"Sorry, I'm not trying to be confusing—"

"No reason to apologize. Really." He looks around. "Can we play some music?"

"Oh, I—sure." My butterfingers kick back in as I fumble for the Bluetooth speaker.

"Allow me." He takes the speaker from me. Deftly, he pulls his phone from his pocket and frowns as he syncs it with the sound system. Within seconds, bright horns and congas fill the room.

"What's this?"

He studies my expression as I listen. "You like Cuban music?"

"I don't know. Is this Cuban?"

"Yes, a kind of rumba. Do you know?"

I shrug. "I've heard of it."

Gently, he takes my hand and pulls me from my stool. He places one hand firmly between my shoulder blades, holds the other hand palm out, elbow bent, arm raised. I put my right hand in his, unsure of what to do with the other.

"Like this." He takes my left hand and arranges my fingers on his right hip. His grin's the sort you'd offer a skittish child, easy and warm.

He moves to the music, taking me with him. I watch his feet as we step side to side.

"Yes, good. Slow, quick-quick, slow." He starts out simple. When he sees I'm getting it, he gradually adds more flare. "Eyes up!"

I raise my head. He watches me as we continue moving. I look over his shoulder, concentrating. The horns and the percussion build, the singer's voice going rough and emotional. *Mi amor es tan fuerte y loco,* the singer cries.

Raul's body moves with the muscular certainty of someone who has done this all his life. Though I'm not usually much of a dancer, in his arms I feel light, slender, bendable. He twirls me, moving with an expert's ease. I remember this feeling with

Pablo—the reassurance of all that confidence, like stepping into a strong river; all I have to do is surrender. He'll take care of the rest.

Is that what I'm doing here? Looking for a Pablo replacement?

Jesus, no. It took me months to patch up the stab wounds Pablo left in me. His betrayal was so visceral, slicing to the bone. I'm barely stitched together as it is. Whenever I think of his affair with Esmeralda, I want to kill someone. Anyone. The rage threatens to choke me as I push it back down. *Mi amor es tan fuerte y loco.*

"Don't tense up," Raul murmurs into my ear. His breath against my neck is hot. Instead of exciting me, something deep inside recoils. My rage about Pablo mixes with my ambivalence about tonight. I can feel myself becoming stiff and wooden beneath Raul's deft fingers. Why can't I just fuck this guy? What's wrong with me? He's pulling out all the stops, yet I'm warm and pliable as steel.

Like a hunter sensing his prey is about to flee, Raul tightens his grip and pulls me closer, quickening his pace as the music speeds up. I yank myself free.

For a moment we stare at one another. The congas and the claves beat out a furious rhythm. I can see in his face mild astonishment. Irritation, too. He probably doesn't hear no very often. He's smooth, I'll give him that. Tonight I'm just not in the mood for smooth.

I shake my hair back, trying to gather my thoughts. I stalk to the counter and turn off the music.

"I'm sorry." He says into the sudden silence. He doesn't sound sorry, though. "I thought—"

"I've been through a messy divorce," I blurt.

"Yes, Zoe said—"

"You should go," I say, cutting him off.

"What? Why?" He looks bewildered.

"I'm damaged, okay?" I gesture at myself. "Not open, not receptive, not ready."

A tender smile lights up his face. "Of course. I understand completely."

Walking him to the door, I want him gone more than anything I've wanted in a long time. He hesitates in the foyer, and I fight the urge to scream.

"Call me." That empathetic, slightly pitying smile still lingers on his lips.

I want to slap it off. Instead, I nod, swallowing back my anger, knowing I'm being a *puta loco.*

"When you're ready," he adds, touching one finger to my nose.

Finally, mercifully, he's gone. I close the door and lean against it. Closing my eyes, the tears burst out of me in two quick, gasping sobs. Then I take a deep breath and head upstairs.

SAM

Wednesday I'm in the library, rereading *Pay Dirt*. I'm in my favorite carrel on the third floor, just past the Medieval History section. Nobody ever comes up here. The gray light seeping through the birdshit-streaked windows is barely enough to read by, but it's quiet. I'm poring over the scene where your protagonist, Nora Clay, finds the first body. I take a pencil and lightly circle each verb, marveling at your nimble sentences. You eschew adjectives in favor of muscular, active verbs. Soon I lose my clinical distance and surrender to the scene. I am Nora as she takes in the details—the victim's torn, bloody dress, the carnage between her legs. I smell what she smells, feel what she feels.

"Always with your nose in a book."

I'm so deep inside your story, the sound of her voice makes me jump. I look up and see Vivienne. Even though the third floor's a wasteland, I glance around to make sure nobody's watching. Instinct, I guess.

"What the fuck are you doing here?"

She rests her bony arms atop the carrel's particleboard divider. She's careful to keep the track marks turned away from me. Her pupils are tiny pinpricks in the vast brown craters of her eyes. "I miss you, baby boy."

I grind my teeth. "Are you stalking me?"

"Don't need an excuse to see my son!" She raises her voice, but her vocal chords are so singed it comes out raspy.

I imagine wrapping my fingers around her stringy throat and squeezing. There's so little left of her. It would be easy. Her windpipe would collapse like soft sand beneath the pressure of my thumbs. It would be an act of mercy. She stinks of cigarettes and the musty residue of whatever crusty couch she's calling home. When I was a kid, Vivienne always smelled of sage. She used to make these smudge sticks and burn them every new place we went, part of her Cherokee tradition. She liked sweetgrass best, but that was hard to get, so she'd gather white sage from the litter-strewn shoulders of country highways. She said sage drove out bad spirits, and sweetgrass welcomed good ones. That was before she got so fucked up on scag she couldn't tell the difference.

"What do you want now?" I demand.

She stares out the window, glazed confusion dimming her expression. When her gaze meets mine again, she looks lost. In spite of everything, a thin wisp of sympathy curls through me like smoke.

I soften. "Do you need money? Want me to buy you a meal?"

Her chapped lips grimace in confusion. She's got no fucking idea why she's here. I wonder when she last remembered to eat. She's worse than I've ever seen her, and that's saying something; her once strong, slender frame has turned on itself, leaving only a husk, desiccated and leathery as beef jerky. What a nightmare, to be Vivienne.

"Something happened to Eva." Her unfocused gaze drifts out the window again.

That douses my brushfire of sympathy like a bucket of cold water.

"What are you talking about?" I keep my voice calm and even, but inside, a dust devil's spinning in crazy circles.

"Eva." She bites her lip. Tears tremble on her dark lashes, threatening to spill. "You loved her. I know you did."

"Why do you always have to bring her up?"

"What did you do to her?" She widens her eyes, her words loud in the stillness. She's got that weird, vacant quality, like a sleepwalker; her attention keeps wandering to some distant horizon only she can see.

"It was years ago," I snap.

"You stopped being Waya."

"Yeah. So?"

"When you . . ." She trails off, glancing down at the jagged scars on my wrists.

I force myself to breathe. "You're high. You know how confused you get when you're high, Vivienne."

"I'm your mother." It comes out a weak, pathetic bleat. "Doesn't that count for anything? Can't you tell me the truth?"

She's not my mother. Not anymore. I severed that tie seven years ago.

Standing outside your office, I try to slow my pulse. You're in there. I can hear you; I can see the muted light through the glass pane in your door, which you've covered with layers of filmy scarves. I knock three times and try to stop fidgeting.

You crack open the door and peer out. When you see me, your face lights up. This is a stock phrase, something people say, but this time it's literal. Your blue eyes and your pale, creamy skin are as translucent as the scarves behind you; it's as if a spotlight's been switched on inside you. You glow like a pearl. To think I'm the cause of that radiance makes my mouth go dry.

"Sam. I've just finished reading. Your timing's impeccable." You let me in.

I take a seat across from you. I sent you my novel a week ago, the very same day I finished it. Maybe that was rash. Most people would let it sit a week or two, re-read it, revise it a few times. I'm not most people.

The truth is, Kate, I know it's good. I feel it in my bones. Now, seeing your face, I'm certain you know it, too. Something inside me releases. I've been holding my breath all week and didn't even know it.

A delicious confidence flows into my limbs, warm as whiskey. "So, you read it. What did you think?"

Your smile's ten thousand watts of pure sunshine. "To be honest, I was terrified I'd hate it."

"But you didn't."

"No." You sound surprised, but I'm not offended. "I loved it. After I threw you at Maxine, I felt terrible."

"You didn't think I was ready." I lean back in your visitor's chair and cross my ankle over my knee.

"You heard me. No need to throw my words back at me." You try on a stern tone, but you blush like a little girl. It's all I can do not to wrap you in my arms and squeeze until you squeal. "But Sam, it's fabulous. Sure, a little rough around the edges, but the story's all there."

"Thanks. That means a lot."

"I mean the narrator is just so creepy. Chilling, really. And the voice, the dramatic tension, the slow burn to the climax. It's . . ." You hesitate. "Amazing."

I believe you. The energy in your voice—in your hands, which stir the air like a conductor—everything about you says you're sincere. I've gotten compliments on my writing before now, but none of it's ever meant as much as this moment. If I could bottle the liquid joy in your eyes, I'd live on that elixir for the rest of my life.

You push a stack of pages between us. It takes me a moment to realize it's my manuscript.

"I've made a few suggestions," you say.

"Of course."

Your fingers flip through, looking for something. Your nails are unpainted, trimmed and neat. I like that. So tidy, unadorned.

Simple. I'd like to put each of your fingers into my mouth, one by one, taste the shape of them.

"Most of my notes are self-explanatory," you say, not looking up, "but this one in chapter seven, I want to go over."

You slip on your glasses and lean forward, scanning the page. I fucking love you in glasses. They disguise your angelic radiance with an intellectual air. Twin lines of concentration appear between your brows, the faint quotation marks that mean your brain is kicking into gear.

I scoot my chair closer. My entire body's electric. The whiskey-warmth of my relief is eclipsed by your proximity. I lean toward you, breathing in your smell. No perfume or scented lotion for you, Kate. You're not trying to disguise yourself as a strawberry. You're the cold of October. You're musk and radiance, pure animal heat.

Your hair falls forward, revealing the back of your neck. Your skin is milk and moonlight, the curve of your spine graceful as a ballerina's. I lean a few centimeters closer. The subtle knuckles of your vertebrae are so near I can almost taste them, can imagine the salt of your skin. Every part of me is wide-awake, coiled. I'm getting hard just looking at you. Do you sense me breathing you in, or are you really that engrossed in my words? The light pools in your hair, on your skin. I have to touch you. Your white neck beckons. You're a wild animal that must not be startled. I watch your hands turn the pages, your fingers caressing my words.

"You have beautiful hands," I say.

You're surprised. "I never really look at them."

"And yet they do so much."

You breathe out an embarrassed laugh. "Let's see yours."

I watch you.

"What?" Your eyes spark with a challenge. "You can study mine, but I can't study yours?"

I put both hands out in front of me. Slowly, checking my face for signs of protest, you turn them over. When my palms are faceup, my wrists exposed, you take a long moment to drink them in. Jagged pink scars run like lightning along my veins.

"What happened?"

"I had a really bad night."

"You don't have to talk about it."

"I'll tell you anything you want to know." The air grows thicker around us, dense and humid. "Anything."

You run a finger along the raised ridge of one scar. "Did you really want to die?"

I consider this, though it's difficult to concentrate on anything except the texture of your skin against mine. "Honestly? I don't remember."

There's a knock at the door. It's so damn loud in the silence. Even as the intruder's rapping for permission, they're turning the handle and pushing their way in. I want to hurl myself at this person, whoever it is. I want to tear their jugular out with my teeth.

You and I both flinch at the sound, turn toward it. Standing there filling the doorway is a bony woman with frizzy red hair, reading glasses pushed into the haystack atop her head. Her beady green eyes go wide with surprise. She narrows them to slits, honing in on how close we're sitting, the look on my face.

I'm pretty good at controlling my expressions. In the third grade my teacher told Grandma she should have me tested for autism because I showed so little emotion. From that day on I spent hours in front of a mirror, forcing my facial muscles to convey every human sentiment from joy to despair. This red-haired goblin caught me off guard, though; no doubt I look drunk. She sniffs, like she can smell my longing.

"Sorry to interrupt." She says it through a mouth so tight and pinched, in a tone that's not sorry at all. What a fucking bitch. Forget about her jugular—I want to tear her face off.

"Frances!" You swivel your chair all the way around to face her. Your hands fold into your lap like a schoolgirl's. "What's up?"

She eyes you with hostility. "Wanted to make sure you got that email. About the meeting."

"Oh, yes, Tuesday, right?" You are composed, poised. I'm so proud of you. A subtle nectarine flush along your throat is the only sign you're flustered.

The goblin nods. "If you can just accept my invitation through Meeting Maker . . ."

I'd like to shove Meeting Maker up her withered ass.

"No problem." Your smile's so warm. How do you do it? You glance at me. "Sam, have you met Frances Larkin? She's chair of the department, an award-winning poet."

I almost laugh out loud. The thought of this wretched little frizzy-haired orc writing a poem! Instead, I school my features into one of the many expressions I've mastered: starstruck.

"Wait, this is Professor Larkin?"

There's a brief, confused beat, during which nobody seems to know what to say, but then you step in. "None other."

I want to stand and reach to shake her hand, but I'm hard despite the total buzzkill of her intrusion. Still seated, I try to make that work for me, gazing up at her gnarled face like a peasant addressing the empress.

"Your work's amazing. The whole reason I came here was to study under you and Professor Youngblood." I shake my head, like I can't quite get over the honor of being in her presence.

She's mollified. Her red slash of a mouth still turns down at the corners, though, like she's just sucked on a lemon. "That's nice. Kate, I'll see you Tuesday."

The door closes, thank fucking god, and we're alone again.

You don't deserve this shit. You and I belong in the pulse and throb of Manhattan. Our days will be filled with words and our nights with glittering parties, and we'll reinvent what it means to be bohemians in love. You'll never have to accept a Meeting Maker invitation again, and Frances fucking Larkin can suck my dick.

KATE

When Frances is gone, I take a shaky breath.

"You okay?" His eyebrows pull together in concern.

"We should—" I scoot my chair in, tapping the pages of his manuscript "—get back to this novel of yours. Sorry for all the distractions."

"Did I lay it on too thick?"

"What do you mean?" My heart goes on racing. God, what's Frances thinking right now? Was I still touching his hands when she barged in, or had I already jerked away like a kid caught stealing candy?

"About coming here to study with you and her. In my defense, half that statement's true."

I shake my head, willing myself to breathe normally. "You didn't come here because of me."

"I did." His face goes abruptly serious. "I love your work."

"You don't have to do that."

"I'm not doing anything." His expression is even more solemn. "I'm your biggest fan. Don't you know that?"

I don't know how to react. To cover my confusion, I stand, go to my filing cabinet, and pull it open. "I meant to share this short story with you—it's similar to the mood you're evoking in your novel."

Suddenly he's behind me. I can feel him there. The heat of his body presses against me, though he's standing a few inches away. I don't dare turn around. He traces one finger down my spine. An involuntary shiver works through me.

"I need you to understand." He kisses the back of my neck so lightly—the touch of a raindrop, a swath of mist. "I think about you all the time."

"Sam." It comes out hoarse. I clear my throat. "We can't."

He turns me around, his hands on my shoulders; the heat of his fingers presses through my blouse. "We can."

"No. This is not going to—"

He's kissing me. I'm kissing him back. He pins me against the file cabinet. The cold metal presses against my skin and this is bad, so bad, but I can't stop. I have to stop.

After way too long, I find the will to push him away. I give him a helpless, pleading look. "I really can't do this. Not here."

"Where?" He stares at my mouth.

"No, I'm not saying . . ." I want to kiss him again so badly, I ache. "This can't happen. It's too dangerous."

He looks at me with sudden patience. "It will happen. But I can wait."

"Sam—"

Already he's walking out the door, though, leaving me breathless and bewildered.

It's five o'clock on Wednesday, and I'm drunk.

Not just tipsy or buzzed—pretty much wasted.

After my meeting with Sam, I drove straight home and yanked a bottle of Bombay Sapphire from my liquor cabinet. I filled a highball with ice cubes, poured gin until the glass was half full. A splash of tonic, a wedge of lemon, and it was down the hatch.

On the second and third, I didn't bother with the lemon. Or the tonic.

I don't usually drown my sorrows. When I do drink, it's a couple glasses of wine with dinner or cocktails with Zoe. We've definitely gotten drunk together more than we should, usually inadvertently, once or twice with grim determination. Those are special occasions, bona fide disasters: when she found out her dad had cancer, for example, or when I caught Pablo fucking his child whore in our bed. Now, though, with Zoe all pregnant and pious, I'm left to my own devices.

This is not a bona fide disaster. It's not even a full-on train wreck.

All I know is, when Sam walked out of my office, something inside me snapped. I knew right then I needed to get drunk. My long, elaborate to-do list transformed into one word: "drink."

I really did start out with teacherly intentions. Before Frances walked in, I was wading deep into his sentences, trying to formulate the exact way to phrase my critique. Usually, my notes fall on the harsh side. Students need to hear the truth if they're ever going to improve. I get flack for it, especially from the entitled babies who've never heard anything but praise. I don't back down, though.

Sam's different. In spite of his controlled exterior, his ability to project any emotion he deems appropriate in the moment, I sense he has a volatile inner life. It's in his writing. In the dark shadows that sometimes pass over his face, like storm clouds sweeping over sunlit fields. My respect for his work means I'd never lie to him. Still, my fear of discouraging him at this early stage has turned me uncharacteristically cagey.

His novel is good. It's raw and pulsing with angsty power. It's also just a draft, though. He makes an amateur move in chapter seven, one that Maxine will hate—a ham-fisted foreshadowing that pretty much ruins the ending. I sense a stubbornness in him I don't want to engage. Making him see what needs to be changed without pushing him away feels important. Monumental. Like the first and only significant moment in my teaching career.

I sip my fourth drink, leaning against the balcony upstairs. I can see into my unkempt, leaf-strewn yard, over my fence, which is heaving under the burden of passionflower vines. I see into my neighbors' yard. Their son's playing a game with a red fire engine, driving it through their immaculately groomed garden, making a siren sound. Fabricating an emergency.

Is that what I'm doing? Making up a disaster so I'll have a valid excuse to get blind drunk?

I relive the scene in my office. Me dithering over his pages, trying to arrange my words just so. Him there beside me, so close I could hear him breathing, could feel little currents of air on the back of my neck. My desire to guide his revisions with the deft precision of a great teacher was so strong, so overwhelming. Desperate.

But if I'm being totally honest—four drinks in, I lack the ability to delude even myself—I wasn't just thinking about his revisions. I wanted to kiss him even before he kissed me.

And then, after Frances left. God, the energy between us. That kiss. The way everything disappeared around us. Those eyes. Those hands. How long can I resist the magnetic pull he exerts on me? I'm like a swimmer paddling in a panic as a muscular riptide pulls me farther and farther out to sea.

Falling for Sam wouldn't just be tenure-wrecking; it would be career-ending. Okay, that might be overly dramatic. Technically, there are no laws against getting involved with adult students. I just don't see myself getting tenure if my committee suspects I'm dating an undergrad. That's a serious scandal. If they don't give you tenure, they get rid of you. A dismissal after seven years at Blackwood, tepid or even hostile references, the rumors. Not good. I could kiss the possibility of a respectable academic career goodbye.

Ha! Kiss it goodbye. Very nice.

Underneath this realization, there's something even more disturbing, something I can only bear to face good and drunk. If he hadn't walked out of my office when he did, there's no telling how far it would have gone. The heat rolling off him. It was like sitting next to a bonfire. All that impulsive, tormented energy. I felt more alive than I've felt in a decade.

My doorbell rings, making me jump. Who the hell is that?

With the blithe, insouciant confidence only four G & Ts can inspire, I swig the rest of my drink and head for the door.

"Hi." I lean against the doorjamb, feeling light-headed.

Raul stands before me, looking strong and handsome and age-appropriate. His suit is so impeccably tailored, he could be the romantic lead in a Bellini film. "You okay? You seem a little breath-less."

"I was upstairs." I roll sideways against the wood, rub my spine against the frame like a cat. God, I'm so drunk. This is bad. "What are you doing here?"

His smile's easy, open. Not rehearsed, like Sam's expressions. I swear, he's so calculating. Why am I thinking about him right now? It's wrong. Maybe I'm having a midlife crisis. *Must be nice, being worshiped all day by guys like that.* Zoe's words echo in my head. God, I'm so depressingly typical.

"Thought I'd stop by," Raul says. "Is that okay?"

I step away and open the door wider. "Of course. Come in."

As we make our way into my kitchen, I try to decide if I should confess about how drunk I am. Probably he can tell, right? But what kind of loser gets wasted alone before dinner on a Wednesday? I busy myself tidying up, putting dishes in the sink, straightening a tea towel. I pointedly ignore the big bottle of gin, now half empty, sitting on the counter.

"Do you want something to drink? Maybe coffee or tea?"

He tilts his head, glances at the gin, eyes sparkling. "Maybe something stronger?"

"Oh, sure. I didn't know if you had to work or—?"

"I'd love a beer, if you have it."

I pull a Heineken from the fridge, start rummaging for an opener.

"I've got it." His key chain has a bottle opener on it. It's silver, with the distinctive open mouth and lolling tongue of the Rolling Stones. He applies it deftly and flips the discarded top into the garbage.

I look for my glass, remember I left it upstairs. I go to grab a fresh one and almost drop it.

"Seems like you may have already started." He puts his hand on my waist. Only then do I notice I'm swaying.

I cover my face with both hands. "Jesus. I'm so embarrassed."

"No! Why?" His hand is still on my waist, I note distantly.

"I never do this. I had such a wretched day. As soon as I got home, I started on the gin." I throw my head back and groan. "I swear I'm not an alcoholic."

"Of course not." He leans closer, staring down at me with those dark chocolate eyes. "Anyway, you're cute when you're drunk."

"I'm not! My face gets splotchy and sometimes I cry."

He touches my nose gently with one finger. "Your face is beautiful. If you cry, then you cry. So what?"

"You're not afraid of tears?" I can feel myself spinning into his orbit. It's ugly and wrong, but I need to distract myself. *This man will not get you fired,* I remind myself. *This man is yours for the asking.*

"Remember our friend Pedro Calderón de la Barca? 'If love is not madness, it is not love.'" With that, he leans down and kisses me.

He's hesitant at first, his lips trying to find how they fit with mine. Once he's sure I'm kissing him back, though, his mouth becomes firm, muscular. Insistent. He pushes me against the kitchen island. I feel my spine pressing against the edge. Before I know what's happening, he's lifted me up onto the tiled surface, his fingers cupping my ass. He spreads my legs with deft hands, pushing against me. I can feel how hard he is through the fine Italian wool of his suit.

This is a man, I tell myself. *A man who wants you.*

I try to concentrate on that—just that.

Every time I remember Sam's eyes unwrapping me, his fingers offering me a cigarette, I force myself to kiss Raul harder. My lips feel bruised with the effort.

But I don't stop.

SAM

The law favors poor impulse control when it comes to homicide. In Ohio, first-degree murder will get you life. Second-degree murder—you couldn't help yourself, you stupid fuck—draws as little as fifteen.

This might lead you to believe that spur-of-the-moment homicide is somehow preferable to a homicide that's planned. As if spontaneity proves you're a better person.

If you want to get away with it, though, you've got to think it through.

I'm a very good premeditator.

Raul leaves your home with a smug, self-satisfied grin. Through my binoculars, it's easy to see him shooting his cuff links like a gigolo. I watch the bastard, my jaw tense, my stomach churning. He strolls down the sidewalk. The dickwad's singing something in Spanish. God, I hate people who sing on the street. So gay. His limbs are loose as he climbs into his Range Rover. I hate people who drive Range Rovers. From my position in your narrow side yard, I tighten my binoculars on his profile. He's sitting behind the wheel, grinning at the windshield like a man who has just been fucked.

The sick, twisted feeling in my gut gets worse.

It's true what they say about the first one being the hardest.

Eva bothered me for weeks. My insomnia, a looming threat even in the best of times, became intolerable. I went forty-eight-hour stretches without sleeping. Her face haunted me. Her voice—soft, imploring—echoed through my nightmares.

This time, I'm confident I'll enjoy myself.

When he pulls away from the curb, I dash for my Honda and follow him. It takes me a minute to catch up, but soon I'm trailing him through the deepening dusk. He wasn't at your place long. He didn't have any stamina. The guy just had sex with you—without any style, from what I could see—and took off. I take cold satisfaction in knowing you didn't enjoy yourself. These guys, with their big cars and their tailored suits—they don't have any idea what to do with you.

The first time I fuck you, Kate, I promise it will take hours.

The second time we'll take even longer, and you'll wonder how you ever put up with the Rauls and the Pablos of this world.

He rounds a corner toward downtown. I leave one car between us, but it's a Mini Cooper, so it's easy to see his hulking tank lumbering up ahead. Even the way he drives pisses me off. He's texting. His swerving inattention's proof. Either that or he's drunk. Eliminating this guy should earn me a medal. I'm saving the lives of Ohio motorists and their innocent children.

When he pulls up in the parking lot of The Woods, I groan. What a cliché. He samples the finest piece of ass in a thousand-mile radius, then he heads for Slutville, hoping to get another blow job from some BAG. Dude's your classic player. He doesn't deserve to live.

I'm going to love offing this guy; the truth fills my broken heart like a shot of heroin.

I'm doing it for you. I hope you know that.

And it did break my heart. There's no getting around that. Today, in your office, I know you felt it. The dark heat that pushed down on us both, pinning us to the moment. The humid pulse of the air. The thick silence that descended as my hand floated toward your neck. When I kissed your mouth I felt you writhe beneath me, your whole body stiff yet supple. You understand what it is between us. You felt it.

You had to feel it. And yet you fucked this sorry excuse for a man.

I'm disappointed in you. I thought you were making progress. Your judgment showed slow but steady improvement.

This is a big step back.

I'm going to fix it. For you. For us. I'm going to fix everything.

Raul's inside the club now. I think through my plan, double back to the trouble spots, go over it again. I make revisions. You're always saying revision is key.

KATE

I smoke a joint on my balcony. I rarely allow myself to smoke. Right now I feel so drained, I need something to smooth my pulse, steady my breath. I pinch the blunt between two fingers. I'm wearing slippers and a bathrobe, cradling a G & T. I feel like a 1950s housewife coming down from diet pills.

Raul is the first person I've had sex with since Pablo. My breathing isn't ragged because of pleasure. Far from it. It's because of the gasping emptiness inside me.

I've never had sex with anyone I felt so profoundly disconnected from.

Sex with Pablo meant wrestling, biting, struggling for dominance. I loved the muscular dance of our limbs, the sweaty aggression of it. At the center of it, no matter how hard we fought, we loved each other. At least I think we did.

Sex with Raul was more like making a long-distance phone call and getting nothing but static.

My thoughts drift stubbornly back to my office. Sam's body so close. The moment before Frances walked in. The delicious silence that fell around us like snow. The taut suspension between us. How he smelled. Sweat. Lemons. Sap. The scent of fresh new life.

That kiss, so rich and textured. If Raul's kiss was a long-distance call, Sam's kiss was a thick voice whispering in your ear. His hands felt so hot through my blouse, as if he intended to brand me. I take another drag off my joint. His eyes, so blue—dragonfly wings and icicles, delphinium, flames.

The impossibility of my situation looms before me. I'm falling for someone I can't fuck, and I'm fucking someone I can't fall for.

SAM

After Eva, I had terrible dreams for six nights. They were bad, I don't mind admitting. I'm sensitive, as I said. On the seventh night, though, after barely sleeping all week, I got drunk, passed out, and woke up fifteen hours later in the hospital, my wrists sewn with jagged Frankenstein stitches. Since then, I almost never dream of her. She's a faint scar on my psyche, a blemish so razor-thin it's invisible.

She had to go. I knew that.

I suppose she could be called innocent. That was just it, though. Her inability to perceive evil, to fathom the depths of human depravity—that was her crime. Her childlike naïveté is what doomed her.

Raul drinks at The Woods for a couple hours. He makes out with an ugly cow, another BAG, for half an hour in the parking lot. Then she drives off in a pickup truck, and he climbs into his Range Rover. I'm relieved to see him head in the opposite direction. If he followed the BAG home, I'd have to wait around some more, and I'm almost out of patience.

Fog winds around the trees as I follow his taillights out of town. I don't bother keeping a car between us now that it's dark. Even if he does notice me, it's not an issue. Dead men tell no tales.

There's a sickle-shaped moon in my rearview mirror. I roll down the windows and breathe in the damp, grassy air. Out here, driving through fields, the world seems far away. The fresh, cold air, the stars, make me think of Eva. Her gypsy-black eyes. She had a favorite spot at the very top of the tallest hill. She called it Mount Mercury. It was the darkest place on a moonless night. From there, the stars were so vast and clear, so close, it felt like you could reach up and pluck one from the void.

Like the gods wouldn't even notice.

They do notice, though.

Eva was so in love with me. I was in love with her, too. The night she told me she hadn't bled for two months, and what did it mean, and could I help her—that's what changed things.

I believed the baby was mine. That's what she wanted me to think. We'd had sex just once, and it seemed unlikely, but of course it was possible—these things happen. I was deep in that magical state, that first-love bliss, when everything about this person seems made for you, and everything they say is ripe with significance.

Then, one moonless night, I went to her yurt, hoping she'd walk with me to Mount Mercury and look at the stars. We needed to plan our escape. I knew we had to leave. She could have the baby, or she could get rid of it—whichever she wanted. Either way, we needed to ditch the Mercury Ranch and its web of anarchic danger. All these aging hippies, these radical burnouts, were dragging us down. I had a guitar. We could busker at first, work bus stations and make our way out to New York. She had this thing about New York. She'd been there once as a child, and she'd grown up watching an old VHS tape of the movie *Fame*. She believed in New York. She'd get a job teaching dance, start her own dance company. I would write and tend bar, and we'd worm our way into the sweet, fleshy center of our Big Apple–flavored dreams.

That night, I stood on her rotting redwood porch for a long time, listening to the sounds within. Their yurt had canvas walls, so I could hear everything. There was the tinkling bell of her childlike laughter. Then the low, grunting sound of her mom's boyfriend, Troll. His nickname was earned. Hearing him in there with her made me tense up right away. I never trusted the frenetic light in his pale blue eyes, the wiry power in his thick arms, his short, stunted legs. He was only about five feet tall but there were rumors he'd killed a man twice his size using nothing but a shoelace. I believed it.

I listened, my stomach clenching, as Eva's laughter grew more hysterical. Soon I could hear the distinct, rhythmic pounding, the whining bedsprings of sex. I didn't want to believe my ears, but the evidence was undeniable. When I couldn't stand it any longer, I burst through the door. Eva was on all fours atop the bed. She arched her back as Troll thrust into her from behind. I clawed at his shirt, tore him off her. Then I grabbed her by her nightgown, which was damp with sweat, and tried to pull her outside, into the cool night. I had a vague notion we could make our escape right then.

"What are you doing?" She looked mystified.

"He was raping you." It was part answer, part question.

The look she gave me was full of pity. Like I didn't understand anything.

That's when knowledge crashed over me like a terrible wave. This wasn't the first time Troll had done this to her. The baby growing inside her was his, not mine. I'd provided her with a convenient scapegoat, someone to deflect the shame of giving birth to a troll baby.

It's ridiculous that I'm the one who could go to jail, when she's the criminal. She's the one who burrowed into my heart like a ferret, rodent claws scratching away until she found my darkest pit.

That darkness is mine. Nobody can force their way inside it.

Someday I'll share it with you, Kate. Until then, it's off limits.

Raul's black beast lumbers through the fog. My hatred for him seethes through me, a tingly sensation. Pleasure and pain compete inside my body. It's like that moment when you know you're going to come, but you put it off as long as you can, riding the edge. Raul's taillights dance before me, trying to get away. It's obvious I'm following him now; he turns onto a small country highway, and I stick close.

When at last he pulls up to a solitary house at the top of a steep driveway, I stop right behind him and put the Honda in park. This is not a complicated plan. It's simple. Since nobody's here waiting for him and his closest neighbor's at least half a mile away, it's even simpler. No need to lure him anywhere. I couldn't ask for a better spot.

The house is very eighties, with big ski chalet windows and a killer wraparound deck. Bet he's had some sick parties here. This is the kind of place where coke flows without restraint. The A-frame's built into the hill, with a spectacular view of Black-wood Valley. A hot tub steams in one corner of the deck. Not a bad place to crash.

He gets out of his car and regards me. I get out, too, feeling loose-limbed and drunk on adrenaline.

"What's going on here?" His voice sounds tight. The pussy. "Who are you?"

"Name's Sam. This where you live?"

He looks from the house to me, his big forehead creased with confusion. "Yeah. Why?"

I don't hesitate. My fist hits his face with such bone-splintering force, he goes down on the first punch.

For you, Kate. Because he was a lousy fuck.

When Raul opens his eyes, I have him duct-taped to a chair. It's an arty, pretentious chair, the kind nobody ever wants to sit in. It's made of cowhide and its seat is so narrow, I can barely squeeze him into it. Why some people feel compelled to pay extra for qualities that render a thing useless eludes me.

"Do you know who I am?" I'm crouched in front of him, hands on my knees.

His dark eyes regard me with dazed fear. "I saw you at The Woods."

"Very good. Do you have any idea why I'm here?"

He thinks about it. Shakes his head no.

"You just had sex with Kate Youngblood." Saying the words out loud makes me see red. That's a very real thing, by the way—seeing red. Maybe you know what I'm talking about. Maybe you don't. It's like a dark red stain over your vision. A pounding in the ears. It makes you light-headed, makes everything seem like it's happening underwater.

A look of slow realization seeps through the terror in his eyes. "You're her student—from that night at the play. Look, if you want her, she's yours."

I slap him hard across the face. He reels backward. He almost falls over, but the ugly chair rights itself. I pace around his expansive living room. It's like a stage, with the massive windows and the deck stretching out into the darkness. I imagine the audience out there, watching us. They know I'm doing this for you. I'm the good guy.

I lean forward until my face is inches from his. I wait until he opens his eyes. "Kate Youngblood is not yours to give away."

"No! Of course not." He tries to seem contrite. It's not a good look on him. "I am sure whatever I did to offend you, we can discuss. I don't want trouble. Kate is a lovely—"

"Don't fucking say her name." My voice is quiet, almost a whisper.

He flinches. "I'm sorry."

"Here's how it's going to work. I'm going to give you a chance to make me hate you a little less. Give me three reasons you should continue to inhabit the planet."

He squints in confusion.

I sigh. "Why should you live? Don't think about it, just tell me."

"Because I love my daughters very much. They will miss me."

"Okay, fine. Number two?"

"Because they need my support to get through college, to pursue their dreams." He looks so earnest, so eager, like a child trying to find the right answer.

"Other than your daughters, you got nothing? Because, news flash! They'll inherit all this." I sweep my arm around the house. "They can probably manage to squeak through college on the sale of this place alone."

"I am in debt."

I study him. He looks smaller than he did in the club. Like he's shrunken two inches since I taped him to that chair. "Is that your third reason? You're in debt?"

"My girls will inherit only debt." His eyes fill with tears.

I shrug. "Scholarships. If they've got their shit together, they'll figure out a way."

"I don't want to die," he whispers. "Please."

I pull my gun from the waistband of my pants and point it at his head. I'm a Glock man. Everyone has their go-to weapon. "Sorry, Raul. I'm afraid those answers are insufficient."

"Please," he whimpers. "*Madre de dios, por favor.*"

"You can start over. Clean slate."

"Start over?"

"In death. Everything starts over in death."

"*Ay, por favor!*"

I click the safety off, watch his eyes as I take a step closer. The muscles in his face twitch with fear.

This is for you, Kate.

You'd want it to be quick. Your heart is tender and fresh, alive with empathy. I've seen it in your writing, the way you layer your characters with so many shades of humanity. They're never all good or all bad—they're complicated, full of contradictions and flaws. Because of that, you wouldn't want Raul to suffer. You could never see him the way I see him. For you, he's another character with infinite complexities, a cocktail of nobility and depravity.

Lucky for you, I'm a Glock man.

Sure, strangulation is quieter, tidier. You don't even have a weapon to dispose of later if you do it with your bare hands. That takes serious cojones, though. I don't mind admitting I'm too sensitive.

Poison, on the other hand, is a coward's way out. You could slip something in the guy's drink and walk away, never even witness his writhing agony. I'm not a big enough pussy for that. Besides, it could all go wrong, fall into the hands of someone innocent.

Whatever scruples I lack, I do have respect for innocent lives.

No, man, give me a Glock any day of the week. It's powerful, direct, efficient. You can stand far enough away to get some perspective, but you've still got to look at the guy when you do it. It's the perfect balance between accountability and distance. You can't shoot somebody and not know it. Still, it won't fester in your brain, forcing you to relive it for the rest of your life.

Don't worry, Kate. This will be over before you know it.

Raul's a test, plain and simple. He's my chance to prove how much you mean to me—how far I'm willing to go to ensure you're mine. Because you are mine, Kate. Already, the delicate tendons of our souls have started weaving themselves together. We won't be pulled apart.

This man can't live. He's in the way. His very presence in our story illustrates my level of commitment. My love for you is so pure, so focused. I'm willing to kill without hesitation to prove it.

"Say your last words," I say. "Make them good."

"Holy fucking shit!" he cries.

I shoot him in the head.

"Wouldn't be my choice," I say into the silence. "But hey, it's up to you."

KATE

Zoe's got a baby in her arms. She's been in labor for what seems like days. It's morning, and everyone's exhausted-drunk and giddy. Zoe screamed, just like in the movies. Somehow that surprised me. I thought that was pure fiction. I usually fast-forward through those scenes, bored by the endless high-angle shots of a woman grunting and sweating, her loved ones gathered round, shouting encouragement like spectators at a baseball game. Come to find out, it's real. Worse, because there's shit and viscera and all kinds of horrors they edit out.

"Look at him." I lean over and touch his tiny nose. Drew. My godson. He gazes up at me with unfocused eyes, a shriveled old man. He's wearing oversized mittens on his hands to keep him from scratching himself with his tiny nails. "What a perfect little terror you are."

We watch as he raises one eyebrow, exactly the way Zoe does. We both gasp.

"Did you see that?" I whisper.

She nods, laughing. "Oh my God, that's such a trip!"

"Un-fucking-believable."

"You're crying." Zoe blinks at me. Her hair's a tangled rat's nest, but she's gorgeous.

"Of course I am. This shit's emotional. We've been up for twenty-seven hours. I'm a wreck."

"*You're* a wreck?" She scoffs. "My vajayjay's a crime scene."

I touch Drew's face with the tips of my fingers. He's so miniature. So impossibly soft. It's hard to imagine someday this delicate creature will walk around, talk on a cell phone, drive a car. "This little monster clawed his way out of there."

"Do you think his ears look like mine?" she asks with a yawn.

"Definitely. Poor guy."

She shoves me, but weakly. "Where's Bo?"

"Went to make a call, I think." It's been a good half hour since the doctor snipped the umbilical chord. There are nurses bustling around, the same ones who whisked Drew off to get cleaned up, then brought him back in a tidy little blanket. Bo slipped out during all the commotion, scowling at his phone.

Five minutes later, he's standing at the foot of Zoe's bed, his face white.

"What is it, sweetie?" Zoe grips Drew a little tighter. Her words come out hoarse with fear. "Is there something wrong with Drew? Did the doctor say—?"

"No! Nothing like that." He doesn't smile, though. The muscles in his shoulders are bunched tight, his lips pursed as if trying to hold something back.

For a long moment, we wait. Bo walks to the window and stares out, saying nothing.

"Do you want me to leave?" If he says yes I'll never forgive him. I've been with Zoe through this whole thing; he disappeared at every opportunity. Pretty sure I caught him playing "Angry Birds" between contractions.

His gaze falls on me, and something shifts in his expression. "No. You should hear this."

"Hear what?" Zoe's voice is sharp. Drew squirms in her arms.

He hesitates. "I'm not sure I should tell you right now."

"Just say it!" She's threadbare, tense.

He leans against the windowsill, his gaze darting from her face to mine and back again. "It's Raul. He's . . ."

"What?" Zoe prompts again, agitated. "He's what?"

"Dead."

A stunned silence fills the room. The last of the nurses bustles out, leaving an even more profound void. Zoe and I continue staring at Bo, trying to understand. She opens her mouth, closes it again.

Finally, I find my voice. "How do you know Raul?" It's not the first question that occurs to me, obviously, but I'm not sure I'm ready to hear how he died. Zoe never mentioned a connection between Bo and Raul. It seems like a good place to start.

"We were roommates in Chicago." Bo runs a hand over his face. The light from the window hits him directly. I notice his bloodshot eyes, his chalky white complexion. "We shared an apartment for a couple years. Sorry, I'm having a hard time taking this in."

"What happened?" Tears stream down Zoe's face.

Bo looks at his shoes, then locks eyes with me. "He was murdered."

SAM

I've always liked Halloween. The ghouls' holiday. I wander the streets of your neighborhood, enjoying the wintry twilight. The breeze tastes like snow. Decorations adorn staid houses. The big Colonial on the corner of Cherry and Walnut splashed out for blow-up ghosts, plastic tombstones, and hairy spiders. Most of your neighbors have more class, though. They opt for gauzy spiderwebs, dried-leaf wreaths. As I walk, jack-o'-lanterns leer at me from tidy porches.

Vivienne used to say the veil between the living and dead is thinnest on Halloween. Just one example of her pseudo–new age, watered-down Indian mysticism. I wonder about that as I walk, even though I'd rather not. I study the shadows for signs. Nothing's stirring. The dead stay dead.

I hear footsteps behind me and turn to see Vivienne limping in my wake. I shake my head in disgust. She's always had a gift for appearing when I think about her too much, one of the many reasons I try not to think about her at all.

"How's my baby?" She looks marginally better than the last time I saw her. That's not saying much. She was week-old roadkill that day in the library—buzzing with flies and crawling with maggots. Now she's month-old roadkill, just desiccated enough to be tolerable.

I shove my hands deeper into my pockets and walk faster. "I thought you were going to stay away for six months. Wasn't that your promise?"

"I got a friend in town. Staying at his place. I like it here."

It's hard to believe there are still Motherfuckers, given the state of her, but I guess some guys are just that desperate.

"Can't help it if I run into you sometimes." She's limping hard, swallowing the pain.

I slow down. Something about this woman still gets to me. "What happened to your foot?"

"Nothing. Sprained ankle."

"You should go to the clinic. Have it looked at."

"Waya—"

"Sam!" I snap.

She starts to protest, stops herself. "I had a dream about you last night. Not a good one."

"Yeah? Thought your dream catchers were supposed to take care of those."

"I'm serious." She stops walking. "It was just like the one I had when Eva died."

That stops me. I turn to face her. There's a vein throbbing in her forehead, a thin, blue pulse. Her dark eyes hold mine. Vivienne's grandmother was a medicine woman in South Carolina. Her *elisi*. Vivienne claims both she and her *elisi* were "born without their veil broken." As far as I can tell, this means she deludes herself into thinking she's psychic. She doesn't like that word, though. Her particular brand of Native mysticism eschews such labels. It's all bullshit. Right now, though, I don't like the look in her eyes—pure animal fear.

"I'm sorry you had a bad dream," I say through clenched teeth.

She picks at a scab on her hand, her fingers working like pinchers. "What have you done, Waya? Tell me."

"Nothing." I look around, take a step closer. "Stop following me. I'm fine."

"I know you." Her dark eyes harden, the fear solidifying into something else. A threat. "The *anisgina* follow you every-where."

I heard the word enough as a kid to know what it means: ghosts.

I grab her bony arm. Like everything else about her, it feels breakable. "I don't want to see you. Ever again. You under-stand?"

She wrenches free of my grip and hobbles a couple steps back, almost tripping on the curb. "You can't run from them."

"Shut up, Vivienne." I shake my head. "How much?"

She chews her lip, says nothing. God, this woman.

I run a hand through my hair, growling in frustration. "Jesus! How much? Just say it."

"A hundred?" She gets the look she always does when it comes to handouts—meek but rapacious, like a starving kitten.

I pull out the eighty-three bucks I stole from Raul's wallet. I'll get more pawning his shit, so I can spare the cash. Stuffing it into her scarred hand, I lean in close, forcing her to look into my eyes. "This is it. No more. Leave town. You got it?"

She squirrels away the cash and nods.

I get Maxine's email the first week in November. A Tuesday. Elec-tion day.

When I fire up my laptop and see her message sitting there, my gut twists in a prophetic cramp. It's got a neutral-enough subject heading. Still, the words strike me as cold, inhospitable, a snowy plane in Greenland.

From: Maxine Katz
To: Sam Grist
Subject: Your manuscript

Dear Sam,

Your novel has been read by my assistant and myself.
We agree it is too dark for my list. I wish you luck in
finding the right home.

Best,

Maxine Katz
Literary Agent

I stand and pace the room. This is crazy. My book is good. I
know it's good. My sweat is in that manuscript, my guts, my
heart. It's a work of fucking art, and this bitch-faced cunt says
it's "too dark"? The fuck does that mean, "too dark"? Did she
even read it? Or is she trying to say her cunty little assistant
(her name has to be Hannah!) read it while playing a game of
"Grand Theft Auto" with her boyfriend? I can see Hannah so
clearly. Hot, but in a slutty-nerdy way, the chick who'll smoke a
bowl and let you fuck her in the ass. She wears glasses and she
reads graphic novels, so she's kind of bookish, but she also has a
vibrator in her nightstand and she does Jell-O shots with her
girlfriends, and she totally had an affair with her roommate
back at Yale. This is the little trust-fund bitch who read my book
and said no. She barely got past the first page, but her boyfriend
wanted her to smoke another bowl and she was losing at "Grand
Theft Auto," so she scribbled "pass" on a Post-it note and got back
to her debauchery.

I would line up all the Hannahs of this world and shoot them,
if only I could. Ridding the planet of Hannahs would be a definite
step in the right direction. An act of heroism. The line would be
long. Hannahs live in every city around the world. There's at least
one in every coffee shop. They multiply like cockroaches at Har-

vard and Stanford and Brown. There's an army of Hannahs out there. They all deserve to die.

I slam my laptop shut and pace some more. The walls of my studio feel too close, too white. The air's thick with failure. The dirty dishes crowding around my sink glare at me in reproach. Did you and Maxine plan this? Is it some kind of test, like Raul? Am I supposed to prove once again how much I want into your world? Is this my cue to launch some grand gesture, something public and over-the-top, the writer's version of John Cusack standing outside Ione Skye's window with a boom box blaring Peter Gabriel?

No, you can't be part of this.

It's Maxine. The lazy whore. She didn't even read my manuscript. How dare she call herself a professional? It's Maxine's skanky little assistant, a lazy cum-dumpster with no taste and no real passion for literature, just an Ivy League education she slept through, and a trust fund that allows her to survive in New York "working" for Maxine Katz, not reading manuscripts and venturing opinions about them anyway.

The picture that forms in my mind makes my skin feel too tight, makes my brain pulse inside my skull. Hannah, sipping an overpriced latte, hungover, still a little high from her wake-and-bake session with Trent, her mouth-breathing boyfriend, handing over my manuscript with a bored expression. "It's too dark for your list," she says. "Readers don't want to be that depressed."

Every relationship has tests. Ask anyone. No matter how much you love someone, there will be moments that force you to work harder, to prove your dedication. Someday, you and I will laugh about this. You will have a new agent, and I will have the Best Agent in Town, someone young and hungry and brilliant, with sharklike instincts and beautiful young assistants who know what they're talking about. Maxine will be a homeless crack whore we sometimes give money to when we run into her in Central Park, and Hannah will be dead. We'll lie in bed in our spacious loft, spreading jam on toast, drinking coffee and laughing about that day when Maxine rejected my debut novel. You'll frown a little as you chew, thinking of how far she's fallen, and say, "Poor Maxine." But I'll show no mercy. "Fuck her. She's got no taste." You'll cover your mouth, trying not to spray toast crumbs everywhere as you giggle, and I'll dive on you, kissing your creamy white neck, losing myself in the porcelain planes of your body.

I can't stay here right now. I need to be near you, near your things. I check your email, make sure you haven't cancelled class. You've got Modern American Literature in room 5233. You'll be there until two. I grab my keys and hurry out the door.

I'm staring at your fridge, which is plastered with photos. They're almost all of you and Zoe. There are a few of you wrapping an arm around an old man. That must be your father. I've gleaned from your books, your bio, your interviews, that your mother died when you were twelve. You were raised by your father and a series of stepmothers, none of whom made the cut for your fridge.

Zoe's the main person in your life.

From your emails, I know Zoe had her baby a week and a half ago. You've only seen her once since then. She's overwhelmed. You don't like babies. All of your protagonists eschew motherhood in favor of other, more selfish pursuits. This is just another sign we belong together, since I would rather hammer nails into my cranium than suffer a screaming infant.

You're alone. You feel abandoned. I can sense it in your home. There's a sad, crooked quality to the way the dish towel hangs from your oven door. The food in your cupboards is meager, spare, a sure sign you're avoiding the grocery store. You're living off take-out Chinese and frozen ravioli. I want to cook for you, make you my grandfather's Irish stew and buttermilk biscuits, a meal so hearty and life-affirming, you'll eat three bowls and ask for more, sop up the last of it with your second biscuit slathered in butter.

We're not there yet. I'm getting ahead of myself. Love can't be rushed. If you came home and found me in your kitchen stirring a pot of stew, you'd call the cops. That's the crazy, backward shit that makes me want to break things, you know? You let Raul in here, let him fuck you, even though he's got no idea who you are or what you need. Then I show up, just wanting to feed you a decent meal, dying to soothe your aching solitude, and I'm the criminal. I bet I know more about you than your own father. I know what you need. Yet, I'm an intruder in the eyes of the law. Even in your eyes, until I can prove otherwise.

I can't think about that now; it makes me too sad.

For now, I have to satisfy myself with the little things—roving your home like a ghost while you lecture in McKinley Hall. I can see you commanding the room, telling stories, weaving your magic. Meanwhile, I'm here, touching your counters, fondling your couch, stroking your two cats. They like me, especially the black one. Her long, slender body shimmies against my hand as I bend over and caress her. I know from your emails with your vet they're called Emily and Charlotte. After the Brontës. I'm guessing the black one's Emily, the tabby Charlotte. Only a black cat could dream up *Wuthering Heights*. The tabby's more of a *Jane Eyre* type.

Emily follows me as I make my way upstairs and into your bedroom. She leaps onto the bed. I run a hand over your white cotton bedspread. She slinks behind me as I open the door to your walk-in closet, run my fingers over the silks and cashmeres, the wools, the denims. When I reach into your hamper and pluck a pair of black lace panties from its depths, Emily blinks up at me. I hold the cotton crotch close to my face and breathe in, never breaking her gaze. She gives me a baleful look. I stuff the filmy fabric into my pocket.

Back downstairs, I glance at the antique clock on your mantel. It's almost three. Where did the time go? Jesus! I take one last, furtive look around. An orchid in your kitchen window catches my eye. One of its petals floats to the floor, a plaintive shedding. I take that as a sign. It's parched. Neglected. Abandoned. Like you, it needs to be saved. You are not a nurturer, Kate. When we're together, I will do the cooking, I will care for the plants, I will buy Emily and Charlotte their treats. You'll be the naughty child, the one who leaves her coffee cup in the laundry room, just a few sips left in it, enough to grow mold. I will enjoy spoiling you. Starting right now.

I forage in the cabinets until I find a glass. I fill it halfway and pour a bit of water into the orchid's pot. It perks up a little. The tiny flower face smiles up at me, grateful. Your orchid and I share a moment of camaraderie. I pluck the fallen petal from the floor and carefully secure it in my shirt pocket. Your orchid knows I belong here, just as Charlotte and Emily know. It's only a matter of time before you know it, too.

I search in the cupboards until I find a bag of food. I pour just a few bites into the cats' bowls. They fall on the food, chomping like savages. I stroke Emily as she eats, enjoying the sinuous feel of her spine beneath my fingers.

There's a key turning in your door. Adrenaline shoots through my body so fast I get a head rush.

For a second, my impulse is to stand my ground. I long to greet you and welcome you in and cook for you and ask about your day and massage the kinks from your taut shoulders and scold Emily for jumping onto your lap when it's *your* turn to be petted, to be loved.

But of course none of that can happen, not yet. If you find me like this, I'll be suspect—worse than suspect. I'll be caught. And even though I know in my heart there's nothing sinister about my presence here, you don't. You won't see it that way.

I don't blame you. My impatience with the distance between us grows more intense every second, though.

You're in the foyer now, closing the door. Any moment you'll turn and see me. My heart pounds against my rib cage like a crazed dog throwing itself against a fence. I dash up the stairs, willing my boots to stay silent. If you could see me now, you'd be impressed. I've got stealth. My criminal instincts are honed. The good girl in you can't help but be turned on by that. Maybe if you catch me, you'll find it sexy.

But no. Not going to happen.

You can't see me.

I have to disappear.

Everything's riding on this. My pulse races.

Without thinking, I run into the first room at the top of the stairs: the bathroom. Your smell is heavy in here, a tropical storm of Kateness. I creep inside the tub and, careful not to make a sound, pull the shower curtain closed.

I hear you walking up the stairs. You're humming. It sounds like "Wild Night" by Van Morrison—one of my favorite songs. That has to mean something.

There's a preoccupied cadence to your footsteps. I picture you flipping through mail, your brow furrowed in that tiny apostrophe of concentration. You probably have your reading glasses perched on the end of your nose. I ache for you. I peek around the curtain just enough to catch a glimpse of your slender bare feet reaching the top of the staircase and making a left toward your bedroom. I hold my breath, letting the curtain fall back into place.

Why didn't I slip out when I had the chance? If you find me here, everything's fucked.

I let my cockiness get out of hand.

From now on, I resolve to be more careful.

You're in the bedroom, still humming. Definitely "Wild Night." I close my eyes and lean my head against the cool, white tile. My heart continues to race. My breathing's ragged. I can hear you searching through drawers. You must be looking for your yoga pants, your wife-beater. Your humming turns to singing in the bedroom. There's the sound of coat hangers clicking against one another. Your voice is husky and rich.

Out of nowhere, a ripple of calm washes over me. This is how it will be when we live together. You'll be in the next room singing while you change clothes. I'll step out of the shower, wipe steam from the mirror. I'll walk into the bedroom, a towel wrapped around my waist. You'll glance over your shoulder at me, your face lighting up as you pull your tank over your head. I'll sit on the bed and rub my damp hair, caught between the need to touch you and the simple pleasure of watching you from across the room.

You drop something—your phone? The sound jolts me back to the moment. I need to go right now, while you're still in the bedroom.

I can't, though. With your scent in the air, your off-key song in my ears, there's too much anchoring me to the spot. We're so close right now. I'm in your world, and even though I haven't been invited, your nearness fills me like a drug.

Oh, god. You're in the bathroom. You turn on the faucet at the sink. Fuck, this is torture. You're so close.

So fucking close.

I listen to you brushing your teeth. Smell the minty freshness of your toothpaste. You gargle. Spit.

My breath catches in my throat as you fall silent. What are you doing now? You're motionless. Are you eyeing the shower curtain? Maybe it's not as opaque as I thought. You can see my silhouette. You're standing there, still as a tree, holding your breath, staring at my outline in the pearly white curtain. Any second now you'll yank open the plastic and—

Oh, god, I can't stand it, I'm going to—

Wait. You're leaving.

I exhale in dizzy relief as your bare feet patter back into the hallway and down the stairs.

When I hear NPR come to life in the kitchen, I decide it's now or never. The stairs end in the downstairs hallway opposite the kitchen, so it's risky. I have to chance it. Let's pray you're in the pantry or at the stove, your back to me. I lift first one foot, then the other, out of the tub, moving like a mime. Every step requires extreme control. My system's still flooded with adrenaline; my muscles ache to take the stairs at a dead run. In spite of the radio, the oak planks will make way too much noise if I hurry. There's a window at the landing. I catch sight of your neighbor's children in the side yard—two little girls. They're playing a game involving plastic guns. Like marionettes controlled by the same hand, their tiny blond heads swivel toward me. We stare at one another through the glass for a long moment.

I need to get out of here.

Now.

There's a bad moment at the bottom of the stairs. You're not in the pantry. Not at the stove. You're at the sink. All it would take for you to catch sight of me is a quick sideways glance.

Again, the crazy injustice of our situation hits me. I know you better than anyone, Kate, yet I'm forced to run away like a thief.

I hurry toward the front door.

Just as I'm closing it behind me, lunging for the porch steps, I hear you say, "Hello? Is someone there?"

As I slip away, head bowed, hoodie pulled up, one of the little girls next door cries, "Bang-bang! You're dead!"

I offer her a weak smile and stride toward my car.

KATE

Sometimes I see my life in the form of a book jacket blurb—the pithy hook on the back, a paragraph or two distilling the novel's essence. They're much harder to compose than you'd think. There's a lot of pressure. I used to write them fresh out of college, interning at a small press in Boston. You've got a hundred words to convert the casual browser into a committed buyer. It's like trying to stuff a bag of squirming cats into a hatbox. All the characters seem too important to leave out, every subplot clamors to be included. It helps if you haven't actually read the book.

Back then, while churning out back-cover copy, I thought I'd be an agent or editor. I never really considered writing novels myself.

Then the idea for *Pay Dirt* hit me—struck me with such force I knew I had to write it. I felt like a cartoon character bludgeoned by an anvil. For seven weeks I did nothing but write that book. People often marvel that I wrote the entire novel in so short a time. I doubt they realize how long seven weeks can last when you do nothing else for twelve hours a day, seven days a week. I was a woman possessed. I didn't see anyone. I didn't venture out. I lived on crackers and cigarettes.

Ever since my internship at Briar Press, book blurbs frequently shape the way I think about my life. I'll observe something I'm doing, a choice I'm making, a person I'm being, and imagine how it would be described in that tiny, confining box. I consider which verbs to pluck from my dusty collection, which adjectives to stir in.

As I poke around the kitchen after class Tuesday, NPR droning in the background, I hear Carl Kasell's crisp diction narrating my life.

Kate Youngblood, professor of English at a small liberal arts college, has lost everything. Her husband's left her for a younger woman; her best friend's left her for an infant. Now, she's finally had sex with someone new, a suave restaurant owner, and he turns up dead. Will Kate discover the killer before she becomes his next victim?

Not my kind of book. There would be pounding hearts and chilling revelations. Endless interviews with red herrings. I don't have the patience for that sort of thing.

Plucky professor Kate Youngblood has everything: a steady teaching job, a thriving career as a novelist—and a taste for young male scholars. When her eye falls on the promising, and gorgeous, Sam Grist, she realizes she has to choose: risk her teaching career, or risk never knowing what it's like to be in his arms.

God, I'm on a roll. I can't believe I'm living this shit.

A rustling movement from the front of the house yanks me from my thoughts. What was that? A latch catching? A door shutting? I look for Emily and Charlotte. They're both right here, staring up at me. Charlotte meows with the chiding disapproval of a neglected old lady and swipes at Emily for no good reason.

There it is again—something—what? Footsteps on the porch?

I reach for the cashmere poncho draped over the back of a chair. Gooseflesh stipples my arms. Wrapping myself in the wool, I creep toward the front door. Before I leave the kitchen, almost as an afterthought, I seize a cast iron skillet. It's not much as weapons go, but it will have to do. I feel silly, paranoid.

Entering the front hallway, I could swear I see a blur of motion outside the wavy glass panels flanking the front door. When I finally get my glasses on, though, it's gone. I look around, gripping the skillet, remind myself to breathe. Nothing seems disturbed. Probably just my imagination.

Charlotte rubs against my ankles, blinks at me.

"It's not time for dinner yet." I scoop her up and cradle her in my arms. Her warm bulk comforts me.

I flash on Zoe holding Drew, and a jolt of embarrassment shoots through me. She's clutching a living, breathing human being, someone she made from her own flesh. I'm holding a judgmental cat that would eat my face if I died.

There's some other emotion under the humiliation. It takes me a moment to name it: envy.

Not that I want a baby—God forbid! But to have someone who needs you that completely? It must be intoxicating. Nobody's ever felt that way about me. I value my independence, but at what cost? What part of the human experience am I missing out on entirely?

I go back to the kitchen, put the skillet on the stove, and pour myself a glass of wine. I check my phone to see if there's anything new online about Raul's murder. He's been dead twelve days; the police don't have a clue who killed him. They've questioned me twice. I was probably one of the last people to see him. Unless you count being drunk alone in my house, I don't have an alibi. The lead detective has an especially suspicious manner that makes me sweat whenever he looks me in the eye. Maybe when you're a homicide detective, everyone's a potential murderer. I'm not used to people sizing me up like that, trying to peer into the darkest corners of my heart.

Another shiver passes through me. I go to the thermostat on the wall, turn the heat up a couple of degrees.

That's when I notice it: the bag of cat food sitting on the counter.

I know better than to leave that there. Emily once chewed through a cardboard box to get at the hard little nuggets inside. A flimsy bag like this would be all over the floor by now. Easy work for a couple of skilled feline bandits.

Though I've already been upstairs, I make myself go through every room in the house, eyeing every possession suspiciously. Was that paper clip sitting on my desk when I left? Did I leave that closet door open? I'm no Miss Marple, though. The truth is, I don't pay enough attention to my surroundings.

Still, I sense a thickness in the air, a humid trace of someone's presence.

I consider going to Zoe's but decide against it. Baby Drew scares me more than my imagined intruder.

I lock my doors and go upstairs to take a bath.

SAM

"Hey, Sam." Jess lingers near my table. She's not, for once in her life, thrusting her cleavage at the world. She wears an oversized fleece sweatshirt, no makeup, and a face so sad it's a deflated balloon.

"What's up?" I try to say it with no interest, my eyes only leaving the screen of my laptop for an annoyed couple of seconds. She's so different from her usual self, though; a tiny flame of curiosity flickers to life in my brain. What's with the Sad Girl routine? Did something happen, or is this another ploy?

She looks around the truck-stop diner, takes in the greasy, laminated menus, the men in baseball caps digging into hash browns, the craggy-faced waitresses with feathered hair. "This where you write?"

Is there anything more infuriating than a girl invading your hideout? Eva did it once. She believed I wanted to be found. Her compulsion to know my secrets was a disease.

"Sometimes," I admit. "Depends on what I'm writing."

"It's very Raymond Carver." She catches me off guard with that one. It's not what I'd expect from Cleavage. She strikes me as more of a reality TV fan than a reader.

In spite of my obvious desire to be left alone, she slides into my booth. She fiddles with the salt and pepper shakers like a girl playing with dolls. "I won't bug you. I just can't deal with the dorms right now. This murder thing's freaking me out."

I lower the screen of my laptop half an inch. "What are you talking about?"

"Remember that girl I told you about?" She sighs the words, like she's too tired to speak them aloud.

"No."

"The one who dated that guy at The Woods?"

I keep my expression blank.

She speaks with forced patience, like I'm a child. "That time I saw you at The Woods, you asked if I knew a guy—Raul? Same dude we saw at the theater with Youngblood? Anyway, he used to date a friend of mine. My roommate."

"Right . . . ?"

"Well, he was murdered. They found him in his home, duct-taped to a chair." She licks her lips, drawing out the moment. "Somebody shot him in the head."

I say nothing. Her fruity perfume causes a headache to flair inside my skull. My temples throb.

"That's terrible." I sound okay. A little wooden. I will myself to add some empathy. "Who do they think did it?"

"The cops keep interviewing Sadie. She was still seeing him—more like midnight bootie calls, but whatever. They got in a fight a couple weeks ago in a bar, so now the cops won't leave her alone."

"You're worried?" I try to sound gentle, but I must hit a sour note.

She shoots me a look like I'm crazy. "Um, yeah! She's my best friend, my roommate, and now she's a murder suspect."

"Okay. Don't get upset."

"God, you're weird." She runs her hand through her hair.

This is one of the phrases I hate most in the English language, along with "brain fart" and "warm fuzzies." Those I despise out of principle. "You're weird" I hate because I heard it all too often growing up, before I learned to school my expressions and temper my inflections.

A fat waitress with bad skin offers me a coffee refill. I hold my cup out and watch the black liquid steam into my cup. She asks Cleavage if she wants anything. To my relief, Cleavage shakes her head no.

As the waitress wanders off, I warm my hands on the hot mug.

"You know who else they questioned?" Dark pleasure lights up her face.

I have my suspicions, but I say, "Who?"

"Professor Youngblood." The delight she takes in this pronouncement makes me want to toss my scalding coffee in her face.

"Because she dated him?"

"Yep. It's usually the girlfriend who did it. Especially when he's still seeing other girls on the side." She looks at her phone.

I hate it when people look at their phone in the middle of a conversation. It implies they've got more important people they should tend to. I don't expect to be the most important person in Cleavage's life, but she's the one who invaded my fortress, infected my writing zone with her sticky-sweet strawberry scent. An intolerable bubbling starts up inside my rib cage, a carbonated rage.

She types something and lines her phone up beside the salt-shaker. "You think she did it?"

"Who?"

"Youngblood!"

"No." I sip my coffee. "Of course not."

"What makes you so sure?"

"She'd never do something like that."

"'Cause you know her so well?" Her eyes sparkle.

"I can just tell."

"Her books are pretty violent," she says, her lips puckering in disapproval.

"You've read them?"

"No." She folds her arms across her chest, leaning back in the booth. "But I know what they're about."

"You can't read the blurb and think you know the book."

She scoffs. "Judgmental much?"

"And you definitely can't know the author or what she's capable of," I add, unable to stop myself.

She stares at me, her eyes narrowing to slits. "You're not . . . ?"

"What?"

"Like, into her, are you?"

I raise one eyebrow, refusing to dignify this with a response. She takes it the way I mean her to.

She laughs. "Shit, you scared me there for a second."

"So, what's going to happen with your roommate?"

"Sadie?" She frowns. "I don't know. I feel sorry for her."

"Because she's a suspect?"

She widens her eyes like she can't believe how stupid I am. "*And* she found out her boyfriend was fucking some middle-aged hag."

It takes all my self-control not to stab her in the face with my fork.

KATE

From: Maxine Katz
To: Kate Youngblood
Subject: Your Latest Manuscript

Hello Kate,

I've just finished reading your latest revision of *Blood Ties*. I know you worked hard to integrate my feedback, so thank you for that. I just can't help feeling it's still not working. Forgive me for being blunt, but there it is.

The relationship between the protagonist and her mother feels stilted. The plot still drags, in spite of the shorter chapters. The climax doesn't deliver. The character arcs feel forced, overly cheerful, and illogical.

I know this will not come as a shock to you. There was a note of embarrassment in your voice when we discussed it at lunch. Since you and I can agree this isn't your best work, I suggest you put it aside for a few months. Try something else. Remember that circus thriller we talked about? Tinker with that.

The bottom line is I can't sell something I don't love. I definitely can't back something I actively dislike. We have to be savvy about what we shop. In a year, when you've written something better, you'll thank me for not embarrassing you by sending this out. If you're upset with me in the meantime, so be it. It's my job to be the brains of this operation—the business brains, I mean. It's your job to create, so don't worry about this small setback. I'm confident you'll turn out something amazing in no time.

Best,
MK

A shiver passes through me. I seem to be cold all the time lately. It occurs to me briefly, illogically, that Raul could be haunting me. Ghosts are supposed to bring a chill wherever they go, right? Raul wouldn't choose me, of all people, to haunt, though. The murder investigation's turned up all kinds of random liaisons—with college girls and waitresses, a kindergarten teacher. I feel dirty, tossed together with all of his other conquests. I've never thought of sex as giving something up, not even the first time, but sex with Raul definitely cost me something. My pride. My anonymity. In this sleepy college town, Raul's murder is big news. The fact that my name's been dragged into it will not help my quest for tenure.

And now, just to add momentum to my downward spiral, my agent hates my book.

I hate my book. Why wouldn't *she*?

God, I ache to write the way I used to. When I wrote *Pay Dirt,* I was a whirling dervish, a mad weaver of words. I slept a few hours at a time, like a cat. My eyes would pop open at two, three, five in the morning, and I'd type feverishly in the dark, my brain still marinating in dreams. My dingy little apartment was a wreck, but I didn't care. I wasn't even there. I was off in the Chicago night, riding in cop cars and partying with bank robbers. My characters blossomed uncontrollably—they sprang to life fully formed, like deities. I smoked compulsively and ate only when the pain of hunger grew intolerable. My apartment smelled like a casino. I was deliriously happy.

Now, I write like a sluggish child composing an overdue book report late Sunday night, her frowning mother ridiculing every word over her shoulder.

After *Pay Dirt,* I waited for inspiration to strike again. The right ideas carry a kind of fever. I knew this. I sat around patiently preparing for lightning to flash inside my brain. Nothing happened. I'd signed a three-book deal with Penguin. Maxine emailed me weekly to check on my progress. I had a file filled with sixty thousand words of false starts. Novels I'd begun and abandoned. I knew the electricity in the blood when a premise had promise. The ideas that came to me all sagged and wilted after a few pages, their characters losing steam, wandering off into the fog.

I wanted to die. I'd just gotten my job at Blackwood. Everyone there kept asking about my next book. My fraudulent reputation as a novelist weighed on me heavily. I ate a lot of chocolate. The fear of revealing my barren imagination turned me stiff and formal. Students complained about my classes. Their evals said I was "cold" and "distant" and "lacking in basic human compassion." One of the little bitches wrote, "Work out more, you cow, and don't take it out on us when you're on the rag!!!" Those three exclamation points were daggers piercing my heart. I gained fifteen pounds and wrote nothing.

Then one day I sat down at my desk and just started typing. I had no idea where I was going or what the damn book was about, but I built it, sentence by sentence, like a bricklayer. I called it *Hidden Depths.*

Predictably, it was a plodding, boring tome. *The Blackwood Sentinal* loved it. Everyone else called it what it was: shit.

And now I've written another equally forgettable, overwrought, sentimental waste of paper. Only it doesn't look like it will waste paper, since Maxine won't send it out.

I don't blame her. Some agents might try to sell *Blood Ties* in spite of its worthlessness. She's got more integrity than that. I don't want to publish a bad book just because I can. Authors who ride the wave of one excellent novel only to cruise back into obscurity trailing a wake of mediocre follow-ups are pathetic. Not that I have a massive wave to ride, anyway. *Pay Dirt* earned me moderate praise and a little respect, but not everlasting fame. It won a few modest awards. The German translation sold more copies than the English version. I sometimes wonder about that. Did the translator infuse it with more panache than I'd managed?

I close my email and fold my laptop shut. In the kitchen, I put the kettle on for tea. Before it whistles, I turn off the burner. I don't want tea. I want a drink, but I'm afraid I might be drinking too much. I come from a long line of staunchly functional alcoholics. Statistically, it's probable I'll join their ranks. Being a writer only ups the odds.

I consider calling Zoe, maybe even stopping by her place for a visit. The smell of breast milk and baby powder that fills their house now depresses me, though. I don't think she wants me there, anyway. The switch babies flip in most women—the cooing and beaming button—seems to be broken in me. Or maybe it was never there in the first place. I fear my silence freaks her out. When I hold Drew, I do it awkwardly, stiffly. He always cries. I hand him back immediately, embarrassed.

A huge part of the human experience I'll never understand. I can't make myself want it, but I can't stop missing it, either.

Fuck it. I go to the kitchen and pour myself an extra-large glass of pinot.

SAM

I'm incensed by Maxine's email. To think Aging Cher dares to reject both of us in one week. You and me, the writers who will be legendary. Scrawny-necked, big-haired Maxine will never taste the glory you and I will dine on nightly. She will never have the sex we're about to have. She will never know the thrill of seeing her work translated to the big screen by the Coen Brothers. What am I saying? She doesn't have any "work." She's a peddler, a used car salesman. She sees only numbers and print runs and foreign rights. Her eyes swim with dollar signs. She doesn't create.

You and me, Kate—we create. We are the gods of our universe. Our hands shape beings and infuse them with life.

I have to intervene. You'll be polite and generous, self-effacing, gracious. I plan to be none of those things.

It's times like these when you need a knight. Someone who will swoop in and deal the death blows you're afraid to administer.

You're too kind. Thank god I'm not.

From: Kate Youngblood
To: Maxine Katz
Subject: RE: Your Latest Manuscript

Thank you for your very unhelpful email. A real agent would not suggest I "put it aside" but would offer insightful comments that inspire me to make it better. Your unflagging pessimism begins to weigh me down.

Your services will no longer be required.

The lack of faith you show in my work leads me to believe you are an anchor on my writing life. At the moment I need a hot air balloon.

Kate

After I send it, I delete it from your sent mail. A few minutes later, an email from you to Zoe pops up.

From: Kate Youngblood
To: Zoe Tait
Subject: Yoga

I'm going to Sarah's 6:00 class. Sorry so last minute. Come if you can, or just meet me for a beer after at O'Malley's. Alcohol's more efficient than yoga anyway. xo

I look at the time: 5:25. Zoe will never get her shit together to meet you. But I know someone who will.

The rain's pouring down in sheets. The sound of it on the roof of my car soothes me. I'm parked outside Radiant Yoga Studio, watching middle-aged women and college girls in leggings and hoodies hustle in and out of the glass doors. Next to the studio, there's a church. It has one of those sandwich-board marquees.

I squint through the rain to make out the words: MORALLY BANK-RUPT? GOD OFFERS INSTANT CREDIT.

I feel good tonight. Raul's been a nonissue for more than two weeks. The cash I stole from his wallet and the gear I took from his home have convinced the cops it was a home invasion that went south. I know you've been low-level worried about his death. I've seen your preoccupied frown in workshop when you think nobody's looking. You're not all that upset by his loss, though. That's good. I like a woman who knows how to get perspective.

You'd never admit it to anyone, but you're relieved he's gone.

Here's the thing about homicide: It never pays to make it complicated. Murder mysteries and police procedurals imply you've got to be a tactical genius to get away with it, but the truth is much simpler. All you have to do is choose someone you've got no apparent connection to, find an isolated spot, and leave as little of yourself behind as possible.

Simple.

Add to that the moral high ground of knowing you've done the right thing, and you've got the perfect murder. No pangs of conscience means no chance of saying anything stupid to anyone.

The cops haven't questioned me. Why would they? I'm not even a blip on their radar.

You push through the glass doors. I'm on high alert, one hand on my door handle, the other reaching for my big black umbrella. None of those cheap, fold-up, toy umbrellas for me. I like a sturdy, *Singin' in the Rain* kind, the old-fashioned variety with a solid wooden handle shaped like a candy cane. The kind you can share.

What can I say? I'm a romantic.

You clutch your water bottle and squint out at the rain, which does me the favor of hammering so hard it sounds like marbles on the roof of my car. It's a sign. Even the rain wants us to be together.

You're ill-prepared, Kate. A thin, white tank top, a sweater that will dissolve like cotton candy the second you step out from under that awning.

I leap from my car and thrust open my umbrella. Like a man with someplace to go, I hurry down the sidewalk toward you.

"Professor Youngblood!" I show you my startled face as I draw near.

You break into a radiant smile. The yoga must have been good for you. You're even more incandescent than usual; your alabaster skin glows. "Sam. Miserable out, isn't it?"

"Depends on how you define 'miserable,'" I say. "I love the rain."

You step aside from the door, careful not to leave the shelter of the awning. "You going to yoga? Wouldn't have pegged you as the type."

"God, no." I nod at the pub down the street. "Headed for O'Malley's."

You eye the pub, your face wistful.

"Can I give you a lift?" At your confused frown, I jiggle my umbrella. "Shelter from the storm? I can walk you to your car. Or wherever you're going."

Your hesitation lasts only a second. A fresh deluge decides it. The wind hammers the drops like tiny, fierce fists against the sodden fabric of the awning. Thank you, rain.

"Wouldn't mind grabbing a pint."

I'm careful not to look too pleased. Must play this cool.

I employ my best Irish accent. "To O'Malley's it is, then, lassie."

KATE

O'Malley's is warm and festive. Guess there's something about a good November storm that drives people to the nearest Irish pub. I scan the room for familiar faces. Aside from a few former students, it's mercifully clear of colleagues and acquaintances. I tug my cardigan a little tighter, pull it down over my ass. When I pictured myself meeting Zoe here after class, yoga wear seemed totally normal. Now, though, with Sam, I feel a little naked.

All the booths are taken. Sam orders us a couple pints at the bar, and we sit at a two-top near the pool tables. It's noisy and boisterous. The cacophony of pool balls smashing into one another makes me flinch. A girl playing darts wears a pink shirt that's ridiculously bright. She swims in my peripheral vision like a lurid tropical fish. My senses feel sharper than usual. Could be the yoga. I'm afraid it's Sam's proximity, though. The strangeness of being here with him, outside the classroom, gives me a heightened awareness of everything around me.

He notices me cringing from all the noise and color. His gaze scans the bar like a military officer before landing on a booth with a lone old man tucked inside.

"Give me a second." He stands and crosses the room in a few long, loping strides.

As I watch him consulting with the stranger, I can't help but notice his preternatural confidence. It fascinates and mystifies me—that blithe, illogical faith in himself, unearned and, for the most part, untested.

He returns a few minutes later looking pleased. "Come on. Let's grab the booth before someone else does."

"What about the—?" I glance to where the little guy in the windbreaker sat. He's gone. "Okay. Great."

As we settle in across from one another in the cozy booth, I can't help asking, "How'd you manage that?"

"Not much you can't get if you ask nicely." His smile's so innocent.

I shake my head, amused.

"What?" he says with a laugh. "You don't believe that?"

"It works pretty well when you're twenty-two and beautiful." The words are out of my mouth before I can stop them. To my horror, I feel heat rushing into my cheeks. Dammit, blushing will only make this worse.

His crooked smile makes something in my stomach flip over.

I clear my throat. "So, how did it go with Maxine? Did you send her your manuscript?"

"Yeah." He sips his beer, swallows with a grimace. "She said 'thanks but no thanks.'"

"What? Oh, God, Sam, I'm so sorry." My surprise is genuine. "I really thought she'd love it. Did you make those changes we talked about?"

His brow puckers in confusion. "What changes?"

With a sick falling feeling I realize I never gave him my revision notes. The ones about chapter seven. The clumsy foreshadowing he needed to cut. That day in my office, I planned to explain my suggestion with the clarity and tact of a master teacher. Except then we got interrupted. Frances barged in, with her piggy stare, her suspicious squint. That kiss. Thinking of it, I can still taste the shape of his mouth, can feel his hands on me, the cold, metal file cabinet against my back.

And I fucking forgot. I went home that day and got drunk, had sex with Raul. The next thing I knew Zoe was having her baby, Raul was dead—it all collapsed around me like a sand castle hit by a sudden wave. In the midst of that chaos, Sam must have sent Maxine his manuscript as is, because I never explained what he needed to change.

I take a long sip of my beer to hide my confusion.

He must see something in my face, because he pins me with that icy gaze of his. "Professor Youngblood? Is something wrong?"

I clutch at my head, elbows on the table. "Sam, I feel terrible."

"About Maxine?" He shrugs. "It's not your fault. That's just how it goes."

"But it is—my fault, I mean."

He shoots me a skeptical look.

"I meant to give you notes that day in my office. There's something in chapter seven that needs changing, only we got distracted, and . . ." I trail off, miserable.

"You forgot," he finishes.

"Yes," I whisper. "I forgot."

"Honestly, I don't know if I'm ready." He says this with perfect humility. An actor hitting just the right note. I don't know what it is that alerts me to his performance. I just know in my gut he's not telling the truth.

"You don't mean that."

He holds my gaze for a long moment. I can hear my pulse pounding in my ears.

"I don't. But Maxine Katz isn't the right agent for me." This time there's nothing rehearsed about it. He's raw and honest at last. There's something somber in his tone, like a prophecy.

I can't help feeling a little thrill of victory. So he's more than just a series of calculated performances. He can drop the mask. He's starting to with me.

"It's a wonderful book. You'll sell it easily when it's ready. I just feel terrible about botching your first shot."

"No." His hand lands on mine. It's warm, solid. "You didn't botch it. I did. I'm too impulsive."

"You believe in yourself," I correct him.

His thumb strokes mine. "I'm a cocky bastard. I dive right in when I should proceed with caution. I should have revised more."

"There are so many other agents out there," I remind him.

"You ever think Maxine's not the right agent for you?" The question comes out of nowhere. His eyes lock on mine with unnerving intensity.

I hesitate. "Sometimes. Sure. But every writer has doubts about—"

"She doesn't understand what a genius you are." He traces soft circles around my knuckles. "You should be with someone who gets you."

I pull my hand gently from where he's trapped it, take a long pull from my pint. "I'm not exactly a hot commodity right now."

"Why do you say that?" He watches me with a solemn frown.

"Because I can't write anything worth selling." I put my glass down. It thunks against the scarred wooden table. "That's a big problem."

"You just need the right situation," he says.

"The right situation?"

"You know. Inspiration." He gestures at the air, as if great books can be plucked from the ether. "Your writing's extraordinary. Luminous. You're just looking for the right idea."

I can't help flashing a wry smile. "Is that what I'm doing?"

"Absolutely." His confidence is charming, damn him.

"And when I find it?"

"When you find it?" he echoes.

"Will I even know it? Or will it float right on by?"

He grins. "Oh, you'll know it. When something's right, you know."

I'm not exactly sure what we're talking about anymore. His

smile wraps me in its warmth. As usual, with him, I wonder if that heat is real or manufactured. At this point, I don't know if I care.

"Maxine, what's this about?" I don't bother trying to be subtle. My nerves are frayed, and her mysterious email about the "end of our working relationship" has me mystified.

"What's there to say?" She's cold—glacial, in fact—and my stomach goes wobbly. "You made it perfectly clear I'm of no use to you."

I clutch my forehead, pacing around my office like a caged tiger. "I have no idea what you're talking about."

"Your email."

"I haven't emailed since you told me to put away *Blood Ties*. You're right, by the way, it's not ready, and I don't know if it ever—"

"Don't play games with me." Her voice is so hard, I barely recognize it. "You dropped me. End of story."

"I—what? No! I assure you I didn't," I protest.

She sighs. "Look, Kate, I don't have time for this. I don't do author drama, okay? If you're blacking out, fine, but—"

"I swear to you, that's not—"

"I got an email from you telling me we're through." Her words are like hail, brittle and icy. "As far as I'm concerned, that's all there is to it."

I recoil at the note of relief in her voice. "You wanted to drop me."

"It's not personal." She breathes, tired now, all the fight gone.

"Send me this email you supposedly got," I say.

"Please!" she scoffs.

"Do it," I say, sounding just as bitter and hateful as her now. "I want to see it."

"Fine." I hear a gentle tapping in the background. "Check your inbox. And good luck, Kate. You're going to need it."

The homicide detective circles back to ask me more questions about Raul. This time he comes to my office, which is unnerving. My colleagues treat me with a mixture of curiosity and repulsion, like someone who's contracted a rare and deadly STD. I catch them whispering and casting sideways glances at me in the halls. A part of me savors being the center of a scandal. That's the writer in me, I guess, squirreling away the details for later use.

Detective Schroeder sits across from me in my office. His calm, gray eyes and his long, square jaw were built to intimidate. I can tell he's taking everything in as his gaze sweeps around the room and lands on me. He studies me with a cold, clinical interest, giving nothing away. His expression is as blank and impenetrable as a stone wall. Even though I've done nothing illegal, I feel compelled to confess.

He glances at his notepad. "You and the victim were close?"

"No." I say it too quickly, though, and he squints at me disconcertingly. "We were getting to know each other. A couple dates. Nothing more."

"How did you meet?"

"My friend Zoe set us up."

"Zoe Tait?" His eyes skim his notebook again before meeting mine.

"Yeah."

"And how did Ms. Tait know him?"

"I think they met through Bo. Her husband. I actually didn't know that until the other day. Apparently Bo and Raul were roommates back in Chicago. Funny how you don't always make those connections. I just know Zoe really likes—I mean, *liked*—Raul." Switching to the past tense, I feel even more self-conscious.

He nods, urging me to go on.

"Anyway, Zoe thought we'd enjoy each other, so she fixed us up." The nickname she gave him, Abs Lincoln, pops into my brain; I have to bite back a nervous giggle.

He notices. "Something funny?"

"No, I—nothing. Sorry."

The pause lingers longer than it should. It's an old detective trick—silence. Most people will rush to fill the void, say something they don't mean to say. I can feel myself itching to speak. Instead, I hold his gaze and say nothing.

He gives in at last. "How many times did you go out with him?"

"Only a few times."

"A moment ago you said a couple dates. Was it two dates or three?"

"Um, let's see. Once to dinner, once to the theater, and one time he came over to my house, had a beer."

After another interminable pause, he says, "Was it serious between you two?"

"No, not at all." I stand and shove my hands into my pockets. "You want something to drink? Cup of tea? Coffee? There's a faculty lounge just down the hall. I can make you something."

"No, thank you, ma'am."

The "ma'am" stings. He sees his mistake and backtracks.

"Miss Youngblood, can I be frank with you?"

I nod, not trusting my voice, and sit again.

"We're trying to understand the events leading up to the murder. It seems the victim had a very active—" he hesitates "—social life. We're looking for any connections that might help us piece together what happened."

"You mean he was sleeping with a lot of women?" I suggest.

He tilts his head back and forth, noncommittal. "It does appear he had a number of female friends."

"I only know my part," I say. "We weren't that close."

"Were you aware of his other relationships?"

I bite my lip. "Um, no. Not until recently."

Again his eyes rake over me, that clinical doctor's gaze. I feel myself start to blush.

"You'll forgive me for being indelicate, but were you intimate with the victim?"

"I just said we weren't that close." I try to give him a prim look, but he's not buying it.

His face is that of an exasperated parent forced into asking his teen an embarrassing question. "Did you have sex with him?"

I sigh. "Once. Yes."

"When was that?"

I blink at him, decide there's nothing to be gained by lying. "The night he died."

SAM

I walk a lot when it's dark inside me. The feel of my feet hitting the ground reminds me I'm alive. I like to get my heart pumping, break a sweat. This morning, in the brisk November air, my skin tingles with the cold.

I've made a fatal mistake.

It was impulsive on my part, that email. I'm not afraid to admit it was out of line. You should be free to choose if and when you fire your agent.

Still, come on, the woman was a cunt. Her rejection email was so boilerplate, so unimaginative. And her "feedback" to you? Please! That was a boob-punch, not a critique. I know the agent's the business side of the house, we're the creative, but do you want someone in your corner who sends emails that cold and unhelpful? She takes the English language and turns it into a blunt instrument.

Forget her rejection of me. It's you I'm worried about. She wasn't good for you. A decent agent doesn't tell you to put something away. What the hell's that? You're an artist; you need guidance and encouragement, not judgment. I know I'm not seasoned in the business, but basic human decency requires an agent to support what you're trying to do. You're the genius. She's the hired help.

The point being, she can suck my dick.

Not to be crass, I'm just saying.

I walk faster, trying to ignore the numbness in my face. An icy breeze whips through a pile of dead leaves. They float into the air like weightless ballerinas.

Even if I walk to Canada, I won't be able to distance myself from my mistake.

You have to understand, I did it for you. Except you don't understand. I know you don't.

I'm doing everything for you. Raul. Maxine. Everything.

Crossing Blackwell Park, I reach into my coat pocket for my earbuds. Most of the time I like to stay tuned in to my environment, make sure nothing's creeping up on me, but today I require music. It's a primal instinct, like the need for food or water.

I put my iPod on shuffle, trusting my fate to random chance. "Sugar Magnolia" starts playing. That song takes me right back to Eva. Back to the aching, shivery fever dream of my first love.

We lived at The Mercury Ranch half a year. It was a long time for Vivienne. We didn't stay with Phoenix for more than a month, though. After that, they got bored with each other, and we moved into a one-room cabin inhabited by an old, drunk painter named Gottschalk Breiner, a German dude with a thick accent. Motherfucker Number Nineteen. He was grumpy on the rare occasion he was sober. Only happened once or twice. He was harmless when drunk, given to singing German folk songs and painting with his fingers. He smoked endless hand-rolled cigarettes and drank red wine from a brass goblet. I was re-reading *Lord of the Rings,* and Gottschalk struck me as the perfect hobbit. His cabin even looked hobbity, with its roof covered in green grass and its tiny, crooked chimney.

By March, Eva was three months pregnant, and I was out of my mind. She was still sleeping with Troll on a regular basis. I couldn't reconcile her innocence with her treachery. She had a way of coaxing secrets from me, things I couldn't bear to tell anyone, even myself. Her wild-animal nature leached the truth right out of me. Her flawless face never showed surprise or disgust. She just took it all in, absorbed my evil like a flower takes in rain.

I tried so many times to convince her we had to leave. She had a fatalistic stubbornness. I didn't think she loved Troll—how could she? But she wouldn't leave him, either.

She died on March thirteenth, her sixteenth birthday. It seemed fitting that a creature so feral should die before she had the burden of fitting in. She claimed she wanted to leave Mercury Ranch, but I knew she never would; she had big dreams, lofty and gossamer-thin. She wanted to run a dance company in New York, live in SoHo. She had it all planned out, but only in childlike terms, with zero understanding of the endless obstacles before her. Her black gypsy eyes only saw wonder and possibility. She had none of the rusty, hard cynicism that caked my heart. Years of trailing in the wake of Vivienne and her Motherfuckers had bruised me. Eva's eyes sparkled. Next to her, my dark, brooding intensity looked like what it was: damage.

I was a twisted, burnt can full of holes, and she was a perfect gleaming flower. Even with Troll violating her night after night, she maintained a creamy innocence I could never understand.

Here's what I learned from Eva: It's not healthy to show people the basement of your soul. Keep them upstairs, in the kitchen or the bedroom. Never give them a tour of your cellar, where the air is fetid and dank. Don't point out the cockroaches skittering across the dripping, slimy walls. Don't show them where you've hidden the bodies.

Nobody can forgive you for that.

I took her to an old abandoned well on the edge of the property. We held hands all the way there. I kissed her for a long time, savoring the sweet taste of her mouth. She became obsessed with pomegranates after she got pregnant. You could always tell when she'd been eating them. I remember her full lips were swollen from my kisses and stained red from their seeds.

I shot her with Phoenix's .45—just once, straight through the heart, from about five feet away. It was a mercy killing. I'd asked her one last time if she'd leave with me. Her eyes filled again with that terrible pity, like she knew something I didn't. Like I was naïve. A dreamer.

She toppled backward into the well, making no sound. I peered down at her through the gloom. I imagined her eyes were open, looking up at me with blank surprise, but of course I couldn't see that far down, couldn't make out details in all that shadow.

That's enough about Eva. She's not important now.

I shouldn't have sent that email. Just because I deleted it from your sent mail doesn't mean Maxine couldn't forward it to you.

God, I'm never going to forgive myself for this.

What I do, I do for you. I want to protect you from fucktards like Maxine and Raul. Your skin is much too delicate, too thin and luminous, to withstand their brand of abuse. You need protection. More than that, you *deserve* protection. I know you don't see that yet, but in the end you'll thank me.

Does that sound presumptuous?

It's only because I know you so well that I dare to be bold. I've read both your novels so many times, I've committed whole sections to memory. *Pay Dirt* was, let's face it, about four thousand times better than *Hidden Depths*. I'm not trying to be harsh, just honest. The sophomore novel is always doomed when your debut's so fucking brilliant. It took my breath away. The first time I read *Pay Dirt,* I knew if I couldn't be a writer, I'd kill myself. What's the point of living if I can't make beauty? If I can write something half as true as *Pay Dirt* before I die, I'll go with a smile.

I'm through the park and on the sidewalk now. The Grateful Dead keeps unfurling into my ears, their voices gentle as ghosts. As I pass Forest Books, a poster in the window stops me. It's a big photo of you. You're looking sideways at the camera. Your Mona Lisa grin holds all the secrets worth knowing. *LOCAL AUTHOR KATE YOUNGBLOOD READING TONIGHT AT 7:00.*

You hate readings. I can just tell. You're not one of those tacky publicity whores. You're subtle, private.

I go inside, pulling my earbuds out and stashing them in my pocket. The bell jingles on the door, and the woman at the counter looks up. She's tall, bony, with gray, frizzy hair and a necklace that looks like it's made from children's bones. She glances my way, then returns to sorting through the stack of books before her.

"Can I help you?"

"Do you still have that first edition *Lolita*?"

She looks up. Her gaze assesses my worth, decides I could be harboring a secret trust fund. "I believe we do. Would you like to see it?"

I tell her I would. She leads me to a glass case at the back of the store.

I'll use the money I got from pawning Raul's shit. Soon enough, you'll understand how right we are together. You'll see how hard I've worked to remove all obstacles. Until then, I'll have to be patient. It's not easy, but I've got no choice.

KATE

I hate readings. Why I even do them anymore is a mystery. It's not like many people come. Even the ones who show rarely buy books. Lately, I don't even have anything new to read—nothing I'm excited about. I suppose I'll trot out *Pay Dirt,* read the same old passages I usually choose. I'll behave like some washed-up one-hit wonder, trying to get excited about the number I've played a thousand times, the single burst of inspiration I've clung to for years. The usual suspects will show: a couple students; a gaggle of menopausal women wearing practical shoes and eccentric glasses; one creepy man who will ask bizarre, vaguely belligerent questions; the homeless woman who will tear through the cheese and crackers while the employees agonize about how to get rid of her.

Tonight, though, my dread runs deeper than garden-variety pre-reading anxiety. Cold fear coils in my belly like a snake. It could be Raul's death. I haven't slept well since the night he died. The night we had sex. The next morning, Zoe went into labor. The two events have somehow gotten confused in my mind. In the vast, inhospitable wilderness of my nightmares, Drew's tiny, old-man face and Raul's splattered brains get spliced together like a bad student film.

As I'm trying to decide what to wear, my phone buzzes on my dresser.

It's a text from Zoe.

> So sorry! Bo had an emergency at work
> and Drew's too fussy, don't want him
> screaming through your reading. Sell lots
> of books and bask in limelight for me!
> xxoo, Zoe.

I sigh. This is no surprise. New moms are notoriously unreliable. She swore she wouldn't join the army of women we've known over the years, the ones who could always be relied on for cocktails or a quick coffee—until the first baby came. Then they disappeared, retreating to a shadowy underworld of other moms, where they planned mysterious rituals called "playdates."

Though I've tried to prepare myself for Zoe's inevitable abandonment, her text makes the snake in my belly coil tighter.

I text back.

> No worries.

What a lie. Worrying is all I do these days.

The email Maxine forwarded has me creeped out. I've read it over and over, trying to understand. Clearly, somebody hacked into my gmail, but who would do that? It's not like they spammed my contacts with offers of penile enlargement. Whoever it is obviously knows me, and, for some reason, wants to destroy the tattered remains of my career.

I tell myself to get over it. Could be a crazy fan, a jealous colleague, a student pissed off about a grade. I changed my password to something wildly complicated. Hopefully it won't ever happen again. I'll probably never know who did it, so there's no point obsessing.

It could be Sam. The rogue thought bursts through the static in my brain.

I refuse to believe that. He's my star student. His eyes on me in class are the only thing keeping me going lately. That look he gives me, like we share a secret nobody else in the world can possibly know. It's intoxicating.

Anyway, why would he do such a thing? It makes no sense. Sure, Maxine rejected him. And okay, so that was kind of my fault, since I was too distracted to offer him the feedback he clearly needed. But what does severing my connection with Maxine do for him? Nothing. I'm his mentor. My success equals more opportunity for him. Conversely, my failure means diminished opportunities.

I refuse to believe he wanted to exact revenge. He doesn't strike me as vindictive. Plus he didn't even seem upset about Maxine's rejection. When I admitted my mistake, the notes on chapter seven I failed to explain, he acted like it was no big deal. And, yes, I've seen how calculating he is. The way he arranges his expressions carefully, like an alien impersonating a human being. Still, that doesn't mean he's vindictive.

Sighing, I yank a dress from my closet and pull it over my head. It's not my most glamorous look, but it will have to suffice. Add a simple necklace, tights, boots, a velvet duster, and I'll pass for an author.

Tonight, that's the best I can do.

The reading is predictably underattended and lackluster. Austin Kleeg, the bookstore owner, optimistically sets up a couple dozen seats. Only about half of them are taken.

Sam arrives a few minutes after I've taken my place at the podium. He slips into the back row, not taking his pea coat off. As I read from *Pay Dirt,* he watches me with such intensity, I find my eyes swiveling toward him then veering away repeatedly. He's like a too-bright light I'm both drawn to and repelled by. The vortex of his presence tugs at me relentlessly. It's exhilarating and exhausting. When I do look at him, my cheeks heat up, my heart pounding obnoxiously. One of the women in the front row turns to scan the room; my stomach flips over. I lose my place, have to pause and find it again. It must be painfully obvious how distracted I am by the boy half my age sitting alone in the back row. Do they see in his gaze what I see—all that heat stirring just below the thin layer of ice?

Afterward, a few middle-aged women from my yoga class come over and have me sign their copies of *Pay Dirt*. They purchased them ahead of time, which is bad for the bookstore, but I can't help feeling a little flattered that they already own it. When they've gone, nobody else approaches me. I look around for Sam. He seems to have left.

As if conjured by my thoughts, he intercepts me as I head for Austin to say goodbye. He steps out from the Mystery section, making me flinch in surprise. He smiles and takes a hesitant step toward me, almost like he's asking permission to approach. It could be one of his many practiced expressions, but something feels different about this smile—more authentic. I give a little wave. Fucking idiotic thing to do. He closes the distance between us, eyes sparkling.

"That was amazing." His voice is low, like he's sharing a secret.

I bat a hand at him before I can stop myself. Another stupid move. Jesus, I'm a mess. "Thanks for coming. It's very nice of you. I hate these things."

"I've always wanted to hear you read from *Pay Dirt*. It's my favorite."

"Not a hard choice. My other book sucks." I don't know why I'm going for self-deprecating. The poor showing and the lackluster sales make it obvious I'm pathetic—no need to underline it. Modesty only works if you're a rock star, and I clearly don't qualify.

He shakes his head, his face serious. "It doesn't suck. You just set the bar so high with your first."

"That's generous." I tell myself to say a polite goodbye and leave. It's impossible. The vortex reaching out for me all night now has a firm hold, pinning me to the spot.

When I finally tear my eyes from his, I see he's holding a wrapped gift. "I got something for you."

"What's this?"

"Something to say thank you."

"For what?" I can hear my voice shaking slightly.

"Introducing me to Maxine."

I throw my hands in the air. "Sam, I totally screwed that up."

"No, you didn't." His brow furrows. "You recommended me. That's huge. She's not the right agent for me. It's probably too soon for me to worry about that stuff, anyway. No big deal."

"Really, I don't feel—"

"You believe in me," he says quietly. "That means a lot."

I feel a pang of guilt about suspecting him earlier. Of course he didn't hack my email. This guy is humble and generous. He's forgiving and gracious. Years of working with the deeply spoiled have blinded me. He's not like the others, with their Amex Black cards and their careless dreams of becoming writers even though they barely read. Sam does the work. He understands that art must be earned.

He nudges the package into my hands. It's wrapped in plain, brown paper, bound with a white satin ribbon. There is something elegant yet homemade about it. I take it from him, turning it over and studying it.

"Looks book-shaped," I observe.

"Very good, Holmes."

Carefully, I tug at the ribbon. The silky pull of the satin resists, then releases. Though the bookstore employees are folding up the chairs, putting them away, the moment is strangely private, sensual. I slide my fingers under the edge of the brown paper, feel beneath. Sam watches my hands with the same focused fascination he trained on my face throughout the reading.

Pulling away the wrapping, I stare at the book in my hands. It's old, with a simple, white cover announcing its title in bold, black letters: *Lolita*.

"My favorite."

I open it and hold it close to my face, sniffing. It's something I've always done with books, ever since I was a kid. This one smells of aging glue and musty attics. There's something strangely familiar about it, like an old friend.

"It's a first edition," he says shyly.

"What?" I almost drop it in shock. "No."

"It is. I got it here."

I suddenly know where I've seen this book: in the glass case where Austin keeps his rare books. I've always loved that glass case, the way it's buried in a quiet corner of the store, lit with a soft, gold light like he's displaying the crown jewels.

"Sam, I can't accept this," I say, my voice low.

"Of course you can."

I don't say what's racing through my mind—that he's on scholarship, unlike the filthy rich, talentless hacks he goes to school with. This had to cost at least two hundred dollars, maybe more.

"I really can't." I try to hand it back to him, but my hands won't obey. "It's too much."

He folds his fingers over mine and gently pushes the book toward me. "Consider it an advance."

"An advance?" I repeat, confused.

"I will be able to afford it one day," he says. "Thanks to your guidance. I'm just thinking ahead."

I want to argue, but I stop myself. It's undignified, quibbling over this here; the employees are starting to shoot us sideways glances. I'll figure out a way to handle this later. For now, gracious acceptance is my only option.

"Thank you. It's incredibly sweet of you."

He shoves his hands into the pockets of his pea coat. "Did you walk here?"

"I did."

"Okay if I walk you home? It's on my way."

The hairs on the back of my neck prickle. "You know where I live?"

For half a second he looks blank, a deer in headlights. Then his expression goes casual, insouciant. "Somewhere on the west side, right? I've seen you leave campus heading in that direction."

It doesn't quite work, this explanation. Then again, it's not outlandish. Could be true. Not inconceivable. Uneasiness pools in my stomach. I try to ignore it.

"Let me just say my goodbyes." I fold the brown paper carefully around *Lolita* and tuck her in my bag.

As I thank Austin, Sam goes outside to wait for me. I can't help feeling grateful for his discretion.

Stepping out into the cold, seeing him loitering in the shadows of the awning, giddiness swirls through me. I'm dropping and rising at once, like riding an elevator drunk.

SAM

Passing under awnings, your face swims in and out of moonlight beside me. You're wearing a black dress, very Katharine Hepburn. You've paired it with your sturdy black boots and a long velvet duster the color of merlot. You are exquisite. I want to walk you home forever, the cold night kissing our faces, our boots stepping in sync.

God, you're beautiful.

It's not so much that I love your body—though I do, of course. It's more that I love the magic that inhabits your body. The way your skin shines like a pearl. The way your limbs move, loose and jaunty. The shape your mouth makes when you're talking, laughing, sighing. The way your blond hair sweeps in front of one eye like Veronica Lake's. There is something very Golden Age of Hollywood about you. You're a classic.

"You read well." I'm not kissing ass. It's true. You do. Your voice is just husky enough, your rhythm hypnotic.

"I don't. I rush it."

I grin, nudging you with my elbow. "Why do you keep deflecting every compliment I offer?"

"Guess my self-esteem's a bit low." You laugh. "Anyway, thanks. I'm glad you liked it."

"Do you always read from *Pay Dirt?*"

You stare at the sidewalk, which sparkles with frost. "Not always. Usually, though."

"Why's that?"

The sadness in your face makes you seem much older. "It's the only thing worth reading."

"You're ashamed of *Hidden Depths*?"

"Absolutely." You say it with conviction. "Wouldn't you be?"

This is tricky. I don't want to say the wrong thing. "You can't get it perfect every time. That would be greedy."

"Greedy?" You walk a little slower, looking amused. "Why greedy?"

"There's a finite amount of creative genius in the world. Everyone knows that. If you claim it all for yourself, that means the rest of us have to make do with scraps."

You giggle. The sound shivers up over the rooftops and spreads out into the stars. I'm good at making you laugh. Really good. I do it better than Raul. That evening when we shared a cigarette at the Lacys' I had you laughing so hard your eyes glazed with tears. Now here I am, doing it again. You look so alive right now, so animated, with your head thrown back and your white throat exposed.

"I didn't use *any* creative genius on *Hidden Depths,* so I guess that's good news for you."

The first snowflake falls. I watch it collide with your forehead. You blink, surprised. You stop, hold your hands out, palms up, and peer into the dark sky. It's the "waiting for snow" stance. A flurry of glittery flakes obliges.

"First snow!" You sound like a child.

I reach out and brush a snowflake from your cheek. You start to walk again. It's hard to tell in the moonlight, but I'm pretty sure you're blushing.

"Do you ever feel like all your good ideas are behind you?" you ask.

When I hesitate, you shake your head, a rueful smile on your lips.

"No, of course not. You're just starting out."

"Everyone feels that way sometimes." I'm careful not to sound patronizing. "Pretty much every time I finish something, I worry it's the last good idea I'll have."

"I just miss it," you say, almost to yourself.

"Miss what?"

"Waking up dying to get back to the story only I can tell. Getting out of bed even if I have a hangover because I've got a paragraph inside my head that has to come out. That paragraph turns into a page, and that page turns into a scene, and before I've even made coffee I'm flying through the story, free-falling without a net."

"Is *Pay Dirt* the last time you felt that way?"

You nod. "First and last. I peaked early."

"No."

"I did."

I grab your elbow; you spin toward me like a dancer. "You can't think like that. You've got so many great books inside you. Don't be so impatient with yourself."

"How is it you're so smart about these things?" You look up into my face with an expression of mild wonder. There are snow-flakes in your hair, tangled in your eyelashes.

This is the moment to kiss you. The pull between us is strong. The moon on your face silvers your edges. I lean in, your mouth so near I can feel your breath on my cheek. The seconds tick by, each one bringing us closer.

You pull away, blinking like someone waking. The snow thickens, swirling between us like static.

"I've never—" you begin, then stop.

"Never what?"

"Felt this way." You tuck a strand of hair behind your ear and start to walk again. "About a student."

Yes! I feel like punching the air. I'm good at this, Kate. I know what you want, what you need—I know *you*. There's nothing you can say or do that doesn't fit somewhere in the bright, gorgeous mosaic of what I know about you. Some of it's because I've read your books. Some of it's from watching you. Most of what I know about you comes from instinct, though. Knowing you is like writing for me. It happens without effort. There's a deep pool of knowledge in me that's just there. I didn't make it. I didn't force it into being. It's my birthright. It's who I am.

I hurry to catch up with you, warning myself not to get cocky. "Does that freak you out?"

"Absolutely!" You widen your eyes like this should be obvious. I love it when you do that. It's fucking adorable.

"Why?" I keep pace with you, though you're walking faster. Snow is starting to stick to the sidewalks, the streets, the parked cars.

"I could lose my job, for starters."

"Not if we don't tell anyone."

You shoot me a skeptical frown. "It's a small town, in case you haven't noticed. Small college."

"Small minds?"

"Yes."

"It's not that big of a deal," I argue. "I'm twenty-two. Almost your age."

You laugh loudly, a bark of amusement. "There's sixteen years between us."

"So you've done the math."

You look down. I nudge you with my shoulder.

I want this night to last forever.

KATE

There is nothing as distracting as the color of Sam's eyes. In class, when I catch him staring, the blue haunts me, even when I look away. It's like God took all the blue things in the universe—icy ponds, morning glories, twilight—and distilled them. The color changes, depending on the light and what he's wearing. Some mornings in class they're the luminous aqua of a crevasse. Tonight, in the moonlight, they're almost violet.

He's brushing snowflakes from my hair. I feel like a girl. It's the most indulgent moment I've let myself have in forever. For two seconds, I stop telling myself how hopeless this crush is. I close my eyes and concentrate on the details—the sweet cold on my face, the smell of his damp pea coat, his fingers touching my hair. He finishes sweeping the snow away. When his hand retreats, I want to push my head against it like a cat. *We could run away!* I think wildly. *We could flee to some seaside town with a boardwalk and an arcade! We could get jobs in coffee shops and write novels and live in a one-room studio with a claw-foot tub!*

"What are you thinking?" he asks, tilting his head sideways to catch my eye.

"Crazy thoughts," I say, "with exclamation points."

He chuckles. "You always punctuate your thoughts?"

"Only the crazy ones."

He watches me, waiting for more. There's something deeply erotic about someone who really watches you. Someone who takes you in. The older I get, the more invisible I become. Used to be I had men's eyes on me all the time. Young and old, married or single, they couldn't resist checking me out. I'd walk across a restaurant, and their gazes would turn to me like flowers pivoting toward the sun. Lately, though, I feel their eyes on me less and less often. It should be a relief. Who cares if I've washed my hair, shaved my legs? Nobody's looking. It isn't a relief, though. It's lonely. My life before thirty had a bouncy, upbeat soundtrack, a sinewy bass line with sex at its core. Now I'm in a silent movie.

Sam's eyes search me. He has a writer's way of looking, a greedy hunger to memorize every detail, stash it away for later. Does he see the same gleam in my eye? Maybe I've lost that lean, hungry look. Maybe that's only for the young.

"What kind of crazy thoughts?" he finally asks.

I sigh. We're standing in front of my door. He wants me to ask him in; everything about his body telegraphs this point. He glances at the doorknob, hugs himself against the cold. I want to believe I'm the sort of woman who can let this nice, young man into her home and serve him tea and chat about books, ask about his plans, sprinkle wry bon mots into the conversation like an old lady in an Oscar Wilde play. Someone who will gently push his hands away if they should stray to my knee, my waist, the sensitive skin at the base of my neck. A responsible, sober educator.

I'm not that woman. If I open that door and he follows me in, I'm going to fuck him. It's that simple.

God, I ache to open that door.

"You okay?" He does that thing again, putting his face in my line of sight so I can't avoid him.

"Just tired." I run a hand through my hair, trying not to think about how good his fingers felt there. Why is it never the same when you touch yourself? "Readings exhaust me."

"Do you get nervous?"

"A little. Mostly because I'm afraid nobody will show."

"Where's Zoe tonight?"

"She's at home." I stare at him. "How do you know Zoe?"

"I met her that day at the mall, remember? And then again at that weird party." He shoves his hands deeper into his pockets.

Goose bumps prickle to life up and down my arms. "So you just figured she'd come to my reading?"

He looks cornered. Quickly, he covers the startled look with one of confusion. "You're not best friends? Guess I just got that vibe. It seems like best friends would show up for a reading. Maybe I got her all wrong, though. Are you frenemies?"

That makes me laugh. "No, you're right. We're tight."

"Did she have her baby?"

"Yeah. She did. Drew."

"Did she buy him the denim overalls?"

I smile. "Yep, she took your advice. You're right. They're very manly."

"I know you want to ask me in," he teases, catching me off guard.

I glance behind me at the front door. It's become a portal to another world. A world where I have sex with Sam. Whatever I do, I can't open that door.

"You know I can't do that." It's meant to sound stern, but I lack conviction.

"You can do whatever you want."

I shake my head. The snow thickens around us, swirling gently. "It's not that simple."

"If you were married, I can see that, but—"

"I'm serious about losing my job." I take a step backward, inching toward the door. The trick is to get him to walk away before I put the key in the lock. "I'm up for tenure this semester. If I fuck that up, I'm out of options. Obviously I can't live off book sales."

"What if you got inspired again?"

The lump in my throat won't let me swallow. I don't even try to speak. His eyes hold mine. The moment stretches on. We're hanging suspended, tiny figures frozen inside a snow globe. When he reaches for me, I don't resist.

His mouth closes over mine with breathtaking confidence. Most early kisses are question marks. This one isn't. There's no comma, no ellipses; it's all exclamation points.

We devour each other, the heat of our mouths a tingly contrast with the tiny, cold touch of each snowflake. God, what a kiss.

When I pull away, my brain finally catching up, he reaches for me with such longing I almost give in. Instead, I lunge for my front door and stab clumsily at the knob with my key. I throw a glance over my shoulder at him.

"Don't look at me like that," he says.

"Like what?"

"Like I'm the enemy." His expression is so injured I want to rush back to him, but I force myself to step inside the threshold.

I shake my head. "I told you, Sam, this is career suicide for me. I really can't."

"What are you so afraid of?"

The enormity of this question weighs me down like a mastiff sitting on my chest. It's ponderous. I can't even begin to list the number of alarm bells he sets off in me. The problem is, I can't seem to listen to any of them.

"Let me in, Kate. Please." It's not whiny or manipulative. It's simple, brave.

I reach out a hand and lace my fingers with his. One tug and he's on me, inside my house, shutting the front door and pinning me to it in a single deft movement. His heat presses into me, his mouth on mine. His hands encircle my waist. Slowly, his mouth never leaving mine, he runs his fingers under my dress, up the length of my rib cage. His palms spread against my flesh.

I've never felt so alive.

His hands are exquisite. He touches me like a blind man trying to memorize every curve. There is something savage and also tender about the way he explores my body. I close my eyes and barely contain a moan.

It couldn't be more different from my encounter with Raul. With him, it felt like touching a plane of glass. I could see him, could see my body touching his, but there was an invisible barrier between us the whole time.

With Sam, his fingers are everything. I'm exquisitely aware of their texture—slightly calloused—and their movements. He grips my breasts with such force, I cry out. My head jerks back. He kisses my exposed throat. He makes a sound that vibrates against my skin, half growl, half sigh.

"I've wanted you for so long," he whispers.

"Sam, I—"

"Please don't."

"I can't help it." With huge effort, I push him away. It's like severing a limb. My body throbs with loss. "You could cost me everything."

"I'm worth it." He leans in again, his teeth nipping at my bottom lip.

"I believe you." My willpower's about to dissolve. I have to get him out of here. "But that doesn't change the fact that this can't happen."

He pulls away. For a long second, he just stares at me. In the shadows of my foyer, his face is hard to see, but his eyes glow with an icy light. "You can't pretend this isn't real."

"It's real." I can feel myself melting into him again. With another massive effort, I will myself to wriggle from his grasp. "But it still can't happen."

"I can do things to you, Kate. I know I can." He runs a finger along my cheekbone.

I nod weakly, not trusting my voice.

With one finger he traces a line from my throat to the space between my breasts. "I want to do things to you. I want to make you feel things you've never felt before."

Sweet Jesus, this is impossible. If I don't get him out of here in the next thirty seconds, I'm done. I yank open the door, maneuver him toward it. "You have to go."

He freezes. My hand is on his arm, getting ready to guide him out. He's trying to work out if I'm serious. Whatever he sees in my face, it pisses him off.

He shoves his fingers through his hair, looking away. "You don't have to make this difficult."

"I'm not *making* it difficult, it just is."

"No." His eyes are full of sorrow. "You're fighting it."

"It's not possible."

"This," his hand waves back and forth between us, "is the only thing that matters, Kate. I've known that forever."

I can feel my brow furrowing. "Forever? What are you—?"

He stops me with a kiss. His lips move urgently against mine, his tongue exploring. I tip my head back and give in again, my hands going to his face, feeling the fine architecture of his bones.

After a long moment, I pull away. The taste of him lingers on my tongue.

I shake my head, trying to clear it. "Look, I shouldn't have to defend myself. I can't do this. End of story."

His eyes search mine for a long moment. He's out on my front step. The snow falls in lacy flakes, tiny worlds spiraling all around him.

"I'm good for you, Kate. Sooner or later, you'll get that."

"Please." I take a step back, gripping the door. "Leave it."

"You can't run forever."

"Good night, Sam." I close the door. When I lean against it, I realize I'm panting.

The next morning, I wake with a hornet's nest of dread buzzing just below my rib cage. I hang suspended in the hypnopompic void for as long as possible. I know I've done something wrong, something I can't take back; I just can't remember what it was.

For a few precious seconds I cling to the hope that, whatever it was, I dreamed it. Maybe the acidic tang of regret at the back of my throat is left over from a nightmare. Any second now, relief will wash through me, cool and soothing as a spring breeze. *It was just a dream.*

Rolling over, I see the frost glazing my bedroom windows, and I remember. *Snow.* Lolita. *That kiss.*

Not a dream, then.

I cannot be this woman. I cannot be so desperate for male approval that I'll risk my job, my entire life, just to feel the rush of being wanted.

Of wanting.

That's not me. I've never been that needy. Lust doesn't rule my life. Neither does feeble insecurity. Pablo and I had great sex, yes, and that was part—maybe most—of what kept us together, but with him, it was a fair trade. We were two consenting adults who didn't like each other all that much exchanging simple daily happiness for scalding sex.

This thing with Sam—and I hate to even acknowledge it's a "thing"—feels a thousand times more dangerous. I refuse to trade my security for God-knows-what. It can't be healthy, whatever it is. Surely I'm insane for even letting it go this far.

In-fucking-sane.

I groan, twisting in my sheets, hating how the memory of his kiss arouses me and sickens me at the same time.

Nothing good can come of that.

I have to get a grip.

Normally, I love Saturdays. I often grade until the wee hours Friday just so I can wake up with the fresh, unspoiled weekend spread out before me like a blanket of pristine snow. There's nothing I like more than piling a massive wall of pillows behind me, opening my laptop, and writing for hours, fueled by strong coffee and a pastry from Miette's, the little French bakery downtown.

This morning, though, I can't settle into the rhythm of putting one word in front of the other. I'm too restless, too neurotic.

I don't believe in writer's block. Even though I haven't written anything worth reading since *Pay Dirt,* that doesn't mean I haven't written. In addition to *Hidden Depths,* that embarrassing scrap heap of careful sentences, I've started countless other manuscripts. The only one I showed Maxine was *Blood Ties,* and that one's obviously shit, so I'm glad I never dared show her my many false starts, which were so full of plot holes and stilted dialogue she would have collapsed in horror.

I'm nothing if not prolific, though. For me, writing is a compulsive need, an addiction. Just as a serious smoker would never attempt to face the day without a morning cigarette, I can't stand to go out into the world without at least a thousand words under my belt. No bullshit journaling, either—way too masturbatory. I need to lose myself in the carving out of worlds, the intricate rhythms of dialogue, the puppetry of plotting, the lush layers of setting. Normally, the total concentration required to wrangle amorphous concepts into scenes is as cleansing for me as a morning run or deep meditation.

Not today. I'm all jangly nerves. The light coming through my window, tinged with frosty blue, strikes me as eerie. The scene I'm working on keeps sputtering to a stop in spite of my efforts to push it uphill. Finally I close my laptop and sink into the sea of pillows, curling up on my side.

I can't stop obsessing about Sam. What seemed romantic in the moonlight now seems dirty, embarrassing. Last night, though, it was all puffs of breath and gusty delight. The snowflakes twirling madly, the cars and houses sugared with snow. The way Sam looked at me. Nobody's drunk me in like that for so long. His eyes were hungry, moving over me with feverish intensity. I can't remember feeling so fascinating, ever. It was a balm. After feeling increasingly invisible every day, I found his need to take me in, to touch me, intoxicating. He answered questions I didn't even know I'd been asking: *Am I still here? Do I still matter?*

When I remember my back pressed against the door, my fingers in his hair, my lips parting beneath his, I have to cover my face and groan with a mixture of humiliation and longing.

Fuck. I'm really losing it.

My night of slow-motion, Ambien-soaked dreams has muddled a few things. Somehow Sam's kiss and Maxine's email keep braiding together, no matter how I try to keep them separate.

I sit up and pry my laptop open again. This time I open the email Maxine forwarded. The one that allegedly came from me.

Who would send this? Why?

Whoever wrote it did so much more than hack into my account. He—or she—hacked into my life. The author obviously knows enough about me to understand how much damage they could do by severing my ties to Maxine. It could be the death knell of my career. A random stranger reading my email could easily deduce she's my agent, but why would they bother to interfere unless they'd benefit? Or perhaps they simply wanted to hurt me. The thought makes me shiver beneath my heavy duvet.

In an effort to focus my free-floating anxiety, I grab the notebook by my bed and write out a list of everyone who could have possibly known or cared about Maxine and her role in my life.

Zoe Tait

Bo Tait (I doubt Zoe tells him much about my career, but it's possible.)

Sam Grist

Jess Newfield (Once she asked me about my agent in class. Theoretically, any of the twelve students in that workshop could be added to the list, but Jess is the only one I actually saw scribble it down.)

Frances Larkin (Again, anyone on my tenure team has access to the name of my agent, since it's buried somewhere in the reams of paper I've sent them cataloguing my worthiness. It's just impossible to imagine the other three taking an interest. Even Frances is a stretch.)

Anyone with access to the internet and/or my books, since I thanked Maxine in both of my acknowledgments. I doubt some random fan or critic would take it upon themselves to fire my agent, though. I mean, what are the chances?

I sink back into the pillows and study my list. Outside, a cloud passes over the sun, casting a gray shadow across the page. I snuggle deeper under the comforter and try to parse out a scenario that makes sense.

Pretend this is one of your books. I sip my coffee for inspiration. *Who has access and motive?*

Zoe makes no sense. Sure, she's expressed doubts about Maxine, but she'd never do something like this. Her own agent, a puckish, flamboyant guy named Gus, is much warmer than Maxine. From time to time, Zoe's suggested Maxine's more prickly than is strictly necessary. I figured she's my agent, not my therapist. As long as she sells my work to the highest bidder, why should I care if she sometimes hurts my feelings? Anyway, Zoe never flat-out told me to fire Maxine. Far from it. And she'd never do something so underhanded. Besides, caring for Drew is exhausting; she's got no energy for sabotage. It's absurd. Double ditto for Bo. On the off chance he even knows who Maxine is, there's no reason for him to contact her.

I cross them both off. It feels good, doing something, thinking it through. Just moving my pen across the page feels productive.

That brings us to Sam. I remember his hands cupping my face like he was holding a priceless treasure. I circle his name. We'll come back to him. I'm not ready to think about Sam objectively.

Jess Newfield's a haughty little bitch, but I doubt she's crafty or motivated enough to hack my email. It's remotely possible, but I don't see it. Her snarky barbs and dark looks indicate the usual resentment I get from her brand of student, nothing more, nothing less. These Millennials, raised on ebullient praise from their misguided parents, are usually petty but not malicious. Jess is a deeply mediocre writer; I've never pretended otherwise. Could she be the rare psycho who takes rejection personally enough to lash out?

I consider this, staring out the window. Bare branches lacquered with ice tap at the glass. I can't see Jess working up enough of a grudge to follow through on something this focused and vindictive. To her, I'm wallpaper, not a nemesis. She sees me as the boring adult who stands between her and an A; you don't carry out a jihad against someone you barely notice. In workshop, she's focused on any male in the room who will slather her with attention. I'm the white noise, the TV droning on in the background.

No, Jess is almost as unlikely as Zoe and Bo. I slash the pen through her name with more force than is strictly necessary.

That leaves Frances Larkin. She despises me, no doubt about that. I'm convinced she only hired me ten years ago because she was outvoted by colleagues with more influence. Certainly she'd like to see me fail. But why sabotage my relationship with Maxine? Could she be trying to kick my already ailing reputation while it's down? The modest success of *Pay Dirt* is the primary reason I got this job. If she can prove to my tenure team that book was a fluke, that my writing career is languishing and is unlikely to be resuscitated, perhaps she can get rid of me without looking like the jealous, bitter hag she really is.

God, am I paranoid, or is this starting to make sense?

I draw lines under her name, trying to visualize it. As I turn it over, my Frances Larkin theory immediately falls apart. She's a bit of a technophobe, for starters. Sure, she uses Meeting Maker with passable ease. The thought of her hacking into my gmail account makes me laugh out loud, though. Not going to happen. Farming it out to some student worker would be too risky. And anyway, she could do way more damage working through academic channels, not publishing ones. Blackwood is where she has

the most power and expertise. She's chair of my tenure committee, for God's sake. She runs the department. Surely she could cast
aspersions on my reputation in a less circuitous way. If she really
wanted to get rid of me, this seems a ridiculously inefficient,
out-of-character method.

The anonymous hordes of readers, fellow writers, and all-around
haters out there are too nebulous to consider. If some nutjob took
it upon himself to ruin my life by firing my agent, then I'm in over
my head.

Which brings us to Sam.

I nudge my laptop awake and study the email again.

From: Maxine Katz
To: Kate Youngblood
Subject: FWD: Your Latest Manuscript

Thank you for your very unhelpful email. A real agent
would not suggest I "put it aside" but would offer
insightful comments that inspire me to make it better.
Your unflagging pessimism begins to weigh me down.

Your services will no longer be required.

The lack of faith you show in my work leads me to
believe you are an anchor on my writing life. At the
moment I need a hot air balloon.

Kate

There's something about that phrase, "Your unflagging pessimism begins to weigh me down." 'Unflagging' is a word you don't
hear every day. But I've seen it somewhere recently. Where?

On impulse, I open Sam's novel from the folder on my laptop

marked "Student Work." My heart's racing, though I tell myself
it's from the extra-strong French-press coffee, not fear. Opening
a "find" window, I type in the word "unflagging." I try to breathe
normally as the mysterious mechanisms inside my computer scan
the document.

I catch my breath when I see the search has found five results.

Five!

We're not talking about an everyday word here, the sort nobody can avoid, like "they" or "said." This is a distinct linguistic
choice, just idiosyncratic enough to account for the gooseflesh
spreading up my arms.

As I scan through the pages, one particular result jumps out at
me: "unflagging pessimism."

I stare at those words, deep dread pooling in my belly.

What the fuck?

The violation of it. The invasion. The betrayal.

Why would he do this? My brain races to make sense of it. Like a
cornered rabbit scanning the forest for predators, I need to understand where the threat lies. Does Sam resent me? In spite of his
apparent calm, maybe he's secretly furious about my failure to
secure Maxine as his agent. Did he hide behind a mask of affable
indifference, only to strike back from the shadows?

But he was so grateful and generous. *She's not the right agent
for me. You didn't botch it.*

Still flooded with panic, my brain rejects this possible motive.
I've noticed how often he dissembles, but this time I can't see it.
He's a good liar but not about this. His acceptance of the situation
was too complete. I can see the effort it takes when he forces his
face into the required expressions. When he handed me *Lolita*,
his eyes were shining, unguarded. That was gratitude, not the
effort to seem grateful.

Something else. A faint memory, swimming into focus beneath
the lens of my fear.

You ever think Maxine's not the right agent for you? I close my eyes, finding the thread and tugging until the other words come loose. *She doesn't understand what a genius you are. You should be with someone who gets you.*

Holy shit. Did he think this would *help* me?

Bile pushes at the back of my throat. The nausea I've been fighting since I opened my eyes this morning surges through me with fresh vengeance.

I rush to the bathroom, prop up the seat, and hunch over the toilet just in time. Vomit spews. The force of it can't be contained by the bowl. Some of it splatters onto the floor. I grip my knees and moan. Before I can flush, the sight of my regurgitated dinner makes me hurl again. I hardly ever throw up. I'd nearly forgotten how much I detest it—the rank smell, the violent heaving, the rawness of everything meant to stay hidden flinging itself convulsively into the light.

At last, I wipe my mouth with the back of my hand and flush the toilet. For a long moment I stand at the sink with a cool washcloth. I stare at my reflection, dabbing at my splotchy cheeks, my waxy forehead. I try to conjure some compassion for myself. All I can manage is disgust.

"What are you doing?" I whisper, touching one finger to the mirror. "Whatever it is, you have to stop."

I don't know if I'm talking to Sam or myself.

SAM

Saturday, I open my curtains and stare down at the shops across the street. The dry cleaner's windows are opaque; the painted name above the door is so worn it's almost illegible. In the toy store, a motley crew of teddy bears and puppets gaze at passersby with creepy intensity. The doughnut shop's windows twinkle with light; the sparkle of snow on its striped awning gives its normally seedy, grease-stained facade a sheen of magic.

On the edge of the sidewalk, an old man blows on his coffee. He cradles the Styrofoam cup and watches the street with dead eyes.

Poor, sad bastard. If only he could feel the joy burning bright inside my chest.

The wintry light streaming through my cheap windows does little to improve my studio. It's a pathetic hole. Dirty clothes and pizza boxes compete for space on the single Formica table. My couch, an orange monstrosity I picked up at the flea market for ten dollars, occupies most of one wall. Old milk crates and slabs of salvaged wood form bookshelves.

It's far from extravagant. That's because it doesn't need to be. There is nothing I need to do here except prepare for my life with you. I've always known you'd never see this place—Jesus, the very idea makes me squirm. I retreat here only to sleep and eat and write and make myself ready for my next encounter with you.

Today, though, not even my grimy studio can get me down. Today, it's a priest's cell, a place of worship. Last night—less than sixteen hours ago—I kissed you. Because of that, wherever I go, I'm in nirvana. This stinky little hovel is the Sistine Chapel.

With trembling fingers, I work the combination on the padlock securing my steamer trunk. The Vault of Kate. I got this box at a pawnshop in Iowa five years ago, right after I read *Pay Dirt*. For a few months, that was the only thing in there—my dog-eared copy of your first book. Slowly, I started adding to my treasures. An article about women crime writers from The *Chicago Tribune*. It only had half a paragraph about you, but I clipped it out carefully, anyway. A review of *Pay Dirt* from *The Boston Globe,* another from The *San Francisco Chronicle*. I added a copy of *Hidden Depths* when it came out, more out of loyalty than any love of the book itself. I printed out some images of you from the internet—the one from your book jacket, another taken at a publishing event.

Since I've moved here, I've added more personal items, objects that radiate an aura of Kateness. There's the shriveled petal from your orchid, the one I watered that day at your house. I've secured it in a ziplock bag. In a small wooden box, I keep a napkin. One day after workshop, as you were leaving the room, you dropped it in your wake. It was smeared with your lipstick. I touch it now with one finger, tracing the shape your mouth made against the textured edge. There's a page from the tiny notebook where you wrote your passwords in your office. You'd doodled a raindrop there and a few random words: *proboscis, Matterhorn, indubitably*. Whether you scribbled these because you were trying to spell them or they're part of an arcane ritual, I'll never know. I've kept it pressed inside the pages of *Pay Dirt* ever since. At the heart of the shrine, your black lace panties sit wrapped inside a red silk scarf. I take them out now and hold them close to my face, breathing deeply.

When I've touched each item, felt its weight in my hand, I lock the trunk once again. The ritual complete, I feel even lighter than when I first woke. We belong together. I grow closer to you every day. Five years ago, all I had was your book. Now I have a miniature museum filled with pieces of you, each one more intimate than the last.

I flip open my laptop and log into your email to see if you've written anything about me.

Instead of loading your account, red text appears: *Incorrect User Name or Password.*

The words start an alarm bleating at the back of my skull.

No. Surely, no.

I try again, typing each letter with slow, careful deliberation. My fingers feel like sausages, like meaty, useless appendages, but I manage to make them obey.

The same error message appears.

I stare at the screen, sick.

For a long moment, words refuse to line up inside my brain. There's just white, formless rage.

I have to take several ragged breaths before I try one last time. *Please,* I murmur to the keyboard. *Please, god, work!*

No. I'm out.

You've changed your password.

You've.

Changed.

Your.

Password.

Trust, Kate. We have to trust each other. How can you not see that?

The betrayal, the slammed door in my face. It's too much.

I pick up an empty beer bottle and hurl it at the wall. It smashes into a thousand shards. My next-door neighbor snarls a curse through the wall.

It's no longer a magical day.

———

"I find the dialogue stilted." Jess's lips are extra glossy this afternoon, the tart hue of a tangerine. But no cosmetic can stop the flow of useless shit coming out of her mouth.

"I agree. So unnatural." This from the pierced-face Raggedy Ann who never speaks. Looks like all the freaks are slithering from the woodwork to condemn me.

Jess goes on, frowning at the pages, her brow furrowing. "I mean, when the protagonist asks the guy for his last words? And he's like 'Holy shit!' So our 'hero'"—here she uses air quotes, her orange-manicured nails scratching at the air for emphasis (how I despise air quotes)—"shoots him in the head and says, 'Wouldn't be my choice, but it's up to you'?" She does this part in a fake, deep voice, like a bad guy in a cartoon. "That's, like, straight out of some Clint Eastwood movie."

I sit motionless, watching her with my blankest, most impassive face.

You kissed me. We stood on your steps and I cupped your face with my hands, and your mouth blossomed under mine, and your small, perfect fingers wrapped around my neck. They were freezing cold, and I loved every inch of them. The snow fell around us in soft, enormous flakes, feather light and tinged with moonlight. There is nothing in this world that can take that kiss away from me. Not even this.

"I thought that line was kind of cool," says Todd, the tatted-up vet.

"You would," Jess says, and everyone laughs.

"The thing I had a problem with was motive. Why did the main character kill this guy? Hardly seemed necessary." Todd has an annoying habit of looking to you for approval whenever he speaks.

"Unreliable narrator." Raggedy Ann is hot for Todd. It's sad. "The protag's crazy."

Todd's head bobs. He addresses you again, like you're the only person in the room. "Yeah, but even batshit-crazy people have reasons for doing what they do. Might not make sense to us, but it's first-person, so we should know what's going on inside his brain."

"Good point." You sit at the head of the table, presiding over us like a third-world dictator.

Jess tries to elbow her way back into the discussion. "I don't need the killer's logic, but—"

You cut her off. "Let's explore Todd's comment. How many of you felt there was insufficient motive for . . ." You consult the pages. ". . . Arthur to kill Santiago?"

Everyone around the table raises their hands. Except me, of course. I'm just the writer. I don't get a vote.

You steeple your fingers together and nod. "As Todd says, it's not necessary for us to agree with a character's logic, but we should be privy to it. There's a contract between writer and reader. We're happy to inhabit a psychotic character's troubled mind, but only if it sheds more light on the human condition. That's the difference between violence that's compelling and violence that's gratuitous."

You disappoint me, Kate. It's been a hundred and thirty-three hours since you tilted your cold face to mine and let me taste you. Since then, you've done nothing but shut me out.

I get it. You're scared. You think you need this stupid little job at this lame fucking college. The funny thing is, the sole reason this place even exists is so we could meet. That's it. Everything else about this university is pointless. The elegant spires and gothic cathedral are nothing more than backdrops for what's happening right here—you and me coming together. Except now you won't even look at me. That's fucked up. You admitted this place is full of small minds. Who knew yours would be one of them?

I retract that. Your mind is not small. It's massive. You're recoiling from fear, like a sea anemone pulling inside itself. I want so much to show you there's nothing to be afraid of. There's nothing anyone here can do to us, as long as we have each other.

And if we don't have each other, there's nothing here worth saving.

KATE

Marching across campus, a cup of coffee in one hand, my bag slung bandolier-style across my chest, I remind myself to breathe. There's nothing wrong with what I'm doing. It's sensible. Professional.

So why do I feel like a world-class shit?

I'm warning my department chair about a student's erratic behavior. It's not personal; it's prudent. In an era when campus violence has become commonplace, it's my responsibility as an educator to report even subtle warning signs. If it turns out I'm overreacting, I'd rather be safe than sorry. Sure, it feels like betrayal, but that's only because of a reckless kiss.

Yeah, more than one kiss.

The shared cigarette on Abby Lacy's patio. *I'll tell you anything you want to know.* The muted, wintry light inside my office. Whisper of lips against the back of my neck. Snowflakes swirling. Hands under my dress, fingers spanning my rib cage. *Let me in, Kate. Please.*

I can't let a passing attraction interfere with my duty to protect my students.

God, I hate this. I feel like a whiny, self-righteous bitch, not to mention a hypocrite—impulsive slut one second, pious vigilante the next. Talk about an unreliable narrator.

I reach into my leather tote one more time, touching the envelope filled with manuscript pages. Sam's latest workshop manuscript. Ever since I read it last week, a cold ball of dread has sat heavily inside my chest, a tightly packed snowball trickling ice water into my veins.

"Cold Blooded" is the story of a clean-cut, cherubic-faced college student who calmly kills people in his spare time. That's not so unusual. Brett Easton Ellis inspired millions of imitators, young men intent on penning the next *American Psycho*. If I had a dime for every murderer's POV short story I slogged through with my red pen, I'd be rich enough to retire that pen forever. My books are dark, so the students who flock to my workshop usually lean toward the macabre. Like attracts like.

The story shouldn't have bothered me. But it did.

The scene where the narrator kills "Santiago" unnerved me like nothing I've ever read. It's difficult to pinpoint why. Was it the glassy-eyed narrator, his medicated, numb approach to everything? The narrator duct-tapes his victim to a chair before shooting him in the head. Something about the scene was deeply visceral in spite of the character's distance from everything he did.

Of course, it's crazy to assume Sam is capable of such violence in real life. That's not what I'm saying. If writing about murder means you're likely to commit it, then I'm a killer ten times over. Besides, if he planned to act out his dark impulses, why would he write about them? Wouldn't that just implicate him?

There's something else that bothers me about the story, though. It bears at least a passing resemblance to Raul's death. While police haven't released the details of his murder, I do know it happened in his home, just like the scene in Sam's story. Of course, Sam's manuscript might be inspired by Raul's death, nothing more. Maybe he read about it in the paper or heard people gossiping and felt compelled to imagine the scene in more detail. A sleepy college town trundling toward the depths of winter has little else to talk about. It's not all that odd that the incident caught Sam's attention.

But then there's the rust-eaten Honda. I saw Sam tear away

from campus in it the other day, jerking the wheel and swerving around a minivan. For hours, I couldn't figure out why it seemed so familiar. Finally, in the middle of the night, it hit me. When Raul took me home from our first date, that same Honda sat parked down the street from me, the windows opaque in the night. I remember how its silhouette tugged at me like a song you half-recognize.

The cold dread in my chest won't go away. I have to take action.

Even if this is the adult thing to do, it's still ugly. No matter how violated I felt when he hacked my email, there's still that part of me that leaned in every time for his kiss. It's like a dark twin I carry inside me. My wicked self wants to hole up with him in a hotel room, live on room service, cigarettes, and sex. My responsible self knows I have to cut ties, be professional.

Besides, if he really is violent, someone should know. After I talk to Frances, I should probably call Detective Schroeder. That's a little further than I'm willing to go, though. It's one thing to send out academic smoke signals, let the tribal leaders know there's trouble. It's something else entirely to involve the police. Sam might be mentally unstable, but that doesn't mean he's a criminal.

Reaching Frances's office, I tap lightly on her door. Part of me hopes she won't be here. No such luck.

"Come in," she calls.

I push open the door and poke my head inside. "You have a minute?"

"Sure." She gestures for me to have a seat, though she's still typing. Without turning away from the screen, she asks, "Did you have a good Thanksgiving?"

"Yeah, it was fine. You?"

"Tolerable. What's up?"

I balance on her wobbly visitor's chair. "I want your advice."

She spins away from her computer, eyeing me over her glasses. "Okay. I'm listening."

"I have this student." I search her book-lined office for the right words. There's a large cobweb in the corner, near the window. A black spider dangles from its center, waiting calmly for victims.

"That's always where the trouble starts," she says wryly. "Everyone knows this place would be paradise if it weren't for the students."

I chuckle. It's obligatory. Frances and I have terrible chemistry. Always have. It's not like there's anything in particular I dislike about the woman; we just don't gel. The feeling is mutual. Once I overheard her discussing me at a holiday party. "Kate's a mystery writer," she'd said, with obvious distaste. "Genre fiction has its place, of course, it's just not the sort of thing I read." I considered going to someone else about this, perhaps the dean of students, but I knew if Frances found out I'd bypassed her, she'd take offense. With her chairing my tenure committee, I can't afford to piss her off.

I press on, trying not to think about how much her orange, frizzy hair resembles a clown's. "He's very talented. Actually, he's the most talented student I've ever had. It's just . . . well, I worry he may have some mental health issues."

"Mental health issues," she repeats, her tone neutral.

"Yes. I'm no psychologist, but something just feels a little . . . off."

"Can you be more specific?"

I sip my coffee, gathering my thoughts. "He turned in a story to workshop last week. It's probably nothing, but the violence in it made me uncomfortable."

She breathes out a quick laugh that startles me.

"What?" I have a feeling I know what she's going to say.

"Isn't that the pot calling the kettle black?" Frances is from Birmingham; every once in a while, like right now, I hear a bit of that southern twang.

"I'm afraid I don't know what you mean."

"Both your books—*Pay Dirt* and—what was the other one?"

"*Hidden Depths*," I mumble reluctantly.

"*Hidden Depths.*" She hits each syllable like she's savoring some delicious irony. "They feature a lot of gratuitous violence, you must admit."

"Not gratuitous," I say, then immediately backtrack. "Well, not *Pay Dirt,* anyway."

"Regardless, it seems a little absurd for you to take issue with *violence* in a student's work. Am I right?"

Last year, Frances published a whole book of poems about insects. They're supposed to be metaphors, but I suspect she missed her calling as an entomologist. She creates such clinical, dry images, carves them out like a surgeon. I can't expect her to understand the difference between what I write and what Sam's writing. I barely understand the distinction myself.

I pull the envelope from my bag and place it on her desk. "It might be nothing. It's just, with all the active shooter incidents—"

"Are you saying he might actually *be* violent?"

"I don't know." I hate how small my voice sounds. "Probably not."

"So why do you want me to read his story?"

"Look, there's something else."

Her eyebrows float toward her hairline. "Yes?"

"I have reason to believe—" I hesitate. I hadn't planned to tell her this "—that he hacked into my email and sent a message to my agent."

This gets her attention. "What did it say?"

"He basically fired her on my behalf." Admitting to losing Maxine as an agent could cast shadows over my chances at tenure, but Frances's steadfast refusal to take me seriously pulled it out of me.

"That is rather serious." She studies her hands before meeting my eyes again. "Do you have proof?"

"No. Not really."

"Not really?" A whiff of impatience enters her voice.

"Just idiosyncratic word choices," I say.

She grimaces. "I'm afraid that's pretty thin. And, frankly, we can't afford to fling accusations at students without rock-solid proof."

I sigh and stuff the envelope back into my bag. "Good point. Sorry I wasted your time."

"I'm just trying to understand what you want from me."

She's an efficient woman, I'll give her that. "Did you ever have a student who unnerved you?"

"Of course."

"How did you handle it?"

"I drank a bit more but, thank God, every semester comes to an end."

I stand and take a couple steps toward the door. "Guess I'll stock up on booze and pray for finals."

"Kate . . . ?"

I turn back to face her, one hand on the door. "Yes?"

"This isn't about that young man I met in your office the other day, is it?"

"Same one." I order myself not to blush. My body's a damn traitor, though. Heat rises to my cheeks. I long to melt into the floor.

She studies me over her glasses. "Interesting."

"How so?" The question's out before I can stop it. I should just leave well enough alone, escape now, but it's too late.

"Sometimes we're our own worst enemy." There's that drawl again, the wise southern lady issuing a hard-won truth. Her piggy eyes stare hard. I can feel them stripping away my pretenses, peeling me until I'm naked.

"I'll remember that." I yank open the door and practically dive into the hall, anxious to escape her knowing gaze.

After my meeting with Frances, I feel so defeated the only cure is a dark chocolate, cream cheese–stuffed cupcake. Logically, I know I can't fill the crater inside me with carbs, but fuck it, I owe it to myself to try. I consider texting Zoe to see if she'll meet me at

Miette's, but a quick glance at the clock tells me she won't be able to join. It's naptime. In the old days—well, last year—Zoe and I would drop everything for an emergency cupcake. I'm the interloper now, the one who has to schedule in advance.

As I push my way into the steamy warmth of the bakery, a potpourri of chocolate, vanilla, and coffee wraps around me like a hug. It's cold out today, frosty and clear. The small café buzzes with students and legal types taking a break from the nearby courthouse. I order at the counter and nab a table near the window. After a few minutes, a girl with blue hair brings me my fix. The latte is creamy, and the cupcake's ebony black. Its sunken center holds a deep swirl of cream cheese. I study it, breathing in the aroma, feeling something like happiness for the first time all day.

When footsteps stop near my table, I tear my gaze away from my beloved cupcake. Maybe some telepathic miracle has delivered Zoe. No such luck. Instead, I find myself gazing at one of the sickliest women I've ever seen in my life. She's tall, with lank, gray hair that's been haphazardly dyed. She's so thin I can see the ridges of her cheekbones; tendons stand out like cables in her neck. She hovers over my table, watching me. There's something at once magnetic and repulsive about her.

"Um, hi," I say cautiously.

It's all the invitation she needs. She drops into the chair across from me and stabs her bony elbows into the tabletop. It wobbles under her awkward, jerky movements. My latte spills milky foam into the saucer. She doesn't seem to notice.

"I seen you with my baby." She's the sort of woman who looks unnatural without a cigarette. Her teeth are a mottled gray-brown, almost tortoiseshell.

I'm so hypnotized by her ugliness it takes me longer than normal to register what she's said.

"I think you might have me mixed up with someone else."

"You're his teacher." She says it in a flat voice that somehow conveys just how unworthy I am of this moniker. "His name's Waya."

"I have hundreds of students, but I don't recall anyone named—"

"You wouldn't know him as Waya," she says, impatient. "Waya means 'wolf'—you know that?"

"No, I didn't." I can feel people peering at us, wondering. The blue-haired girl behind the counter looks uneasy, like she's worried she might have to interfere. I glance at my cupcake, still untouched. I've no desire to eat it with her here. I sip my latte instead, mopping the bottom of the glass with a napkin.

"He's Cherokee. Like me. But he won't tell you that. He goes by Sam. Stupid name." Her mouth turns down in a bitter frown.

"Are you talking about Sam Grist?" It's almost impossible to believe. Sam's in perfect shape. Could he really come from this broken-down shell of a woman?

She just nods, though it's obvious the name pains her.

"Right, okay, Sam is my student." I smile, but it feels stiff, fake. I abandon it immediately. "He's very talented. One of the best writers I've ever worked with."

For a split second, I see another woman entirely. It's like that optical illusion—the one that shows both an old crone and a young woman, depending on your perspective. The beautiful girl she must have been swims to the surface, visible for half a heartbeat. Her dark, cavernous eyes shine with pride, and a fragile smile transforms her features. Then it's gone, and she's a wraith again.

She leans forward as if sharing a secret. Stale cigarette smoke wafts from her. I glance down at my cupcake once more. I'm worried spittle will fly from her decaying mouth. Then I feel ashamed. I'm a bleeding-heart liberal, an artist. Here's a broken woman I should want to help, and all I can think about is protecting my fucking cupcake?

"He's into something. I know he is," she whispers.

I shouldn't encourage her—university policy says we're not supposed to discuss our students with their parents—but a dark, insidious curiosity has me riveted. "What do you mean?"

"First there was Eva. Now . . ." She looks past me, her face so haunted I almost glance over my shoulder to see what she's looking at. I know whatever she sees, though, won't be visible.

"Sorry, I don't know anything about Eva."

She looks frightened, as if I've accused her of something. "I'm not going to say. But right now, he's like he was with Eva, maybe worse."

I finally manage a thin layer of professional distance. I shrug apologetically. "I'm not supposed to discuss students with their parents."

"He's into something." She ignores my effort to end the conversation. Her hands fly to her temples, and she winces. "I get headaches when he's like this. Black pain."

"I'm sorry." It sounds ineffectual—two flaccid, meaningless words. I do feel sorry for her, my bleeding heart throbbing to life at last. More than anything, though, I'm horrified that Sam has such a broken, damaged mother. What was it like, growing up with this woman? Maybe he got funneled into foster care. I don't know much about hard drugs, but I don't think you turn into this overnight. Either way, Sam's dim view of the universe makes more sense now.

"You're his teacher. Watch out for him." She pins me with imploring eyes.

"I'll do my best."

She looks unconvinced. Her face convulses in pain, her scabby, gnarled hands clawing at her hair. Without another word, she stands and stumbles out the door.

I look at my cupcake. My appetite's vanished.

SAM

The Tuesday after Thanksgiving, you look tired. There's a pale, papery quality to your skin, a new sadness in your eyes. I'm in the bell tower. It's easy to get up here—simple trapdoor at the back of the cathedral, rusty ladder, nothing locked. Typical campus security. I watch you with binoculars as you stride across the quad. You're trying to walk with purpose, letting the cold infuse you with briskness, but I can see the leaden quality to your limbs, the sluggish drag in your step.

I spent the endless weekend walking around Blackwood, refusing to feel sorry for myself. You went somewhere. I don't know where, because you changed the password on your fucking email, Kate, and following you around the airport was too risky. Also, I didn't have money for parking. Everything I stole from Raul is long gone. Vivienne hasn't tried to contact me since that day in the library. Guess I can be grateful for that. Maybe I'll hit the jackpot, and she'll amass enough drugs to OD.

The holidays are always a slap in the face.

I don't long for "normal" parents, siblings, a cast of zany aunts and uncles. My loner status suits me. It's my natural state—for now. There's a reason just about every successful children's story starts by killing off the parents. Our favorite heroes are all orphans—Oliver Twist, Harry Potter, James with his giant peach. I know my story starts this way for a reason.

All I long for is you.

By next Thanksgiving, you and I will be in New York. We'll live in our loft in the Meatpacking District. Our bed will be enormous. We'll host boozy parties that will make Truman Capote's Black and White Ball look like a church social. When we finally stumble to bed at 5 A.M., we'll laugh so loud our neighbors will throw things at the walls. When I undress you, I'll pop the buttons on your shirt in my haste; you'll throw your head back and laugh even louder.

On Thanksgiving, we'll eat takeout Chinese and drink dirty martinis. We'll go to an off-off Broadway production of a new play written by a Polish lesbian. We'll walk the streets of the city, taking in every detail with our writers' eyes—the Greek family arguing outside Grand Central, the homeless man with a piratical eye patch, the prostitute in electric blue spandex haggling over prices with her frail john. Our eyes will store it all like cameras; later, when we're lounging in our enormous bed, we'll fold these details into our novels, mix them in like spices. In yours they'll taste sweet, tangy; in mine they'll turn bitter as coffee beans. A hundred years from now, doctoral students will study our texts side by side, noting the parallels, digging them out like Easter eggs and marveling at the evidence of our bound psyches.

Today, though, it's Tuesday, the last Tuesday in November. The sky hangs low and ominous. Fat rain clouds creep over campus like an army of bloated ghosts. You look tired, and I feel cold. A chill radiates from my bones. We're so far away from our life in New York. The joy that awaits us there is a phantom looming on the horizon. It's not real to you yet; you can't even see it. Because of that, any pleasure I take in it feels small and cheap.

I watch you cross campus, your hands shoved deep into the pockets of your kelly green coat. I love your clothes. Everything you wear has a whiff of the past. You don't don stupid retro costumes like the chick with the pierced face in our workshop. You're not into costumes, just quality. Everything you wear is cut with the tailored attention of a bygone era. You radiate 1940s, handcrafted quality. In an age of disposable shit, you shine like a pearl amid gaudy, glass beads.

You stop to talk to that disgusting little desiccated poet. What's her name? I pry it from my memory. Larkin. I bet her pussy smells like cat piss and fermented cheese. I bet her poems smell like she pulled them from her fetid cunt. You look more tired than ever as you listen to whatever she's telling you. Your mouth forms a pretty little bow as you purse your lips and endure her words. When you reply, your breath steams the air, delicate as lace.

Then it hits me with such force, I almost drop my binoculars.

You won't be mine until you're free of this place.

New York won't be real for you until you let go of this cramped little life. A bird in a cage doesn't long for a sky it's never seen. I need to show you what you're missing. Why this never occurred to me before now, I have no idea.

The plan forms itself with effortless clarity. It's like one of those plots that comes to me in a dream, a novel played out in minutes, perfect and whole.

I have vision. My knowledge of our future runs bone-deep. I can see where we're headed. You can't, and that's okay. I don't blame you. There's nothing sinister about your ignorance. You just don't understand.

Once you're free of this mess—the redheaded goblin, your narrow, stuffy job—you'll see it, I know you will. New York will beckon. I'll be there, showing you the way, giving your hand a squeeze when you get scared. I'll lead you to our sunny loft apartment, our spacious bed, our fresh new life.

This is just one more test, like Maxine and Raul. I'll prove myself, Kate. I'll be the knight that deals the deathblow you're too timid or naïve to deal yourself.

Leave it to me. Leave everything to me.

———

I find her in a large corner office. Dust motes float in the gray sunlight. She is dwarfed by the large cherrywood desk, but then, she'd be dwarfed by just about anything. That's what happens when you're a dwarf. The smell is just what I'd imagine—cheese, mildew, ass, decay. Her book-lined shelves give off a musty, antebellum aroma.

"Professor Larkin?" I step inside, not giving her the chance to turn me away.

She looks up, startled. "Young man, you should learn to knock."

"The door was ajar," I lie.

She frowns, takes off her glasses, and scans me from head to toe. "Can I help you?"

"There's something we need to discuss." I pierce her with my baleful stare. "You're the chair of the English department, right?"

"I am."

"So I should come to you with concerns?"

She eyes me. "What sort of concerns?"

"About Professor Youngblood." I hesitate, every muscle in my body communicating distress. I read somewhere that 93 percent of communication is nonverbal. All my life, I've worked hard to convey meaning with my hands, my face. I don't feel things the way most people do, but I've learned how to embody the full range of human emotions.

The silence fills the room.

"You're the one I saw in her office that day." A light's dawning in her orc-ish little face.

"That's right." I take a seat. Her visitor's chair is small and hard. It wobbles. She enjoys making her guests uncomfortable. It also sits a couple inches lower than hers. As if anyone's going to feel inferior to this decaying orifice on legs. Fucking amateur.

She leans forward, her bony elbows resting on the desk. She's trying to seem objective, neutral. It's easy to see the greedy gleam in her eye, though—a sparkle of schadenfreude. She can't wait to get her grubby little hands on information with the power to destroy you. I bet she's waited for this moment ever since you glided into her office for an interview.

"What's your name?"

"Sam Grist."

"Go on then, Sam Grist. What are these 'concerns'?"

God, I despise her. The way she pronounces "concerns," her voice dripping with skepticism. The way her small, puckered mouth turns up at the corners, like she finds me amusing. How can you stand to kiss this goblin's mephitic ass, Kate?

I loathe the idea of giving her the ammunition she craves. For a second, I waver. Then I remind myself: I'm doing this for you. Making this gnome happy is just a necessary evil. You must be cut free from the brambles of Blackwood College. Only then will you see our future.

Only then will you be mine.

With great precision, I school my face into a look of anguish. "I don't want to get her in trouble."

She inches forward. "You just tell me what's going on, let me decide what to do about it."

"I'm struggling in her class." I look at the ceiling, make my lip quiver. "She offered to help."

"No law against that," she says.

"When I went to her office for our appointment, she locked the door." I avoid her eyes, then meet her gaze with effort. "She tried to kiss me. Said I could get a better grade if I only . . ."

"If you only . . . ?" she prompts, so rapt it's obscene.

"If I'd, you know, have sex with her," I whisper.

She blinks at me. "That's a very serious accusation, Sam."

"Like I said, I don't want to get her in trouble," I say in a rush. "But I don't want this to happen to other students, you know? My uncle's a lawyer. One of the best in the state. I don't want to involve him, but I also don't think she should be allowed to manipulate young people who are just trying to get an education."

"Of course not."

"I think you should know what's going on in your own department," I add, my voice full of reproach.

"There will be no need to involve lawyers," she says.

"Good. It's not something I want all my friends knowing."

"Naturally." She stands. "If it comes to it—and it won't—but if it did, you'd be prepared to tell your story, say, to the Board of Trustees?"

I recoil. "Why would I—?"

"Like I said, it won't come to that. The point is, I need to know you're serious about these allegations. I can't act on hearsay."

I look her dead in the eye. "I swear. That's what happened."

"There's no doubt in your—?"

"Why would I lie about this?" I let my voice break, tears in my eyes.

She nods, her face full of resolve.

Your career here at Blackwood is over, Kate.

I know you won't understand, not yet. It's my job to pave the way to our future. Everything, even this, I do for you.

KATE

I have to pee. Desperately. As I look around at the faces of my tenure team, I can think of nothing else. This is the most important meeting of my academic career, and it's all I can do not to wet my pants.

Finn Hobbs, with his ridiculous waxed mustache and his ever-present fedora, eyes me with distaste. Beside him, Eileen Cooper, the spitting image of Judi Dench, flips impatiently through her phone, scowling furiously. Next to her, Lilly Smith, the tiny child genius who specializes in seventeenth-century French poets, perches lightly on the edge of her seat, looking like she might take flight. One of her eyes is a slightly different color from the other, giving her an unnerving, lopsided intensity. Frances Larkin shuffles papers at the head of the table. We're in a windowless room in the humanities building; the walls feel as if they might squeeze tight at any moment like a trash compactor.

My bladder aches for release.

Asking for a bathroom break when our meeting's barely begun is unthinkable. I'd have to trek across the building and up two flights, making them wait. Not an option.

I cross my legs, willing myself to be a grown-up for once.

Frances clears her throat. Lilly, who is easily startled, flinches.

"As you know, this committee has been charged with determining your readiness for tenure." Frances takes off her reading glasses and tucks them into the pocket of her blouse. "It has not been an easy decision. The Board of Trustees will receive our report, and our recommendation will go into effect immediately upon their approval."

I nod, squeezing my thighs together tightly.

Frances glances around at the other committee members. She takes me in with an expression I can't read. Her face is as hard and grooved as a peach pit, her eyes blank. "Let me end the suspense and tell you now: the committee has decided not to recommend granting you tenure."

My mouth goes dry. I try to speak, but nothing comes out.

"There are many factors in a decision like this, naturally," she continues, shuffling the sheaf of papers before her. "I assure you every aspect of our recommendation is documented here."

I stare at the other committee members, still too bewildered to speak. This can't be happening. Everything they asked me to do, I did. The endless syllabus revisions, the massive stacks of paperwork documenting my pedagogy. I served on every committee, went to every department gathering. How can they look me in the eye and tell me I don't deserve this?

Actually, they're not looking me in the eye. Finn stares fixedly at his hands. Eileen's staring past me as if reading a dire message on the far wall. Lilly watches Frances with the nervous attention of a lapdog waiting for a walk. Only Frances seems capable of meeting my gaze. The expression on her face is one of glacial disdain.

I swallow hard and force myself to speak. "Perhaps you'd be so kind as to summarize the key points from your report." My voice doesn't sound like mine.

"Certainly." Frances glances at the papers again, flipping through them at random. "The committee took issue with some of your student evaluations."

"A few negative comments from students with low grades, but—"

"Some of your work on the Student Success Committee was late," she continues doggedly.

"I missed one deadline." I can barely breathe. The pressure in my bladder is more acute than ever.

"Inappropriate student contact was another factor." Frances's tone implies she didn't want to bring this up, but my unreasonable questions have forced her hand.

"A major factor." Eileen finally lowers her gaze so it's level with mine. Her Judi Dench nostrils flare in distaste.

I gape at her. "Inappropriate student contact?"

Frances shoots Eileen a sharp, censorious glare. "That was one factor among many."

"What does that mean?" I enunciate each word carefully. My mouth is numb. The top of my head feels like it's disintegrating.

"It means you crossed a line," Finn says primly. Finn Hobbs! The man who's slept with so many male dancers on campus they could form a chorus line! Is he seriously slapping me with accusations of misconduct?

"I'm sorry." I struggle to remain calm, but my heart flutters like a trapped hummingbird in my chest. "I'm still not sure I understand. What specifically are you referring to?"

Frances sighs, clearly disappointed the conversation's taken this turn. "There were allegations of sexual harassment. I'm afraid they were quite serious claims. The committee felt, in light of such—"

"Allegations?" It comes out too loud, my voice booming around the small, airless room. I force myself to speak more softly. "Who accused me of what, exactly?"

"We're not at liberty to disclose that." Frances puts her glasses back on, a note of finality in her voice. She's obviously eager to wrap this up. She pushes a single sheet of paper at me, brandishing an expensive-looking silver pen. "Of course, you can refuse to sign our recommendation, but I wouldn't advise that."

"Why not?" I force through clenched teeth.

Her condescending pity makes me wince. "If you intend to find another job in academia, going quietly is the only course of action open to you."

"Going quietly?" Finally, the full weight starts sinking in. I see the boulder rolling downhill just before it flattens me. "Let me get this straight. Not only are you denying me tenure, you're firing me?"

"You can finish out the semester," Frances says. "After that, your contract is unlikely to be renewed."

"Unlikely?"

"I recommend you start searching for a new position immediately," she clarifies.

My stomach drops like an elevator with its cables severed. "I don't understand."

"Sign here, and you may have a shot at another job." She speaks slowly and carefully, a patient adult explaining something to a dim-witted child. Again, she offers me the pen. "Refuse to sign, and you'll never work in academia again."

With numb, clumsy fingers, I take the pen from her. I stare at the paper before me, but the words swerve and dance like they're drunk. Some distant voice in my head urges me to consult a lawyer, but I'm too far gone for such responsible behavior. I glance again at the circle of faces around me. They're all staring at me now, watching the pen in my hand, waiting to see what I'll do. It's like I'm seeing them through the wrong end of a telescope; they're tiny and distant, miniature. They all wear matching expressions of embarrassed fascination.

I sign my name. Anything to get out of this room.

SAM

I march through the frigid twilight to your house. It's fucking arctic. I tuck my chin and huddle deeper into my pea coat. I'm Odysseus closing in on Penelope. My feet keep slipping on the frozen sidewalks, but I plow forward. It's ten degrees out. Black ice keeps sending careless drivers fishtailing into the gutters. Wreaths adorn every other door in your neighborhood. Though it's not even December, white lights line the peaked rooftops and twinkle beneath the glowering sky. Even a few smug Christmas trees glisten from behind picture windows. Our pathetic human attempt to stave off winter with tiny lights and pagan symbols.

When I get to your place, every window is aglow. I stand on the sidewalk in the deepening shadows, taking in your two-story bungalow.

Will you miss this life when we move on? I doubt it. The urban pulse of New York will get into your blood, its staccato rhythms invading your psyche. We'll order takeout dishes from every exotic outpost in the city—fig-and-olive tapenade from Iberia, grilled octopus from Hokkaido, fried tarantula from Skuon. We'll spend days on end writing, seeing no one but each other, living on leftovers and martinis and the fumes of our imaginations.

What aspects of this sad, solitary life in Ohio will call to you then? Nothing and no one. You'll dive into our new existence headfirst and never look back.

The tricky part is getting you there.

I try to detect your mood from out here on the sidewalk. Are you angry? Defeated? Relieved? My senses spread out like tentacles, probing your windows, trying to get a read on your state of mind.

Then I see you. You're wearing an oversized sweatshirt and pajama bottoms. The light catches in your hair as you stand in your picture window, framed by the half-open curtains. The look on your face is hard to identify. You're backlit, a silhouette.

It takes me a moment to realize you're looking right at me.

There's no point in trying to hide. The need for secrets is over. It's time to act.

I march up to your front door. Adrenaline spikes through my body. Every single minute of my life has led to this one. Every breath, every thought, every word was a prologue to this.

You open the door just as I reach the top of your porch steps. I see now the sweatshirt you're wearing is loose and slouchy. Your collarbones are exposed. The strong, slicing lines poke out from beneath your neckline. Your feet are bare. I stare at them. They're lily white, with pink, unpainted nails. One foot rubs against your ankle. The gesture stirs such tenderness in me. Your body is an offering, a chalice. You knew I would come to you—there's not even the slightest hint of surprise in your face as I move toward you.

I picture you trying on different outfits and settling on this one, because it's casual and rumpled without screaming *fuck me*. You're not a negligée woman, and I love that about you. When we live together in New York, you'll wear clothes just like this all the time as we lounge around our apartment, fucking and writing and fucking some more. When we go out, you'll put on offbeat, quirky combinations that somehow work—sequins with leather, fur with army fatigues. Tonight you're not wearing a bra, and I can see your nipples hard and tight against the cotton; I want to tear that sweatshirt off you, rip your white pajama pants to shreds. Are you even wearing panties? The pale cotton is whisper-thin; the drawstring waistband hangs on your hipbones, half an inch of flesh just visible.

Our breath forms little clouds in the air. I keep walking until I'm a foot away from you. We stare into each other's eyes; emotions cross your face like storm clouds chasing each other across the sky.

"You sent Maxine that email," you say without preamble. It's not a question.

It's not what I expected. I take a moment to consider, decide refuting the accusation is futile. I nod. "Yes."

Your knuckles turn white as you grip the doorframe, like you're holding yourself in place. The air grows thick around us. Your glare is a knife at my throat. You are seconds away from slamming that door in my face. If you do, I know I won't get another chance.

"Don't look at me like that."

"Like the enemy?" You throw my words back at me. "You are the enemy."

I smell gin on your breath. Your neck goes red and splotchy. The crest of your sculpted cheekbones are pink. I've never seen you furious. You're magnificent, a Viking goddess preparing to launch yourself into battle.

"Do you have any idea how invasive that is? The damage you've done?"

"Let me in," I say.

"Why would you do such a thing?" you demand, your voice rising, ignoring my request. "Why? What could it possibly do for—?"

"Please, don't be angry." I reach a hand out to touch your shoulder, but you shake me off.

"Don't be *angry*?" You're incredulous. "This is my fucking life, Sam."

"Just let me in," I repeat. "Give me a chance to explain."

"Are you crazy? Tell me why you did it."

"I wanted to help."

Your eyes widen but not in surprise. You've just had your worst fears confirmed. You're a child checking the closet for monsters, and now you've found one. "Jesus. I thought you understood me, but you're out to destroy me."

"I do understand you. I'm looking at the big picture here."

You make a sound somewhere between a laugh and a shout. "You see my 'big picture'? That is so arrogant!"

You're in pain. I see that. A tiny whorl of anger twists inside my chest; I take a deep breath, searching for patience. I saw your tenure team gathered in the humanities building, heard them talking in low, scandalized murmurs. I watched you fleeing the building like it was on fire. My huge, crushing love is bigger than your abuse. I can endure anything.

"Can we talk inside?" I ask.

You launch yourself from the doorway and get in my face. "Did you tell them I sexually harassed you? Is that what happened? You're systematically tearing down my life, brick by brick. Why, Sam? What did I ever do to you?"

"I can explain."

"What kind of psycho pulls this shit?"

You're in so much pain. Tears glisten on your cheeks. Were they there when I arrived, or did you shed them without me noticing? My heart is swollen and sodden inside me, heavy as a waterlogged corpse. "Come on. Let's go inside and talk."

"What can you say? What can you possibly say to make me forgive you?" You whirl around and stomp back into the house. The door starts to close. It's swinging shut with the finality of a guillotine.

I shove my foot inside. I should feel pain as you try to slam the door shut, but it doesn't register. "Please don't do this."

"Why would I let you in?"

"If you send me away, I'll kill myself." I say it simply, without emotion. I'm not threatening, just stating a fact.

In the shadows of your foyer, I see your face crease in bewilderment. "What are you—?"

"And then you'll never know what happened or why."

Right away, I know I've hit my mark. You're such a writer, Kate. You need to know. Character motivation is everything in your world.

For a moment, you look like you might still refuse, just to be cruel. Your face is livid, your entire body animated by rage. I can almost hear the sparks hissing and crackling off your skin.

Then something shifts. A look of resigned recklessness comes over you. "Fuck it." You walk away from me, into the house, leaving the door hanging open. "I've already lost my agent and my job. What more can you take from me?"

I follow you inside, close the door behind me. The shape of your ass in those sheer, white pajama bottoms is mesmerizing. In the light of the hallway, I can almost make out the crack, can see the roundness, the curves. You stride toward the kitchen, anger putting a jaunty spring in your step. You're exquisite like this. Pure, radiant, electric.

I can't help noticing my plan is already working. Yesterday I watched you cross campus, docile and sluggish. You were like the straggler gazelle, the one who falls prey to the lion. When you talked to that hideous leprechaun Larkin, your body language screamed *victim*. Now you swagger.

The added bravado makes me love you so much I fear my heart might explode.

It's working, Kate. I've cut you free from your bonds, and you're thriving. Yesterday, you were frightened and meek. Today, you're scrappy, ready to kick ass. This is what we'll need to forge our life in New York. We can't go there seeking approval. We have to go ready to conquer, stripped of pretense. We have to be wild animals unleashed from captivity.

When you reach the kitchen, you snatch the bottle of Bombay Sapphire off the counter and pour a double shot into a highball already half full of ice. Then you splash some tonic on top of that and swig.

"You going to offer me a drink?" It's cheeky, but I suspect you like it.

You glare at me. "This is not a joke, okay? I'm watching my entire life unravel, and you seem to think it's amusing."

I raise my hands, palms out. "Fair enough. You're mad. I get that."

"I'm so far beyond mad." The gin seems to make your diction more precise. "Mad was a truck stop I passed a hundred miles back."

"I'd never do anything to hurt you."

This elicits a harsh bark of laughter.

I go on, my voice even. "I saw the email from Maxine, and I wanted to protect you."

"Protect me?" You stare at me, wide-eyed with disbelief. "By firing the best agent I'm ever going to land? You arrogant little—"

"She wasn't supporting you the way a good agent should." I refuse to let your scorn derail me. "I want more for you. We have to surround ourselves with people who take us seriously."

"What the fuck do you know about it?" you yell. "You had no right!"

I go to the cupboard and take a glass out, pour myself some gin, and drink it straight. Just one shot to calm my nerves. Your rage is thrilling, but I need to stay rational. Only I can talk you down from this precarious ledge. I need to make you understand the enormity of my love for you. If you can see that, everything else will fall into place.

"I know this might sound strange, but every single thing I do is motivated by my deep respect for you." I want to say love, but it's too much too soon. You might laugh at me.

You stare at me like I'm a stranger. Your eyes fill with some new emotion. It's not anger anymore. It's something else. Fear.

"How do you know where I keep my glasses?" Your voice is so quiet I almost can't hear you.

I force my expression to stay neutral. "Just a lucky guess."

"You've been here before," you whisper.

"What? Of course not." I look at you like the very idea's insane. "I mean yes, I walked you home the other night, so I knew where you lived, but—"

"You fed my cats." You're white-lipped now, gripping the counter as if it's the only thing keeping you upright.

The air around us thickens, the tension so palpable I can taste it.

"Your cats?" I give you my best bemused look.

There's a slow light coming on behind your eyes, a dawning clarity. You blink a few times, like someone waking from a dream.

"You've had too much to drink." I put a hand on your shoulder. "Rough day. A lot to take in."

The bottle of Bombay Sapphire sits on the kitchen island between us. You stare at it, your eyes wild. It's almost empty. For a second I wonder if you're thinking of doing something stupid—smashing it against the counter like a sassy barmaid in a western. Brandishing the jagged remains, jabbing them at me. As if I pose a threat. As if there is anyone on this planet who cares more about making you happy or keeping you safe.

You look so pale I think you might pass out.

"You need to sit down." I steer you toward the couch in the living room. I take a seat beside you. I want nothing more than to hold you in my arms, but I keep a careful distance, not wanting to spook you. In the last five minutes you've gone from livid to terrified. Now I sense you're rounding the bend to something else.

"There," I say. "That's better, right?"

"What did you mean, about killing yourself?" You're quiet now, watchful, trying to understand. Your rage and fear are still there, rippling like fish skimming the surface of a lake. You're trying to calm down, though. You're searching for answers. "Why would you say that?"

"Because it's true." Everything in me begs you to understand. I ache for you to know how empty my life is without you. Love, Kate. This is love. Not the paltry, shriveled bouquet Raul offered, or the pathetic heat you got from Pablo. My love is fierce and complete; it's driven everything I've done and thought and wanted for the last five years.

"I don't understand."

I take a deep breath and try to explain.

"I read *Pay Dirt* when I was seventeen. That was *the* book for me, you know? The one that made me fall in love with words. I knew right then: if I couldn't be a writer, I might as well die."

You're very still, watching me. Your hands grip your knees, like you're prepared to flee at any second.

I don't touch you, though I want to with such excruciating intensity my skin throbs. "I really did come to Blackwood so I could work with you. Without you, I'd have nothing to strive for, nothing to work for. You're perfect in every way."

I see you swallow. You're still tense, rigid, but I think I see the slightest softening in your shoulders, a loosening in the set of your jaw.

"I hacked your account because I wanted to know everything about you." I look down, then back up again. "It was wrong. And the thing with Maxine—that was out of line. It was a crazy impulse. I wanted to protect you. I lashed out in your defense. But you're right. It was arrogant to seize control like that."

"Fuck yes, it was."

"It wasn't my call." I lick my lips. I've never felt so vulnerable. Even with Eva, when she burrowed into my heart like a rodent, I never felt this naked. I pray you can see me. Please, god, I need you to look past the flimsy, insufficient words I've offered.

I need you to see the enormous underground network that connects us. "I'm sorry. So sorry."

You lean back against the cushions. Your hands release their grip on your knees. You're not done being mad, but you're relaxing a little, and that's good. That's great. Trust happens slowly.

When you speak, you sound stern but also exhausted. "This obsession of yours might cost me my career. You do understand that, right?"

"You have to believe in yourself more than that, Kate. You're a genius. You'll find a better agent, someone who will help you hone your ideas and rework them. And Blackwood? Frances Larkin?" I scoff, trying to make it clear just how beneath you she is. "Fuck her. If they don't know how lucky they are to have you, they don't deserve you."

Your smile is sardonic. "So kind of you to give them the ammunition they needed to shoot me down."

"Come on. You're bigger than this place."

"It's one thing for me to make that call." Your anger's back, crackling to life. "It's something else entirely for you to orchestrate my downfall."

"Not your downfall. Your release."

"That's not up to you." You glare.

I get it. I do. You're independent, in charge of your own life, and I took that away from you. Maybe I've been in too much of a hurry. I know I can be rash, impatient. I try to find the words that will bring you back to me. There's nothing I want more than to soothe the jagged rage that's causing you so much pain, like shards of glass running through your veins.

"I was wrong." I swallow hard, but my voice still cracks. "Like a little boy lighting your house on fire so you'd run into my arms."

"That's so fucked up."

"Yes," I agree.

"I can't possibly trust you." You say it like someone stating the most obvious fact but expecting an argument anyway, like a scientist telling a fundamentalist the earth wasn't created in seven days.

"Yet."

You breathe out a soft, incredulous laugh. "Who are you, Sam Grist?"

"The impetuous fool who worships you." I grin.

"No. Don't try to charm your way out of this."

"If you throw me out right now and never speak to me again, I'll understand."

"You will?" Your voice turns arch, challenging, like you might take me up on that offer.

"Yeah." It's my turn to state the obvious. "I'd shoot myself, but I'd understand."

"That's not funny."

"I'm not trying to be funny."

I know we're both remembering that day. The heavy silence in your office. Your finger tracing the shape of my scar, searching my face for answers. You wanted to know. I'll try to tell you.

"When I did it before, I don't remember much." My voice sounds small. "I just know the emptiness was burying me alive. I remember thinking, 'This is what it must be like in an avalanche. Getting suffocated by cold, heavy nothing.'"

You tilt your head, considering.

"You're the point, Kate. Without you, there's nothing."

It's a testimony to our connection—our bone-deep bond—that you don't protest. You stare into my eyes, and I know you believe me. There's no pretense anymore. You see me for who I am, and you don't flinch.

KATE

This is crazy. I'm certifiably insane.

This boy has taken everything from me. He's arrogant, willful, probably a sociopath.

And still, I let him into my home.

He's admitted to all his crimes against me, and I haven't kicked him out.

Who am I? What the fuck is wrong with me?

Is it because I'm drunk and lonely and so empty right now I'll take anything I can get? I'm a refugee fleeing my war-torn village, the blood of my family splattered across my face, pausing for a friendly chat with the conquering army.

No, that's not right. I'm Patty Hearst clinging to my gun-toting captor.

It's a bad habit of mine. When my life's falling apart, I find solace in just the right metaphor. When I caught Pablo in bed with his jailbait mistress, I remember trying to decide with clinical precision whether it was more like getting kicked in the chest by a horse or getting impaled by a rusty meat hook.

Meanwhile, as I try to select the precise simile to describe my exploded life, Sam continues looking at me with hungry fascination. For a long, stupid moment I let myself return his gaze. Even when we first met, Pablo never looked at me like that. After the day I've had, with the gin turning my inhibitions paper-thin, Sam's intensity is like a drug. I lean against the cushions of the couch, my fingers inches from his. All it would take is one touch. I pull my hand back and hug my knees.

He knows how to play me. *If you send me away, I'll kill myself.* What the hell is that? He already knows way too much about me. It puts me at a disadvantage. Maybe I can even the playing field—lure him into thinking we're good, then find out what he's planning. If I've got any hope of defending myself, I have to understand why he's trying to destroy me. Keep your friends close, your enemies closer.

"Maybe getting out of here will be good for me," I say, testing the waters of normal conversation.

His face lights up. "Of course. Blackwood's stifling."

"I've never felt completely at home here."

"Where are you from?" He angles himself on the couch so he's facing me more directly.

I get the eerie sense he knows the answer to this question; he's only asking to draw me out. Anyone who's read my full bio would learn where I grew up, so it's not that weird, but shivers crawl up my spine just the same.

"Northern California."

"I lived in Boonville for a summer. You know it?"

I nod. "Yeah, that's close to my hometown. What were you doing there?"

"We moved around a lot." His smile is rueful. "I had what you might call a colorful childhood."

"That can be good for a writer."

"I guess."

I remember that day at the bakery. His mother, with her mottled, gray teeth, her wild eyes. *I seen you with my baby.* Life with that woman couldn't have been pretty.

My instincts tell me to approach his past with care. Though

I know half the answer, I ask the question that seems the least threatening. "Where are your parents?"

"Never knew my dad." His face goes tight with things unsaid. He searches the air. "As far as I'm concerned, my mother's dead."

As I suspected, not a happy childhood. I try to find a question that will strip away the casing, show me the gears and sprockets under his careful shell. Everything I hit on seems too ham-fisted, though, too clumsy and obvious.

I decide to go with simplicity. "Why's that?"

"She killed herself." A muscle in his jaw jumps. "She's still walking around, but the mother I knew is dead."

A silence falls over us. I wonder if I'm pushing my luck. Turning the camera onto him defies our usual dynamic. From the very beginning, it's always been his eyes on me, not the other way around. I'm afraid he'll see through my efforts to unmask him. If he thinks I'm digging, he'll clam up. Can he see me sweating? It's like facing off with a cobra. One wrong move and it will strike. I should just kick him out now and lock my doors.

"Please don't ask me to leave," he says, reading my mind with uncanny accuracy.

I unclasp my knees and scoot a few inches away from him. "Sam, you know I can't—"

"I promise not to ask for anything." He fixes me with that searching gaze of his. "You shouldn't be alone right now."

"I could call Zoe."

"She's got an infant," he says gently. "She might not be able to—"

"I *know* that." It comes out sharp, accusing.

"You feel abandoned." His expression goes placid. He's much more comfortable talking about me. "She was your best friend."

"She still is." I sound like a child.

"Yes, but it's not the same."

"No." I swallow, fighting to think straight. How did we get

back to this, with him the cool observer and me wriggling under the microscope?

"Everyone needs one person they can count on. Zoe was yours. Now she's not."

"We're still close," I say weakly.

He backs off a little, a mischievous smile playing at the corners of his mouth. "She's pretty funny. I like her. 'Gregory Pecs'?"

In spite of—or maybe because of—all the tension coiled inside me, I laugh too loudly. So he was listening that day at the mall. "You heard that?"

"You said I was hot." He stares at me hard, peeling my layers away with those eyes of his.

I give him a warning look. At least, I think that's what it is.

"You need a friend tonight," he says softly.

"You're my student," I remind him.

His smile is just the slightest bit wolfish. "Not for long."

I give him a look. "Really? You got me fired and now you're—?"

"I'm sorry." He holds his hands up.

I sigh, rubbing my forehead. "You should go."

Those eyes. Those blue, haunting eyes.

"When's the last time you ate?" he asks, smoothly changing the subject.

That stops me. "Breakfast."

"That settles it. I'm ordering pizza." He reaches for his phone.

"No, that's not—"

"I'm not leaving until I watch you put away at least three slices of Luigi's Meat Lover's Delight. You're wasting away."

Maybe I can dissemble long enough to ferret out what the hell he's trying to do. If I don't at least try, I might never find out. Nothing gets under my skin like an unsolved mystery. This time, though, it's not just niggling curiosity. If I don't know what's driving him, how can I defend myself?

"Fine," I say. "But after that, you go."

"We'll see." His calm assurance fills me with dread.

SAM

I order pizza and pour us both gin and tonics, making yours extra strong.

Thank Christ, Luigi's takes forever. They employ the slowest delivery boys in the western hemisphere, and I could kiss them for it. They must stop seven times en route to get stoned. Slugs show more ambition than these guys. Most of the time, this would make me apoplectic with impatience, but tonight it's the sweetest blessing ever. I telepathically urge them to smoke another bowl, to drive off into the night and straight through to Kentucky. Never has anyone loved stoner pizza boys the way I do tonight.

I pair my phone with your Bluetooth speaker and hit a playlist called *Kate*.

You tell me about growing up in Mendocino, about the salty fog and diving for abalone and a beach covered in sea glass and distant seals barking you to sleep at night. I tell you about moving every few months with Vivienne, making it sound like a playful adventure and not the dark motherfucking nightmare it was. Your eyes shine as you listen, and your hair moves around your shoulders as you stretch out on the couch. You're still not wearing a bra, and though I refuse to gape like a frat boy, if I soften my gaze I can look into your eyes and still see the hard, teasing tips of your nipples straining against the fabric of your sweatshirt in my peripheral vision.

When we live in New York, you'll never wear a bra. Other men will gaze at your exquisite breasts as they move under your clothes. Sometimes I'll want to kill them, but I'll quell the urge with a witty, cutting remark aimed in their direction. They'll back off like betas bowing before the alpha. They will smell the bone-deep satisfaction you'll radiate. You'll be mine, and they'll know it.

Even now, you're mine, Kate.

You don't know it yet. The way you hold back only makes me love you more. The distance you keep between us on the couch is adorable. As if sixteen inches of linen cushions could keep us apart.

I'm dying to hold you, taste your mouth, stroke your hair away from your face, and let you cry. Of course I don't dare. You're delicate, wrung out by the day and the gin and the accusations. You're frayed and threadbare. Usually, fragile people make me nervous or annoyed, but you're different. Most people weaken under pressure. You're a turbulent cloud collapsing under its own gravity, gathering into a hot core that will soon become a star. I savor the tension sparking between us like static electricity. It's excruciating.

Just being here is incredible. Everywhere I turn I'm surrounded by your things: your shelves lined with books, all of them dog-eared and well-loved, none of them there for show; your fern hanging beneath a skylight, the tips of each frond a little crispy (will you never learn to water your plants? You're hopeless, and I love you for it); the bright yellow rain boots by the back door, crusted with dirt, evidence you're still a little girl stomping through mud puddles. Your home is so you, and I want to explore every inch of it. This is nothing compared to our loft in New York, though. It will be you and me combined, our treasures and detritus blending until it's impossible to tell where you end and I begin.

"What about Jess? Aren't you two dating?" It's a non sequitur, coming off a conversation we're having about memorable family pets. I can see you realizing how off-topic your question is and blushing. You're the cutest creature that ever walked the earth.

"Why would you ask that?" I flash a puzzled frown.

You shrug one shoulder and pull your bare feet toward you, a casual yogi. "I saw you together that night at the theater."

"Oh, right." I shake my head. "We didn't come together. She insisted on sitting next to me."

"So she is interested?" When I don't answer right away, you clarify, "In you, I mean? Romantically?"

"I guess." I look away, wanting to hit just the right note. A silence falls over us. I let it stretch on, daring you to wonder.

"She's pretty," you offer.

I scoff. "Not my type."

"What is your type?" It's almost a whisper.

I answer without hesitation, "You."

The tension builds to a crescendo so rich I can taste it. Your body pulls at me like a magnet. An Iron & Wine song comes on. The very first time I heard it, I thought of you.

Lay here, my love
You're the only shape
I'll pray to.

I inch toward you on the couch with glacial patience. You're frozen, watching my lips, then my eyes, then my lips again. You might bolt at any second. You're a doe, standing motionless in the forest, watching for signs of danger. I want to reach my hand toward you, let you sniff me, run my fingers through your hair and whisper reassurance. I'm terrified you'll jerk away, spooked. It takes extreme patience to keep from springing like a lion.

That's when the stoner pizza boy rings the doorbell.

I'll shoot the motherfucker.

KATE

There's something oddly comforting about the boy from Luigi's. He's nothing special, just your average, acne-scarred college kid in a baseball cap and a down jacket. When I fling open the door and see him standing there, though, cardboard box in hand, I let out a breath I didn't know I'd been holding. It's like seeing something blessedly normal in the midst of an acid trip.

The cold air on my face slaps me from my trance. I have to get Sam out of here. As much as I want to know what he's really after, letting him stay a minute longer is reckless. He's way too dangerous, and I'm too compromised to take him on.

The delightfully average pizza boy hands me the box. "Here you go. That'll be eighteen dollars and seventy-three cents."

I turn back toward the house to grab my purse, but Sam intercepts me, handing the kid a twenty and a couple ones. "Thanks, man."

"Have a great night." The boy turns and dashes toward his car.

Brilliant. Now I can't kick him out until he's had a few slices of pizza. It would be rude to send him packing when he just bought my dinner. Oh, the irony: I'm worrying about offending the kid who's systematically robbed me of my livelihood and my privacy. Something tells me not to set him off, though. He's a chess player now, calculating every move, but if I push him away too suddenly, there's no telling what will happen.

"Thanks," I murmur, trying not to let my apprehension show.

He smiles and closes the door behind us, sealing us back inside our pressure cooker. "No worries. Least I can do."

I set the pizza on the counter and open the box. The rich, velvety scent of cheese and sausage wafts up, bathing me in aromatic ambrosia. God, I do love a good pizza. Luigi's is amazing, a little hole-in-the-wall run by a skinny old Italian guy and his fat Peruvian wife. Together, they make some of the best pizza I've ever tasted.

A pornographic moan escapes me.

He laughs. "Wow. If I'd known it would get that reaction, I would have ordered three."

"Sorry. Guess I'm hungrier than I thought."

He picks up a slice, carefully severs a strand of mozzarella, and arranges it on top. Cheese oozes along the edges; sausage and pepperoni glisten amid the mushrooms and olives. His hands float toward my mouth. I watch, mesmerized, as his fingers offer the slice, inching it closer to my lips.

I'm buzzed, but not drunk enough to know that feeding each other is not part of the plan. Here be dragons.

"Sam." I manage to infuse the single syllable with warning. It's weak, though. I clear my throat.

His gaze locks on mine. I can feel him gauging my willpower. Whatever he sees there must convince him to back off.

With a shrug, he steers the slice back toward his own mouth and bites into the tip experimentally. "Mmmm. Food of the gods."

I grab a couple plates from the cupboards and two cold Heinekens from the fridge. "Liquor before beer, in the clear, right?"

He pulls a silver opener from the pocket of his jeans and uses it to pry the caps off.

I freeze.

It's not just any bottle opener.

It's a silver key chain. With a mouth on it. Lips open. Tongue lolling. The Rolling Stones logo.

I've seen it before. In this kitchen. Opening Heinekens.

I go cold all over. It's as if somebody just threw the door open and let in a storm front.

"Something wrong?"

I force my gaze up to meet his. He's staring at me with his usual appraising intelligence. Except now there's something different there. Wariness. The predator sizing up his prey.

"No! Why do you say that?" It comes out too bright.

He puts the opener back in his pocket and hands me a beer. Then he raises his in a toast. "To new beginnings."

"New beginnings." I tilt my bottle toward his, willing my hand not to shake. The necks touch with a soft clink. We both drink.

I have to get him out of here. God, my heart's racing. I can feel cold sweat pooling beneath my breasts and under my armpits. What the fuck? How did he get that bottle opener?

He's unstable and invasive and cocky and obsessed. But a murderer?

Is it possible?

Calm down, Kate, I remind myself. *It could be a coincidence.*

I try to imagine myself telling Detective Schroeder what I know. It wouldn't be real evidence, would it? You can't prove murder with a trivial detail like that. It's circumstantial at best. So they have the same bottle opener. So what?

I know it's not that simple. My gut churns. Do I ask him about it? What if he decides I'm onto him? If he killed once, he can do it again.

Fuck, my mind's racing. Thoughts blur past before I can catch hold of them. My mouth's dry again. I take another swig of beer, just to moisten my papery tongue. *What do I do, what do I do, what do I do?*

"Should we, um, eat here or . . . ?" he asks.

"No, let's take it into the living room." I can't go to the police with nothing but a bottle opener. He's got no motive. They didn't even know each other, did they?

Unless.

Oh, God.

No.

His Honda was parked down the street when Raul dropped me off that first night. What if he was watching the whole time? Maybe even—the thought lands like a bowling ball in my stomach—the other time. When Raul and I had sex.

The night Raul died.

The walls feel like they're closing in around me. Panic tickles the back of my throat, a scream trying to escape. I take another long pull off my beer.

There's only one thing I can do. Try to work the conversation in that direction, see what I can get out of him. Maybe the booze will loosen his tongue. A bottle opener's inconclusive, but a confession? That's something else entirely.

I take my plate of pizza, my beer, and follow him into the next room.

SAM

You're trying to get me drunk.

This makes no sense. You're not doing it for the usual reason—to coerce me into having sex—since we both know I'd fuck you against the wall or bent over the couch or out in the middle of the freezing goddamn street if you'd let me. You keep the beers coming, though. I caught you dumping yours in a potted plant when you thought I wasn't looking.

You've got something up your sleeve, but what?

Two can play at that game. I get up several times and dump my beers out in the sink, refilling them with water so you won't get suspicious. Thank god Heinekens come in green glass. I want to know what you're up to, so I pretend to slur my words and lose focus. The key to playing drunk, as any decent actor will tell you, is subtlety. You have to remember that drunk people try to behave like they're sober; you have to keep reining it in, not go balls-out like an amateur. A real drunk will talk with more precision, more concentration, just to be sure his syllables line up. The trick is to show supreme concentration and let the sloppiness leak through.

I'm not a trained actor, have never wanted to be onstage, but I've always embraced the art of artifice. When you grow up with a string of Motherfuckers posing as the authority figure, you learn to prevaricate with your whole body, to lie with such conviction even you begin to believe. I read Constantin Stanislavsky and Stella Adler, and I've watched all the DVD commentaries where the actors talk over the movie and explain what they're doing. My life is one big performance, and I'm proud of that. Some people might fault me for dishonesty, even slap me with the dreaded "pathological liar" label, but I maintain we're all playing a role; some of us just do it better than others.

You, for example, are not a natural liar. In fact, you're bad at it. You're furtive and clumsy, and I love you for it.

It's just one more reason we fit, Kate. When we're together, I will do the lying, and you'll be the childlike innocent who lets every emotion show on her luminous face. Together, we'll be unstoppable. You're transparent and I'm opaque. You're yin and I'm yang. Opposites really do attract.

You're steering the conversation in a specific direction, and I try to oblige you by stumbling into your trap.

"Did you read about the guy who got murdered here in Blackwood?" You've been inching toward this for a good ten minutes, bringing up random tales of small towns where bad things happen—a murder in your hometown growing up, a friend of a friend who was abducted in college. You give me a wide-eyed, innocent look, and I want to laugh at how obvious you are, but I manage to keep a straight face because I'm good at this.

"Outside of town, right? Over in the eastern hills?"

You nod, and I see your throat move as you swallow hard.

That's when it hits me. You've connected me with Raul. You must have stumbled on it sometime tonight since you can't act your way out of a paper bag, and you wouldn't have let me in if you suspected me earlier. Something shifted in you about an hour ago. After the pizza came—that's when you started thrusting beers at me and dumping yours and watching me with the cagey skittishness of a kidnapped child.

Fuck me. I scan everything I've said and done in your presence

in the last hour, replaying it all like a surveillance video on re-
wind. But no, *I've been careful. I've been so damn careful.* I play it
all again, my brain heating up like a cheap computer working beyond its capacity. *What have I done, what have I done?* Everything was going as planned, my life's work coming together, our
escape to New York imminent, *maybe even tonight*—board a train
and never look back, land in Grand Central and walk the streets
until we find a seedy hotel. We'll register under fake names, laugh
about how it's the perfect setting for a thriller. We'll take notes on
all the smells, the suspicious stains, the Band-Aid curled up in the
shag carpet because even the grubbiness will enchant us when
we're together; we'll listen to fights and animalistic grunting
through the paper-thin walls, and then we'll add our own fierce
sounds to the New York night.

I pull free of my fantasy and freeze on a single image: the
bottle opener.

That fucking bottle opener.

Most of the stuff I took from Raul was impersonal and easy to
sell—a stereo, a TV, a video game console. Only the bottle opener I
snagged from his pocket was distinct; everything else I've pawned.
It's the one memento I took to remember him by. My trophy.

I recall feeling the weight of it in my palm, seeing that open
mouth and tongue, a symbol of Mick Jagger's fuck-you sensuality,
his rock-star recklessness. To think this cheap, womanizing prick
with his cologne and his restaurants and his Range Rover and his
blow jobs from BAGs in parking lots carried a talisman of raw,
masculine power—it pissed me off. In that moment, I knew I had to
keep it, the way soldiers in Vietnam kept the sawed-off thumbs
of their kills. I had to remind myself who deserves you. Not the
Rauls of this world, but me. I'm the one willing to kill for you. I'm
the one with a tongue that will fit your pussy like a lock and key—
if only you'd stop dicking around with these cheap imitations of
real men and give me a chance.

For a moment, I'm filled with pure, white-hot rage. You let

Raul fuck you. I watched as he pushed your lily-white thighs apart and stuck his inadequate dick inside you. What is it with you, Kate? Why can't you see that Range Rover–driving asshole never loved you? He didn't know anything about love, not the kind that burns inside me, the kind that's made me your slave for five years, ever since I read the first line of *Pay Dirt*. My love for you has shaped me; it's made me who I am. What kind of stupid bitch doesn't recognize her soul mate when he's sitting on her couch pretending to drink her beer?

The rage recedes. The hiss and whisper of a retreating wave fills my head.

You can't be blamed. It will take time. Everything worth having takes patience and work. All you see now is ugliness and loss. You're staring at a black-and-white picture, honing in on the negative space. You lost your job. You lost your agent. You lost the only guy you've had sex with since Pablo. You're looking at me, the source of all your loss. I can see the terror stirring behind your dilated pupils. You want me, and you fear me. Lust and caution.

It's only a matter of time before you open yourself to me. You'll see my actions for what they are. You'll know I killed Raul to ensure our future.

I can wait. Patience is my strongest virtue.

KATE

"So you did?" I try to sound casual. "Read about the murder, I mean?"

He's been quiet so long I wonder if he's even listening. His stare's far away, preoccupied. The glimmer in his eyes as he comes back to me makes the lump in my throat return.

"Sure. Yeah. Sounded like a random burglary gone wrong?" The statement comes out with a question mark attached.

I shrug. "That's what they thought. Nobody knows for sure. He was a friend of mine. In fact, I think you met him."

"Oh, yeah?" Nothing in his face but mild surprise.

"We dated. A little. Nothing serious." Goddamn it, I can feel my skin heating up like a steamed tomato. I want desperately to dim the lights, but I don't move. My heart's pounding so hard it feels like a drum inside my chest. "That night at the theater, I introduced him to you and Jess. Raul?"

"Right." He nods, his gaze going vacant, like he's rummaging around in his memory, trying to find the right face.

"I didn't really know him that well. We only went out a couple times."

"Still. That must have been rough." He pivots toward me on the couch, his body oozing empathy. "Were you pretty into him?"

I breathe out a surprised laugh. *Please, God, don't let me look as terrified as I feel.* "I barely knew him, really."

"Did you sleep with him?" His voice is suddenly hard.

I have to concentrate on keeping my reply calm. "How is that your business?"

"Come on, Kate. You can be honest with me."

"I don't want to talk about it." My hands tremble as I gesticulate. I still them on my thighs, willing myself to calm down. If he thinks I'm onto him, it's over.

"You're the one who brought it up." He's got that cold, icy stare trained on me, and I can see him weighing his options, deciding how much I know and what to do about it.

"Let's talk about you." My words sound stilted.

We eat our pizza in silence for a moment. I get up and turn on the gas fireplace.

"How's your novel coming?" I ask, trying to sound like I'm breathing normally.

"It's done."

"Aren't you revising?"

He looks hurt. "No. Not really."

"Have you started on something new?" I ask brightly. Too brightly. Fuck, I'm bad at this.

"Of course." He hesitates. "I don't talk about what I'm writing until I'm done with a draft, at least."

"Totally get that." It's a relief to land on familiar ground. "And, by the way, when I suggested you revise, I'm not saying that because it's less than brilliant. It really is amazing."

"Yeah?" He lowers his chin and looks at me from beneath dark brows.

I nod. "Amazing. And you know I'm stingy with praise."

"You're famous for it."

"Guess that makes me a bitch, in most people's estimation, but—"

"Fuck them," he spits, agitated. "Bunch of whiny babies."

So much for my plan to steer the conversation toward Raul. Did I seriously think he'd confess? Now all I've done is put him on guard. Nice work, Kate. Very smooth.

"You're one of the few people I've met who's willing to be honest," he says.

"Thanks." After a pause, I slap my thighs in a gesture of closure. "Well, this has been fun, but I should really go to bed. It's been a crazy day."

He ignores this obvious cue. "What will you do next?"

"About what?"

"Your life." His eyes look darker than usual, almost purple.

I consider the question. During this whole conversation, there's a hamster racing on a wheel inside my heart, frantically trying to escape. "I'll go wherever I can get a job."

"Have you ever thought about New York?"

"What about it?" I ask, surprised.

His shrug is elaborately casual. "Ever thought about giving it a shot?"

"New York City?" I ask.

He nods.

"Not really. I mean, it's always seemed very glamorous, the heart of publishing and all that."

"The heart of the entire world." He says it with such passion I do a double take.

"You've lived there?" I ask.

He shakes his head. "Not yet. But I'm moving there."

"Really?" I'm caught off guard by that. "When?"

"As soon as I can convince you to go with me." His eyes are dead serious.

It takes me a second to respond. "You're joking, right?"

For a long, tense moment we stare at one another, teetering on a precipice I didn't even know was there.

"Kate?"

"Yes?"

His eyes bore into me. "Don't you trust me?"

"Trust you?" I think about it. My brain feels like a frozen pond; my thoughts move sluggishly through ice-cold fear. "In general, you mean, or—?"

"Are you afraid of me?" He moves closer.

"A little."

His fingers brush a tendril of hair away from my forehead. "I would never, ever hurt you."

"Okay."

"Never."

"Sam, I don't think we should—"

He tilts forward as if to kiss me. I recoil, standing up, bumping my forehead hard against his in the process.

"Look, you really have to go now."

SAM

You're so skittish, Kate. Even now, when I've cut you free of your moorings. You're on a sailboat drifting out into the moonlit night, but you're still grasping at the shore, trying to hold on to the lines.

"Why do you keep pushing me away?"

"Look, I get why you'd move to New York. When you're young, the world's wide open, but I'm not in that place—"

"You could be," I interrupt. "You should be. You're not old."

"I have to make a living." You look very tired.

I lean forward, touching my forehead to yours. "Come to New York with me. Tonight."

"Tonight?" You say it like you've never heard the word in your life.

"Why not? What have you got to lose?"

You look lost.

I press my advantage. "It's all I've ever wanted, Kate. You and me in the greatest city on earth. What could go wrong?"

You laugh.

"Don't laugh," I warn you. This is not a joke.

Your lips tuck together as if to hold in your mirth, but it gurgles up from your throat just the same.

"Why are you laughing?" My own voice sounds hard, but I

can't soften it. I tell you what I want more than anything, my entire reason for living, and you laugh? What the hell, Kate?

"I'm sorry." But you don't look sorry. "What would we do there?"

"Live. Write. Become famous. Love each other."

You laugh again. This time there's a thin edge of hysteria in it. I can feel my anger rising, but I force myself to breathe. Out of nowhere, I remember the relaxation technique Motherfucker Number Nine taught me: breathe in for a count of four, belly extends; breathe out for a count of six, belly contracts.

You're not laughing at me, I remind myself. You're just nervous. Overwhelmed. We both are.

Though it's backfired so far, I continue confessing. It's like a vein's been opened, and the words pour out. "We could create our lives anew. Walk the city at all hours and feed our imaginations. We'll record everything we see with our eyes—fuck Instagram, our brains will be our cameras—and then we'll go home and write about it and read each other our pages by candlelight, drinking and laughing, and then I'll go down on you and—"

"Okay, you know what?" You start to pace the room. You're no longer laughing, but this new hardness in your face might be worse than nervous giggles. "You've got one hell of a fantasy going, but I'm not the girl who belongs in that picture."

"Why not?" I ask, mystified.

"Because I'm thirty-eight years old, Sam!" You're exasperated. You throw your hands up in the air, like this should explain everything.

"So?"

"I already went through my move-to-a-new-city-and-reinvent-myself phase. Several times. I'm over it."

You're killing me. "It's not a phase."

"It doesn't feel like a phase when you're living it." You touch my arm, apologetic, distant. "That's the whole point. If I see it as a phase and you see it as your life, we'll always be at odds."

"Why are you doing this?" It takes effort to get the words out.

"I need to get some sleep." You offer a wan smile.

I stare at you, willing you to stop behaving like an aloof, condescending bitch. You need to take a good, hard look at what I'm offering. I've torn my chest cavity open and ripped out my raw, beating heart. The blood's still pouring down my forearm, pooling at my elbow, dripping onto the floor, and all you can think to say is *I need to get some sleep*? Really?

You're scared.

You're refusing the call to adventure.

The reluctant heroine.

I won't back down from this challenge. You're begging to be convinced. I can do this. I can do anything. My life's been one big rehearsal for this moment. Your cynicism's no match for my optimism.

It's obvious, though, we're done for tonight. I may be an optimist, but I'm not stupid.

I shove my hands into my pockets. "Yeah. Okay. Sorry if I stayed longer than I should've."

"It's fine." You smile again, but it does nothing to mask how frightened and tired you are. Your eyelids are so thin and pale they're almost translucent. "Thanks for the pizza."

"No problem." I move toward the door, though it kills me to leave the warm embrace of your living room.

When you open the door, cold air rushes in. "Good night, Sam."

I feel cheap, exposed, empty. "Yeah. Good night."

I'm too depressed to even try for a kiss.

KATE

I call Detective Schroeder as soon as Sam leaves. My fingers tremble so violently I can barely dial. I get his voicemail. My brain freezes after the beep, but I try to find the right words.

"Hello, Detective. It's Kate Youngblood. Professor at Blackwood? Listen, there's something I need to . . ." I hesitate, my thoughts spinning, refusing to find traction. "I need to tell you something about the case you're investigating."

After I hang up, I walk around my house, restless and indecisive. I don't want to be alone here. There's no way I'll be able to sleep. I feel like I've wandered into a nightmare; I can't tell what's a real threat and what's a mere phantom conjured by my overactive imagination.

"Sam killed Raul." I say it aloud, just to see if it sounds crazy. I really can't tell if I'm overreacting or underreacting. Either way, I don't have definitive proof. There could be any number of logical explanations for why he has the same bottle opener. Lots of reasons. Maybe it's a trendy man thing, some sort of masculine fashion statement. Or there was a concert and they gave those away as swag. It doesn't mean anything.

So why am I trembling uncontrollably? Why have my teeth started to chatter?

He admitted to hacking my email, sending Maxine that damning message. He admitted to accusing me of sexual harassment. Someone who invades a person's privacy and fucks with their life without regret—that's sociopathic, surely. When I confronted him, he barely even seemed bothered. Sure, he apologized, but it was obvious he believed in the inherent rightness of what he'd done. Or maybe rightness and wrongness don't factor in for him. There's only what he wants, and what he's willing to do to get it. That's the definition of a sociopath, right? Someone who doesn't give a shit about anyone else. I decide to look it up, just to be sure. Precise definitions calm me.

I pull the OED off my shelf. Just flipping through the pages, I'm soothed, although my hands are still shaking. I find the right entry and whisper the words aloud.

"A person with a personality disorder manifesting itself in extreme antisocial attitudes and behavior and a lack of conscience."

Someone who doesn't give a flying fuck.

If he's a sociopath, that opens the doors to other possibilities. Easy enough to commit murder if you've got no empathy. Can you be a sociopath with a code of honor? Is that even possible? If so, that would be Sam. I'm pretty sure he's got a moral compass; it's just fucking whacked.

You don't really know him, I remind myself. *You're basing all this on his writing and what little time you've spent with him.*

It occurs to me, somewhat tangentially, that I could call Maxine, explain about Sam and what he did. She met him; she read his work. Maybe his peculiar brand of psychosis will make sense to her once I explain it, and she'll see me as the victim here. I try to imagine us having a good laugh over it, perhaps turning it into an anecdote we'll share at cocktail parties—that time when Kate's crazy student tried to sabotage her life.

Even as I'm dreaming this up, I know it's not going to happen. Maxine was dying for an excuse to get rid of me. That's clear. She probably planned to drop me anyway, unwilling to be shackled to a has-been. I bet she felt guilty about it, wanted to find the right moment. Even if she believes me about Sam, she'll probably figure it serves me right for being such a weak judge of character. I introduced her to the psycho, after all. I vouched for him. What does that say about me?

I stop in front of my French doors, caught by my reflection in the glass. I've got my wool throw draped over my shoulders. I look old and frail. My skin's so white it's almost gray. I'm withered, desiccated. I rest my forehead against the cool glass, willing myself to think clearly.

That night, when he walked me home, I felt so young, so alive. The snow and the moonlight, his open fascination. The feel of my back pressing against the door as he pinned me with his body. Even now, knowing what I know—suspecting what I suspect—it doesn't change the chills I get reliving that strange, romantic hour. I pull the first edition of *Lolita* from its place of honor on the top shelf.

My phone vibrates. I look at the screen, surprised Detective Schroeder would call me back so late. It's not him, though. It's Zoe. I answer, swallowing hard before I try to speak.

"Hey. What's up?"

"I don't know." She sounds a little dazed, like she just woke up. "I had this feeling I should call you. Like maybe you need something. You okay?"

That's all it takes. I burst into sobs.

"Come over." It's not a request; it's a command. "Right now."

"I'm on my way." I wipe my eyes, shove my phone into my pocket. I grab my keys, my coat, my purse, and practically run out the door, like someone managing a narrow escape.

It strikes me that the only two men who truly look at me these days make strange bedfellows: a probable murderer and the detective who's investigating said murder. Maybe that's the price of aging. You no longer have to feel naked walking down the street, men's eyes pawing at you like so many hands. In exchange, you disappear, except when it comes to men who need something from you, men with their own twisted agendas.

That's not a very positive outlook. Must be the lack of sleep, the stiffness in my neck, the fact that my life is falling apart.

I stay at Zoe's Tuesday night and meet with Detective Schroeder first thing Wednesday morning. I call in sick to work and don't feel even a little guilty. Fuck them. Baby Drew woke up eleven times. I counted. How do parents do it? I'd brain the little monster. He is cute, though, I'll give him that. Nature's way of ensuring fewer parents give in to their infanticidal urges.

Zoe's a rock. I'm so glad she called. Even if their guest bed is an instrument of torture, and their offspring doubly so, she pulled me back from the abyss. I would have driven myself crazy home alone. Flinching at every gust of wind, hiding under my duvet like a frightened little girl. As soon as I arrived, she poured me a massive glass of wine, and I told her everything. She listened, her expression bouncing from sympathetic to horrified to calm in just the right places. Zoe has always been a great listener. Even now, with one ear cocked for Drew's cries, she can pull the truth from me like nobody else.

Detective Schroeder and I arrange to meet at the station. I've never been to a police station before. I suppose I should have been by now—a crime writer should research these things—but the opportunity never arose. It's completely sterile and devoid of drama, which is disappointing. I didn't realize until I got there that I had expectations; I pictured myself being interviewed on the set of *Castle*, with soft lighting and an elaborate murder board in the background. Lots of cops milling about, talking shop, making jokes, drinking coffee, studying forensic samples. I feel ridiculous when I realize how made-for-TV my assumptions are. I take a seat across from Schroeder in his office, trying not to fixate on his cheap, particleboard desk or the stained Berber carpet.

"So," he presses his elbows into the desk, leaning toward me. "What did you want to tell me, Professor Youngblood?"

"It's about Raul's murder." I bite my lip, trying to think of the best way to frame this.

He studies me with reptilian distance. He reminds me of a crocodile, that predatory stillness. It feels like he's biding his time. At any moment his jaws might snap open.

"So I gathered," he says, not moving. "Go on."

"I have a student. His name's Sam Grist."

He pulls a notebook from his pocket and scribbles something. "Grist. Okay. What about him?"

"He has the same bottle opener Raul carried."

His bushy eyebrows pull together. "The same bottle opener?"

"Yes. With the Rolling Stones logo. You know the one?"

He looks puzzled.

"You know, the lips, the tongue?" I stick my tongue out by way of illustration.

His looks slightly alarmed, but then he gets it. "Oh, right. I know what you mean. Red and black, right?"

"Exactly." I look at my lap. "Sam has the exact same kind Raul had, and it got me thinking: Where did he get it?"

He nods. "How did you happen to see this bottle opener?"

Fuck. I can feel all the blood rushing to my cheeks. "I saw him using it."

"In class? On campus?"

I consider lying, but I know I'm no good at it. "No. At my house."

This time the bushy eyebrows fly straight up. "At your house."

"Yes. He came by. We shared a pizza." Oh my God. Why did I not think this through? Suddenly I feel like the criminal.

He jots something down in his notebook. "Forgive me for asking, but are you in the habit of entertaining students at your home?"

"No." My mouth feels like it's full of sand. "I didn't invite him. He just showed up."

"With pizza?"

"No. We ordered that once he got there." I push my hair away from my face, flustered. "Look, I know this sounds sketchy, but it's not—we're—I mean, yes, he has a crush on me, but we're not . . ." I sputter to a stop.

"I'm not accusing you of anything," he says, more gently than I'd expect.

"It's not like it sounds. I had a very strange day yesterday."

"So, you're not in a relationship with this student?" He asks it in a neutral tone, perfectly reasonable, like it doesn't matter to him one way or the other.

"No. Not like that. Of course not."

He nods. "Did this Sam Grist ever spend time with Mr. Torres?"

"Not that I know of." I consider. "They were both at the party where I met Raul? But I never saw them interact. Oh, and I did introduce them once, very briefly."

"Really?" He looks mildly surprised.

"It wasn't a big deal." Why do I sound like I'm making excuses? "Raul and I went on a date, and Sam was there with a girl—"

"Where was this?" He flips a page in his tiny notebook; his pen hovers over the paper.

"On campus. We went to *Oleanna*."

"Sorry, is that a café or . . . ?"

"A play. David Mamet?"

"Oh, yeah. The guy who did *Heist*?"

I'm impressed. "Exactly."

"So you were at the theater, then."

"Right. I went with Raul—it was our second date—and Sam sat next to us, just by chance. He was with another student of mine, Jess . . . her last name's Newfield."

"Jessica Newfield?"

"Yeah. That sounds right."

He jots it down. "Is she Sam's girlfriend?"

"He says no." I shrug. "I have no way to be sure. She flirts with him in class, but who knows?"

"So, you introduced them—Sam and Raul?"

"Yes. And Jess, too. We made small talk for a few minutes, and that was it." I try not to think about the heat I felt coming off Sam the whole performance, the way just touching my elbow to his made me sweat.

I meet Schroeder's eye and suddenly feel self-conscious again. He's looking at me with steady, searching intensity.

"Was there something else you wanted to say?" He leans forward slightly.

"About that night?"

"Yes."

"No, why?"

His head tilts slightly to the side. "You looked like you had something to add, that's all."

"No." I sound like a teenager evading her father's questions. I sigh, frustrated. "Look, the thing is, this kid Sam is obsessed with me. He hacked into my email, fired my agent."

"Your agent?"

"Pretended to be me, told her we're through." I take a deep breath, steeling myself for my next revelation. "He even told my boss I sexually harassed him, which got me fired."

"That's pretty serious."

"You're telling me! He's ruining my life."

His eyebrows arch, but otherwise his expression remains unchanged. He waits for me to go on.

"I think I saw his car near my house the first night I went out with Raul. A silver Honda."

He nods, barely glancing at his notepad as he jots that down.

"And then, last night, when I saw that bottle opener, which I *know* was Raul's . . ."

"Does it have distinctive markings? Dents or scratches you recognized as unique and definitive?"

"No. But come on. It's unusual, right? How many people have that specific bottle opener?"

"I couldn't tell you." He glances over my shoulder very quickly at the clock.

I stare him down. "I'm not saying Sam killed Raul."

"What *are* you saying, Ms. Youngblood?" It's not a challenge but a gentle invitation.

"That it's possible." Suddenly, to my great annoyance, a sob tries to burst from my lips. I swallow it down like a sneeze.

"Are you all right?" He's solicitous, leaning forward. His squinty eyes study my face.

I force myself to speak in a calm, even tone. "He kind of scares me."

He sets his notebook down and leans back in his chair. "But owning the same bottle opener and meeting that night at the theater—those are the only connections between them, as far as you know?"

The evidence looks threadbare when he puts it like that. I just nod.

"Anything else that makes you think we should look at this young man?"

"He's obsessed with me," I repeat, praying it doesn't sound delusional. "He thinks we're going to run off together."

He considers this for a long moment, his calm gray eyes assessing me. "Are you suggesting he may have killed Raul Torres out of jealousy? Perhaps he saw you and the victim together and became enraged?"

"I'm not sure."

"Do you believe he's mentally unstable?"

"Maybe." I hold his gaze. "He's very bright, talented, but I think he might be a sociopath."

"What makes you say that?"

I choose my words carefully. "He seems incapable of empathy.

Like he'll do anything to get what he wants, no matter who gets hurt."

"Has he ever been violent that you know of?"

"No." I hesitate. "Unless you count his stories."

"His stories?" he echoes.

"He's in my fiction workshop, so I read his work. Sometimes it's pretty violent. In fact, his last manuscript made my skin crawl, and that's saying something. I even told my department chair about it."

"Was he concerned?"

"She," I correct him. "No. Not really."

"Has he ever made threats, either to you or his fellow students?"

"Not that I'm aware of." I pause. "He threatened to kill himself, though."

"When and where was that?"

Great, now we're back to last night. "At my place. Last night. That's the main reason I let him in. He's tried it before."

"Attempted suicide?"

I nod. "He's got scars on his wrists. We've talked about it."

"I see." He nods, completely unfazed. "Anything else you want to tell me?"

I feel lost. Don't ask me what I thought he'd do. Rush to get a warrant? Organize a SWAT team? All I know is, the blank look he gives me feels like a brush-off. I'm on my own.

"No. I guess that's it."

The detective stands. So do I.

He puts one hand on my elbow, steering me toward the door. "Well, Professor, it's an interesting theory. We'll definitely keep it in mind."

"Do you have any suspects? Besides me, I mean?" I try to laugh, but it comes out sounding strangled.

"We're working on it." He gives me a tight smile and opens the door.

I take the hint and step out into the hall. "I know it sounds a little out there. I just have a feeling about this. You know? Intuition."

"Sure." He starts to close the door, a placid smile on his thin lips. "Thanks for your help. We'll be in touch."

SAM

I'm so tired of being right.

Everyone talks about doing what's right, but nobody has the balls to follow through. I'm the only person I know who actually lives by a code of honor. I get that it might not be everyone's code, but it's mine, and I stick to it, day in and day out.

Fuck other people. Fuck legal systems and the ten commandments and everybody judging shit they don't understand.

You're leaving the police station, your face tense with worry. I can tell by the way you slam the door of your Saab you're pissed. It's a scrappy gesture, and it turns me on even though I should throttle you. Guess the cops didn't take your concerns to heart. You went running to them like a whiny little bitch. I bet they laughed at your wild accusations. Thank god for inept law enforcement.

Here's the truth, Kate: Nobody wants you to know how easy it is to get away with murder. Criminals with half a brain, decent impulse control, and a modicum of organization can accomplish a lot and never get caught. It's just too hard to connect someone to a crime if he hasn't left behind any clues.

Yet, you ran to the cops like some damsel in distress. Why, Kate? What I did was justifiable homicide. That guy fucked you, and he didn't deserve you. Not for a second. He was trolling the clubs, and he was an all-round self-absorbed man-whore, just like your ex, Pablo. I had to save you from that. What I did was right. I did it out of love. Out of honor. Nothing that comes from love can ever be wrong.

I follow your Saab, keeping a car or two between us at all times. You're tense. I can tell by the way you drive. You jerk the wheel around like you're a marionette. It takes effort to track you without being seen, but I enjoy the challenge. At one point you run a yellow light, and I fume for a few minutes, glaring at the circle of red, commanding it to turn green. For almost three blocks, I think I've lost you. Just as I'm slapping my steering wheel in frustration, I catch a glimpse of sunlight bouncing off your silver car up ahead, a quick flash before you hang a right. I gun it until I'm in your wake, shielded by a black van.

You careen into the parking lot on the north end of Blackwell Park. It's risky, following you into the smallish lot. I idle on the street for a couple of seconds, willing you not to turn your head in my direction. You get out of your car and slam the door. You're still pissed. When you're striding past the swing sets toward the interior of the park, its secret innards, I deem it safe to park.

As I get out of my car, the weather shifts. The sun goes dark behind a cloud. Wind whips bare branches about. They shake off clinging leaves and send them spiraling. Droplets from the recent rain shiver free of foliage. A gust picks up a pile of leaves and swirls them around your boots. You stuff your hands into the pockets of your green coat, lean into the wind, and walk faster.

I take care to keep myself concealed. I doubt you're ready to see me, and I don't trust myself around you in this mood, but I want to be near you just the same. Scratch that. I need to be near you. Being anywhere else is too desolate.

You laughed at me. You're a fucking bitch. I want so much to forgive you.

The pace you set is a punishing one. You slice through the park like a woman on a mission. I can't imagine where you think you're going. Maybe you're trying to walk off your anger. It's one more sign we're meant for each other. When you feel the darkness closing in, you crave motion. Same as me. My legs work hard to keep up with you. I like trailing behind you, unseen, working to match your pace. You're strong. I can imagine your thighs tensing as you power forward, into the wind. Your hair's whipping around, and your shoulders hunch against the cold.

We leave the playground, where a few harried mothers in down vests chase after wild-eyed toddlers. They're like tiny savages whipped into a frenzy by the promise in that icy wind. The farther we go into the forest at the heart of the park, the harder it is to conceal my presence. I try to keep my distance. You're focused ahead anyway, marching with grim determination. At one point, I snap a twig underfoot. You whip around, tense, watching. In the half-second it takes for you to turn, I duck behind a hedge and hold my breath, count to ten. When I peek through the leaves, you're off again, propelled forward with fresh gusto.

You're so beautiful, Kate. Even now, when you've betrayed me, I love you.

That's my real crime. Loving you so much I'll do right by you, defend you, even if it means killing people.

If you understood that, you wouldn't go running to the cops. You'd believe in me like I believe in you.

I refuse to accept I'm wrong about you.

You veer toward the hillside cemetery. Once we pass through the wrought-iron gates, it's harder than ever to hide. There are only a few trees and hedges dotted among the graves. I give you a healthy lead, then stay low, dashing from one bush to the next. There are a few majestic oaks that make for good cover. It's tough, though, and a couple times I think I catch you looking sideways over your shoulder in my direction. Maybe I'm just being paranoid.

When you stop near a statue of an angel, I find a decent-sized maple to hide behind. You stand there, staring at her white marble wings. Your head's turned away from me, but I can almost see you in profile. There's nobody else around. Rain clouds hover overhead, slate-gray and heavy. The wind is so fierce now the maple I'm clinging to sways, its branches creaking in protest, its leaves whipping off in red gusts.

"I know you're back there," you say, without turning around.

I peek around the trunk. You're still.

"Sam? I know you're following me."

My face is hot in spite of the cold.

At last you turn around. "You're not exactly a ninja."

There's nothing I can do except step out into the open and walk over to you.

"You're good," you say, peeking at me sideways, "but not that good."

"What did you say to the cops?" I blurt, my voice too loud and wooden.

You hesitate.

"What did you tell them?" I enunciate carefully; I sound like a bad actor reciting stilted lines.

"About the bottle opener." Your eyes are sad. You stare at the angel, not looking at me.

"Why didn't you ask me about it?"

You breathe out a cynical laugh. "Yeah? 'Excuse me, young man, but I see you've got the same bottle opener as my murdered ex-boyfriend'—"

"He wasn't your boyfriend."

The fear in your eyes makes me want to hit you. Though, of course, that won't help.

"What do you know about who is and isn't my boyfriend?" Your voice is even, but I can see the ferocity in your face. You're magnificent when you're angry.

"That guy was a piece of shit."

"Tell me you didn't hurt him," you say in a rush.

I shake my head. "It's not what you think."

"Tell me," you repeat, your voice shaking.

A raven caws from the branches of a nearby tree.

"I didn't hurt him." He felt no pain.

You watch me for a long moment. The wind ruffles your hair. Your cheeks are pink with cold. "I'm trying to understand what's happening here."

None of this was real to you before now. I can see your writer's mind struggling to strip the veneer of fiction from all this, the habitual instinct to frame everything as a story, not an actual thing happening now, complete with stakes and consequences. I can see the fear competing with confusion in your face. There's something crucial here you're missing, though. Just because I killed that piece of shit, that doesn't make me a threat. I did it to protect you, to make sure you get everything in this world you deserve.

"You don't have anything to be afraid of, Kate."

You don't look convinced. It's okay, though. Eventually you'll see. You don't understand me, but I understand you. For now, that's enough.

After a while, you turn and walk through the park, with the wind at your back.

KATE

"I don't know how I got through that conversation," I tell Zoe. We're doing laundry at her place, folding an infinite supply of onesies and cloth diapers in the kitchen. I'm too freaked out to go home. Even though Zoe and Bo's place is claustrophobic, a tiny dollhouse with a guest bed that barely clears the stereo, I welcome the overcrowded warmth of it.

"The kid's a total psycho," she breathes, clutching Drew a little tighter. He's latched to her breast, nursing, and I'm trying to ignore how weird it is to see Zoe, the girl I danced with all night, every night, in Madrid for an entire summer, feeding an infant from her body like she's been doing it all her life. The absent-minded intimacy of it stabs at my tender places. I wonder if I'll ever have such a visceral bond with another human being. It's both repulsive and hypnotic. Every now and then he opens his eyes and gazes up at her adoringly. Who will ever look at me with such pure love?

I fold a pair of Bo's boxers, trying to ignore the weirdness of this as well. "Detective Schroeder didn't take me seriously. I probably sound like a paranoid, overwrought teacher who's been working with these monsters so long I figure they're all out to get me."

"That's terrible!" She's incredulous. "You've got to make them do something."

"What, though?"

"I don't know. Search his place? Detect? Aren't they supposed to be professionals?" When Zoe gets worked up, twin spots of color appear on her cheeks, like one of the little girl's in her illustrations.

"Even if they found something—"

"God!" she cries, surprising me with her vehemence. "It makes me so furious thinking of you at that college, so vulnerable, exposed, with this crazy kid stalking you, and they won't do a goddamn thing until he comes after you."

"Innocent until proven guilty." My tone's resigned, but secretly, I love her indignation. After Detective Schroeder's nonchalance, it's just what the doctor ordered.

"Stay here tonight." She tucks a blue baby blanket around Drew that looks soft as a cloud. "I refuse to let you out of my sight."

"It's not that bad."

"It is, though." She shudders. "I hate that he knows where you live."

For a long moment, I fold laundry in silence. The kettle whistles, and she gestures with Drew. "You mind holding him a sec?"

As I take him from her, she cradles his head, protecting his spindly neck. I don't know who's more worried I'll drop him, her or me. By the time he's settled in my arms, the kettle's wailing, and his eyes fly open. She crosses the kitchen to make us a pot of tea.

I run one fingertip along his forehead, his cheek. His skin's impossibly soft. Chubby legs poke out from his striped onesie, rolls of fat bent at frog-like angles. He blinks up at me with grumpy curiosity. I'm sure he'll open his mouth and wail when he sees I'm not his mom. To my surprise, he snuggles closer and lets out a milky sigh.

My heart floods with a muddy sludge of hunger, relief, regret.

When she returns with steaming cups, I hand Drew back. The warmth and weight of him gone, I wrap my hands around my mug, greedy for its warmth. I still feel cold, even though she's got the heat cranked. The chill of that walk through the park, the conversation with Sam, won't leave me. A rime of frost has settled over my bones.

She takes a tentative sip of tea. After a moment, she speaks. "You're attracted to him, though, right?"

"Attracted, yes." I think about it. "But also repulsed."

"Explain," she says in that simple, cut-the-shit way that makes her the best friend I've ever had.

I blow on my tea, watching the steam skitter away. "He sees me. It's hard to explain. Do you ever feel invisible?"

"Of course."

"It's like, after thirty, every day I blend in a little more, become a little more khaki, less golden," I say.

She barks out a bitter laugh. "Try being pregnant. I mean, people *see* you, you're a whale, they have to notice you, but sexually? Might as well be wallpaper. It's so weird."

"Right. Because you're no longer a realistic sexual conquest."

"Yes." She lets her head drop back in despair. "It's so demoralizing."

"So imagine, all of a sudden, waking up and finding yourself in somebody's spotlight."

She watches me, intrigued. Her hands rearrange Drew with expert nonchalance. "Go on."

"Everything you do is fascinating. Everything you say is profound. Every move you make gets recorded and considered." I take a sip of tea. "It's intoxicating. I'm drunk on it."

She looks wistful. "That sounds intense."

"So intense!" I almost knock over a tower of onesies. "I haven't felt anything like it for years."

Her brows pull together in worry. "Tell me you're not in love with him, though."

"No." It comes out defensive, though, and we both notice. Before her expression can get more doubtful, I hurry to explain. "I'd have sex with him in a heartbeat if I thought it might not ruin my life. Even running away with him holds a thread of appeal.

Living in a renovated barn and writing all day. It's like love, in some ways, but—"

"Oh, no," she groans. "No, no, no!"

"Of course I don't love him. Are you crazy? He killed Raul."

She tilts her head. "You really believe that?"

"Yes." I drink more tea, trying to find the right words. "When I asked him about it at the cemetery today, I saw something in his face. Usually he's so guarded and careful, but for two seconds I saw something dangerous."

Her eyes are hard to read.

"What?" I tackle a pile of cloth diapers, suddenly eager for something to do with my hands. "What's that look?"

She glances down at Drew. "I wasn't totally honest with you about Raul."

"No?" I watch her carefully, my hands still folding. "How do you mean?"

"I mean I—" She breaks off, opens her mouth to start again, but nothing comes out.

Something in me recoils, but I know I have to get it out of her. "Zoe? What is it? You can tell me."

"I had a crush on him!" she blurts.

"Well, I figured," I say, relieved it's something so benign.

"And I slept with him," she whispers, glancing furtively at the door.

"You slept with Raul?" I hiss, leaning closer.

She nods, chewing her lip.

I sit there, stunned. I've no idea how to feel about this. "Why didn't you say?"

"We were trying to get past it."

"By fobbing him off on me?" It sounds sharper than it did in my head.

She looks miserable. "You've got every right to be mad."

"I don't think I'm mad," I say slowly, meaning it, "just irritated you didn't tell me."

Her shoulders droop. Drew squirms in her arms, cries out. She jumps at the chance to get out of the conversation. Her arms sway as she carries him over to the Cuddle Cove I bought for her shower. She deposits him gently, coos to him in a cutesy voice I don't recall ever hearing from her before Drew.

I'm still reeling from her awkward announcement. If she was into Raul, why push him onto me? It doesn't make sense. Except, of course, she's married with a newborn, and not exactly free to pursue him. I can't help feeling a little used. It's like I've been thrown into the game as a last-ditch pinch hitter, and nobody bothered to tell me.

Based on the intel Detective Schroeder let slip about Raul's love life, Zoe and I were two among many. Adding Zoe to that crowded roster makes it even dirtier, more sordid. I kind of want to end the conversation, make an excuse to leave, but I go on folding. There are still too many questions that need asking.

She comes back to the kitchen table, her eyes wary.

"I'm not mad." I try to look reassuring. "I just want to understand."

"I know I should have told you. It seemed selfish, though. I really thought you'd fall for each other. I didn't want our stupid one-night stand to get in the way of that."

I slide a stack of diapers into the basket and start another. "So you kept it from me to make sure it didn't interfere with my opinion of him?"

"Exactly." She won't meet my eyes as she grabs a onesie. "I feel like a real shit though, now. Especially after . . ." She stops.

"His death?" I finish.

She tosses the onesie onto the table and clutches her head. The sobs that wrack her shoulders catch me off guard. I hurry over to her and wrap my arms around her.

"Hey," I soothe, "it'll be okay."

"He's dead," she whimpers. "I still can't believe it."

I make her meet my eye. "Were you in love with him?"

She won't answer. It's answer enough.

"But you pushed me at him," I say. "That must have been horrible."

"It was. But I had Drew to think of." She glances at Drew, her eyes frightened. I notice she doesn't mention Bo.

I try to understand. I really do. It's just so foreign to me. I prefer to amputate my exes from my life, especially if I still have feelings for them. When Pablo and I broke up, I wanted to get as far away from him as I could. I would have moved across the country if it weren't for my job and Zoe. The last thing I would have wanted was to draw him into my social circle by fixing him up with my best friend. Then again, whatever she felt for Raul was probably nothing like what I felt for Pablo. We were married almost ten years. Zoe and Raul shared one night, from the sounds of it. He wasn't her ex; he was her secret lover. I've never had one of those, unless you count Sam.

"I don't really get it," I admit. "To be honest, though, my life's such a train wreck, I don't have the energy to make it a big deal."

"I'm still committed to Bo," she whispers.

"Of course." Again, it's "committed," not "in love with," but this is the unspoken truth about her marriage. She hit her mid-thirties and caught baby fever. Bo was there, he wanted a family, she's making it work. She made her choices. I don't feel the need to judge her.

"Are you mad? You can say if you are," she adds.

"No." I shake my head. "Really."

She looks out the window, remembering. "That thing you said. About feeling invisible? And then finding yourself in someone's spotlight?"

I nod.

"That's it. You think you've disappeared, and then someone comes along and says, 'I see you. I want you.'"

"Yes," I whisper, glad she understands.

"It's crack," she says, smiling. "Pure fucking crack."

"Exactly."

SAM

Fuchsteufelswild. That's a word Motherfucker Number Nineteen taught me. The German one. Gottschalk Breiner. Dude had a forehead so big, you could write a novel on it. Germans have the craziest compound words. *Fuchsteufelswild* translates as "Fox Devil Wild." It means you're fucking pissed. Crazy pissed. He used to call me that when I'd get so angry I didn't even know what I was doing. I'd whirl around the room smashing whatever I could get my hands on, my vision blurring under angry tears.

I don't feel much, but one emotion I've always experienced to its fullest is pure, animal rage. I can get *fuchsteufelswild* with the best of them.

I feel it building in me as I walk. The fox. The devil. The crazy fucking fox-devil. It's rising inside me, the color of blood.

You're the only woman for me, Kate. There's one way for this to go. I've worked five years to make it happen. I can't accept another outcome. You will—must—come with me to New York.

If that's not going to happen, then I don't want to live. I don't want anyone to live. If you're not mine, then nothing in this world makes sense. You've got to see this. You've got to know.

The sun's setting. It goes down so early these days. Tomorrow, December begins. Winter's coming. The icy stretch of snow-covered days yawns before us. But you and I won't be here in Blackwood to see it. We'll be in New York.

And if not there, then all bets are off.

I have to make one more effort to convince you. One grand gesture to push you over the edge, tip you past the precipice and into my arms.

All great romances require sacrifice. Think of Juliet drinking that potion, knowing she'd wake up in her family's tomb, surrounded by dead relatives. That had to suck. But she did it.

Of course, it didn't turn out well.

I try to keep my thoughts from veering in that direction. It's necessary to keep my head above the darkness. I can feel it closing in on me. The fox-devil blood swirls through me, a rising red tide. You will be mine. You must be mine.

First stop: the Conservatory of Flowers at Blackwell Park. I must stay focused, stay busy, stay on task. It's got a palatial glass dome at the center and wings that stretch out like a great glass bird. I pick the lock without a problem, harvest what I need in the gathering dusk. I've got a big garbage bag at the ready, gardening shears in hand. I choose the most exotic blooms: bamboo orchids, oriental lilies, African violets, and Chinese hibiscus. After a while I stop reading labels and just snip whatever catches my eye, whatever makes me think of you. The smell is heady—the perfume of violets and lilies and roses mixing with damp soil and sweaty warmth.

I'm heading toward my Honda with the garbage bag full of blossoms when I catch a glimpse of Eva. Her dark hair blows wild around her face, her curls writhing. She fixes me with the exact expression she wore before I pulled the trigger: surprise mixed with disappointment. I used to see her all the time, but not anymore. She's not even a blip on my radar. I turn away from her, letting her sink back into the fog.

I heave the bag of flowers into the passenger seat of my car, slam the door, and walk around to the driver's seat. Just as I'm about to climb inside and drive away, I hear feet pounding against the pavement. I turn to see Jess jogging toward me, emerging from the mist. She's covered from head to toe in spandex, her shiny hoodie unzipped just enough to reveal sweaty cleavage heaving with exertion.

She jogs in place as she greets me, pulling earbuds from her ears. "Hey, Sam, what's up?"

"Not much. You?"

"Needed to move. All this sitting on my ass working on my novel is getting to me."

I know she wants me to ask about this so-called "novel" of hers, to express interest, but I don't.

When she sees I'm not taking the bait, she changes tack. "Did you hear about Youngblood?"

"What about her?" I ask.

"They're giving her the boot. Guess she fucked one of her students." Her eyes gleam with pleasure.

"You sound pretty happy about that."

She shrugs. "She kisses up to hot guys, but to girls like me she's awful. I'm not going to miss her."

"Whatever," I say, wrenching my car door open.

"Who do you think she had sex with?" She does some kind of arm stretch, holding one elbow. "That vet? Or maybe the twitchy dude with the red hair?"

Not for the first time, I want to slam my fist into Jess's face. I remind myself she's beside the point. She's what you'd call a "contagonist"—not a protagonist, not an antagonist, just a character sent to distract the hero from his mission.

"Later." I climb in, gun the engine, and drive off without another word, enjoying the look of indignant hurt on her face in my rearview mirror.

KATE

I wake in pure darkness, my T-shirt damp with sweat. I'm sitting straight up on Zoe's guest couch, panting like a racehorse, adrenaline coursing through my body.

In my dream, Sam was here. I watched as he leaned over Drew's crib, gathered him into his arms, unexpectedly adept in his ministrations. I crept closer, peering through the soft, blue shadows of Drew's nursery. Tenderness tickled my throat, threatened to blossom into a sob. It was painfully moving, seeing Sam's eyes light up with wonder as he gazed down into Drew's tiny face.

"He's beautiful, right?" I whispered, standing beside them.

"Yes." Sam caught my eye. "Like you."

When I looked back down, my breath caught in a gasp. Sam had a knife pressed to Drew's pink throat. Drew squirmed and kicked like the rabbit in Sam's story.

"What are you doing?" I tried to grab the baby away, but Sam was too strong for me.

"I'm doing it for you," he said, his voice flat and calm. "I do everything for you."

That's when I woke.

Why did I drive straight here from Blackwell Park? The risk I put Zoe and Drew in, the hideous danger I dragged to their doorstep—it's appalling. The knowledge breaks over me all at once. *Sam didn't follow me—I checked my rearview mirror—but how do I know he hasn't trailed me here in the past? My car's right out front. How hard would it be for him to figure it out?* My selfishness and naïveté hit me like a slap in the face. *How could I be so stupid?*

I know I have to leave immediately. As my eyes adjust to the darkness, I consider my options. The sterile, anonymous quiet of a Best Western sounds like heaven. Since I'll be unemployed in a matter of weeks, though, such luxuries are out of the question.

After dressing in the dark, I find Zoe walking in circles around the nursery, bouncing Drew gently as he cries. When I push the door open, she jerks around, startled. She's pale, with circles under her eyes as dark as bruises. Seeing the nursery brings my dream back, and I shudder.

"I'm going home," I mouth, not wanting to shout over Drew's wails.

She shakes her head. "I don't want you there alone."

"Don't be silly. I'll be fine."

"Kate." Her voice is thick with warning.

I don't feel like explaining my fear that staying here could put her in danger. She'll wave this off, argue with me, insist I stay. It's better if I take refuge in my usual self-absorption.

"I can't sleep with all this crying." I try to sound grumpy. "Sorry, but I'll take my chances for a little peace and quiet."

She starts toward me, but I blow her a kiss and back away.

I slip out her back door and drive across town toward home. The quiet warmth of my Saab, with only the whir of my heater and the gentle slap of windshield wipers, feels luxurious. Peace at last. Not for the first time, I let out a deep sigh of relief at having dodged the motherhood bullet. As fucked up and crazy as my life feels right now, at least I don't have to worry about dragging another human being through this shit.

Still, the pleasure of my escape is bittersweet. The anchor of a baby sounds oppressive, but the rootless future I now face makes me feel light-headed with something like vertigo. For almost two decades, Zoe's been my one constant. Now, with her planted firmly here, her life wrapped snugly around Drew and Bo, I can already sense us turning into something else. Facebook friends. Christmas-card acquaintances.

I'll have to go where I can find work. New Mexico or Idaho or Mississippi—wherever they'll take me. I might have to make do with adjunct assignments for at least a semester or two. There's something both exhilarating and depressing about the prospect. It's like a second shot at my youth, without the boundless energy and optimism that made the first go-round bearable.

I pull into my driveway and shut off the engine. For a moment, my dark house looks ominous. The opaque, black windows stare back at me impassively, revealing nothing. I remind myself of the deep silence waiting for me inside, the hours of sleep I desperately need if I'm going to face workshop tomorrow. By now, rumors of my disgrace have probably trickled through the department, maybe even reaching the ears of students. It will take serious grit to face them all. Sam will be there, with his icy blue eyes revealing only what he chooses. I'll need to be in top form, well rested, and tough as shit.

Grabbing my bag from the backseat, I ready my keys and head for the back door.

Inside, something strikes me as not quite right. I stare around the kitchen, trying to put a finger on it. The stove's not on, the dirty dishes are where I left them.

No, nothing's obviously amiss. Probably just sleep-deprived paranoia.

As I climb the stairs, I sniff the air. The scent is faint, very subtle, but definitely there. It's floral. Not the cloying, overly bright aroma of perfume or air freshener, but the smell of real flowers. Like a summer breeze, full of fragrant hope.

I open the door to my bedroom and gasp.

The room's ablaze with candlelight. Every surface is studded with candles—tiny votives flickering. And flowers. There are flowers everywhere. Lilies and roses and orchids, a burst of color in my white bedroom. They cover my chest of drawers, my desk, even my bed.

"Welcome home." Sam's sitting in my leather chair in the corner, reclining in the shadows, his face unreadable.

When I've recovered enough to speak, I turn on him. "What the hell are you doing here?"

He frowns, like this is a strange question. "Surprising you."

"Yeah." I clutch at my chest, willing my heart to stop racing. "No kidding. How did you get in?"

"Your house isn't exactly a fortress."

I'm trying to get my bearings, stalling as the room spins around me. "God, you scared the shit out of me."

"Didn't mean to freak you out."

"Well, you did."

"Don't you like it?" He sounds hurt.

Instinct tells me to tread carefully. He's got me on thin ice, and I have to watch where I step. *Lightly, lightly.*

I put down my bag. "Sam."

He gets up, produces a bottle of wine, pours me a glass. It's all so surreal. I wonder dimly if I should threaten him, call the police, report him for breaking and entering. It's like one of those dreams where you know you should scream, but you can't. You know you should run, yet your feet stay planted. I pretend to sip the wine, wondering if he's drugged it.

He stands inches from me, searching my face with that look I've come to crave. He takes me in like a starving man gazing at a feast. I can feel my body responding in spite of my brain, which is screaming warnings like a car alarm. My breathing deepens as I take in the smell of him—earth and dew and violets.

His fingers reach out, brush a strand of hair away from my face. "You're here."

"Yes. I'm here." I look away. "But, Sam, you do get why this is scary, right?"

"Don't patronize." His voice is quiet but edged with menace.

I change direction. *Lightly, lightly,* I remind myself. I pivot on the cracking ice and take a step toward the shore. "You're ballsy, I'll give you that."

This seems to please him. The ghost of a smile appears. "The hero must risk all to win the prize."

"And what is the prize, exactly?" I whisper.

"You, of course."

"Just me, or is there something else?"

He thinks about it. To my relief, he doesn't look angry now. His hand moves to my neck, tracing the skin below my jawline with the caution of an art collector inspecting a precious vase. "Your love. Our life together."

"In New York?" I'm trying to understand. Maybe, if I can see the full delusion, I can find a way to ease him away from it.

"Yes."

"Why New York?"

His brow furrows. "Aside from it being the most exquisite city on earth? It's where we belong."

I make my voice as gentle and coaxing as I can. "But what gave you the idea, originally? A movie? A book?"

He thinks about it. I watch as realization dawns on his face. "A girl."

"What girl?"

"It doesn't matter." He turns away abruptly, and I can feel the ice cracking again.

"Someone who lives there?"

"Just a girl." His eyes are cold when they meet mine again.

I reach up and touch his shoulder. "It's okay. You don't have to tell me."

"She wanted to dance there." He sounds distant, wistful.

I nod. "She must have been very important to you. Was she family?"

"No. Like I said, just a girl." The candlelight flickers across his face as he stares past me, into the distance, remembering.

"I know what it's like to have a dream." *Please,* I think, *let me be convincing this time. Let me be a decent liar for once.*

His eyes snap back to me, wary. "You're not going to tell me how you're thirty-eight and done reinventing yourself, are you?"

"No." I let my fingers wander to his chest, feeling the shape of his muscles, the warmth of his body beneath his T-shirt.

"Good. Because I hate that shit. Mediocrity is the enemy. You and I are going to be savages."

My smile feels thin. Fake. I pray he doesn't notice. "Listen, why don't you give me a second, let me brush my teeth, change my clothes?"

His eyes go on watching me, cagey. All I need is a minute alone to grab my phone and dial 911.

"Could you go to the kitchen, maybe get me a glass of water? The wine's delicious, but I'm so dehydrated."

"Okay," he says at last.

As soon as he's out of the room, I fumble for my bag and seize my phone.

SAM

I stand outside your room, the door ajar. The candlelight casts a thin wedge of gold under the door. I can hear you fumbling with your purse and then a pause, and then your hoarse, desperate voice says, "There's an intruder in my house. Please come right away."

You just kicked me in the stomach.

I know what this feels like. I'm not speaking in metaphor. When you whisper those words, I think I might be sick. Motherfucker Number Thirteen slammed his massive steel-toe work boot into my guts with three sharp vicious kicks one night. He'd warmed up by punching me in the face, knocking me to the floor, hit his stride as I lay curled up in a fetal position on the cracked linoleum. It's a particular brand of motherfucker who enjoys kicking you when you're down.

He broke two ribs that night. It was that first slam to the soft, unprotected flesh beneath my rib cage that hurt the worst, though. Now, standing with my back pressed against the wall, listening to you whisper into your phone, it's the same feeling.

Really, Kate?

Intruder?

You have a serious fucking problem, you know that, lady? I'm the one human being on earth who loves you with every cell, every follicle, every drop of blood, and yet you see me as a threat.

How is this possible? You're standing in a room filled with four hundred and thirty-six fresh, exotic flowers and a dozen tiny candles. I know, because during the three hours you left me waiting here all alone, I had plenty of time to count them—to arrange and rearrange them for optimal romantic value. What kind of "intruder" dazzles you with dewy blossoms and candlelight?

You know what this is, Kate? You're damaged. Deep down, you do understand we belong together. But, somewhere along the way, you picked up this idea that you don't deserve real love. I don't know if it was your decade with Pablo that did it. Maybe the scars were carved into your psyche even earlier—childhood? Whenever it happened, whoever hurt you, it's turned your whole view of men upside down. So many times I've felt the purest part of you reaching out to me, wanting to be seen, begging to be touched. Yet this other part of you, the fucked-up little girl who thinks true love is always suspect, dials 911 the second I leave the room.

I've been worried about your judgment for quite some time now. Fucking Raul. Making do with Pablo all those years. Enduring abuse from Maxine. Putting up with your inadequate little job at a shitty little college, thinking that's all you deserve. I've tried my best to free you from these unhealthy patterns, to pry you up and out of that stuck, scared little space between the rock of mediocrity and the hard place of failure. It's an ugly, small world you inhabit, stranded in the middle of the country. It's obvious from your writing you have the imagination, the vision to break free of this shit. But when I show up and offer you a one-way ticket to a brand-new life filled with all the art and sex and beauty you could ever ask for, what do you do?

You call the police.

I'm so disappointed in you.

"Disappointed" is a tiny, inadequate word compared to what I really think of you. You make me sick. You make me want to destroy this whole fucked-up, backward world. There is no word for what you are to me right now. They say frustrated love turns to hate. I understand what this means now with every muscle, every tendon. The great sea of love I have for you no longer ripples in the moonlight. Now it rears up into a tidal wave so towering, it can wipe out whole cities with one massive push.

There's nothing left in this world for you or me, Kate. If you can't see what I'm offering, what I'm serving up on a silver platter with four hundred and thirty-six perfect hothouse blossoms and twelve tiny candles, then you're incapable of love. I'd like to kill whoever did this to you. Who was it? Who looked into your eyes when you were just a little girl and taught you the impossibility of true romance? Tell me, because I'd like nothing better right now than to off the bastard. I'd like to gouge his eyes out with a rusty screwdriver and force them down his throat until he chokes.

There's no time for psychoanalysis now. It's impossible to probe your past, locate the source of your psychosis, and undo the damage. I'm a dreamer, a romantic, yes, but even I know there are limits to the miracles love can work.

It's time to face facts. If you're incapable of love, then I have no reason to live. If I have no reason to live, then you need to die, too, because I was your only hope. This is not malice talking; this is me taking pity on you. Without my love, you'll crawl off to some other meaningless job at an even more obscure and lackluster college. You'll try to write and fail. Words will pile up, but none of them will mean anything. You'll lose faith that you'll ever have anything meaningful to say. You'll flail and thrash about and drink too much and fuck men with big cars and receding hairlines. You'll shop at Target and eat at Applebee's and go to the movies alone on rainy afternoons. As middle-age descends on you, with its sagging skin and flabby, deflated dreams, you will hate yourself. You'll want to die, but you'll lack the courage to do anything about it.

At least if we end it all now in a showery burst of fireworks, our work stands a chance of being read.

KATE

By the time the cops get here, Sam has slipped out of the house and driven off into the night. He must have heard me make the call. I feel weirdly guilty, imagining him overhearing my whispered plea for them to come right away. Then I feel pissed about feeling guilty. This little psycho invaded my inner sanctum. Yeah, okay, so he came armed with cinematic gestures—flowers and candles and wine—but do those make his break-in any less invasive? No, I tell myself. They do not. Get a grip, Youngblood. You need to get over this ridiculous sense that you owe him something. He's stalking you, plain and simple. It's beyond stalking now. It's breaking and entering. His actions grow bolder every day, his demands more outlandish. He's systematically ruining your life; you need protection.

The officers who show up are a strange pair. One's a woman about my age, mid-thirties; the other's a man in his early twenties, so fresh-faced and chipper it's impossible to take him seriously. I invite them in. My mind's racing in a million directions at once—scanning the dirty dishes in the sink, wondering if I have a beverage to offer, trying to remember if I stashed that bag of weed in the depths of my underwear drawer the last time I rolled a joint. I've never called the cops before unless you count Detective Schroeder, and I feel deeply self-conscious, unsure of protocol.

Once we're settled on the couches in the living room, the fresh-faced kid, Officer Huff, pulls out a notepad and a cheap ballpoint pen, which he bounces against the arm of the couch with manic energy. He's fidgety, the sort of kid who frequently shows up in my classes full of gangly enthusiasm.

The woman, Officer Grodynski, looks tired and unhealthy. Her skin has a slightly gray pallor, and her mouth is bracketed by the parentheses of a heavy smoker. She fixes me with a concerned frown. "Tell us what happened, ma'am."

I try to sound calm and reasonable as I explain the day's events: my conversation with Detective Schroeder, my walk in the park, my discovery that Sam was following me. They listen intently, the kid jotting down notes the whole time.

When I get to the part about staying at Zoe's and waking in a panic, Officer Grodynski interrupts. "You thought he might harm the baby?"

"It seemed possible." I massage my forehead. "Not likely, but possible."

"And you know the intruder how?" she asks.

I answer her question simply. "He's my student."

"What grade do you teach?"

"College. I'm an English professor."

"And, just to be clear, this is the same young man you spoke to the detective about?"

"Yes."

"When was that?" Huff asks, gripping his pen tightly.

"This morning—I mean, technically, yesterday morning, since it's already tomorrow." I know I sound frazzled, but I don't care. It seems impossible my meeting with Detective Schroeder happened less than twenty-four hours ago. My sense of time is twisted, distorted by fear and lack of sleep.

Officer Grodynski's brow furrows. "On Wednesday morning, about ten hours before the break-in?"

"Yes. Something like that."

Her bloodshot eyes sweep over me, assessing. "Why did you go to Detective Schroeder specifically?"

"He's investigating the murder of Raul Torres, a man I sort of dated." I can feel myself blushing. "I have reason to believe Sam had something to do with Raul's death."

"And Sam is . . . ?" she asks.

"The kid who broke into my house tonight." I can't keep the edge of irritation from my voice.

The two officers exchange a quick smirk. It reminds me of students in class, the way they mock me silently with their eyes.

"Is something funny?" It comes out sharp, tinged with panic. I probably seem paranoid. I will myself to calm down.

"Not at all," Grodynski soothes. She offers a condescending, tight smile, and I want to scream. "So, let's get this straight. You came home at what time?"

"Midnight . . . ish."

"And you were coming from?"

"My friend's house."

"Does this friend have a name?" Grodynski asks.

These two are seriously testing my patience. "Zoe Tait. She just had a baby. I was staying there because I suspected Sam was stalking me, and I didn't want to be alone."

"And you came home because . . . ?"

"I told you. I got worried in the middle of the night that Sam might follow me there."

Huff pauses to study me. "That's when you found the intruder?"

"Yes."

"So you came home a little after midnight, and this student was in your house, right?"

"Right."

"Where was he?"

"In my bedroom." My voice breaks on the last word. I can feel my heart racing at the memory.

"I see. Has he ever been in your bedroom before?" Her tone's elaborately neutral, detached, which somehow manages to make the question more insulting.

"No. Jesus, I told you, he's my student. He broke in, okay?"

"Has he ever been here before?"

A sick feeling washes over me. "Yes."

"With your consent?"

"Yes, but . . ." I trail off. But what? I've no idea how to finish that sentence.

They both stare at me, eyebrows raised in expectation.

"It was just once, and I didn't really want him here, but I didn't know how to get rid of him." My voice shakes with defensive anger. "The point is, this guy's dangerous, okay? He hacked my email, and now he's broken into my home. I have reason to believe he's mentally unstable and capable of violence. Are you going to do something about it?"

They stare at me blankly for a moment.

Officer Huff opens his mouth to speak, but Grodynski gets there first. "We'll file a report, look into it. We'll do everything in our power to ensure your safety. You may want to consider a restraining order as well."

"But that takes time, right?"

"It does." She fixes me with an expression that teeters between pity and disapproval. I'm certain she's thinking uncharitable things about me, the professor who lets a student into her home one night and complains he's stalking her the next. Her training forbids her to judge me openly, but the tightness around the edges of her mouth, the reserved skepticism in her eyes, tells me everything. "In the meantime, I'd suggest locking all your doors and windows, installing a security system. You can't be too careful."

I feel like a frightened child who's been sent back to bed armed with the promise that there are no monsters under her bed.

When they leave, I watch the red glow of their taillights disappear like demonic eyes retreating into the darkness.

SAM

Everything I've done for five years got me closer to you. The GED and community college. Working at shitty cafés and bookstores and bars, saving every cent. Not buying music or seeing movies or eating anything but rice and beans so I could afford an apartment in Blackwood. It's a shitty studio, moldy and sordid; the rank odor of cat piss lingers in the green shag carpet. It's so depressing when it rains. The gray light illuminates the peeling linoleum of the tiny kitchen, the trail of ants snaking along the counters. All this I've endured so I could inch a little closer to you. I was sure if I could look you in the eye, land in your orbit, fate would take care of the rest.

I suppose it has. Destiny has its own ideas about where we're headed.

Not New York. Instead, it's the great beyond for us. The mysterious final frontier.

Have I really done all I can do? Is there any hope left? I scrape around in the dark corners of my psyche, trying to locate some shred of optimism.

You're a storm, Kate. You've blown through my life, leaving nothing but windswept destruction in your wake.

I can't help but admire how you've decimated me.

You won't be convinced. I see that now. I have offered you the romance of the century. We would've been epic. That's what kills me, you know? We would have rewritten the classic love story; Henry and June, Mary and Percy, Scott and Zelda—they would have paled in comparison. You're supposed to be a writer, Kate. Can't you see the exquisite story I've handed you? The tale of forbidden love, of dreams forged against the odds. How can you not eat this up? Women flock to rom-coms and devour romance novels with greedy enthusiasm, but what happens when a regular Joe tries to sweep a woman off her feet? I'm the perp here. You stood in a room filled with *flowers* and *candles* and called me an *intruder*.

That's messed up, Kate. I'm just saying.

So, no. The answer is no. Deep in the darkest corners of my consciousness, there is no lint of optimism clinging to the crevices. There's no ray of hope to illuminate my dark night of the soul. You're blind. You've got no idea who I am or what I can give you.

Because of that, I've got my Glock cleaned, loaded, and ready.

And okay, so the answer's not no. It's sort of. I do cling to one hope. I've sent my manuscript to G. P. Putnam's Sons. They were the first ones with the balls to publish *Lolita* in the States, so I figure they earned me. It's got a cover letter that begins, *By the time you read this, I'll be dead. I will have killed many others as well. This is my story.*

Posthumous fame isn't what I had in mind, but like I said, sometimes destiny has its own ideas about where we're headed.

I only wish you could have written something new before we die. Of course, I haven't read *Blood Ties*, but I've got a feeling it's not your best work. It leaves me with an uneasy feeling, knowing the story you send out into the world after you're gone isn't up to your usual standards. I want everyone to remember us by our final, beautiful sentences, as seamless and as sculptural as ocean-battered boulders.

You deserve that. We both do.

I'm afraid there just isn't time. There's no way I can continue walking around with the hope of our shared life extinguished inside me. All my love for you, all that burning-mad desire, now smolders. It's a charred battlefield. I can't carry it. There is nothing but death and destruction in me now.

KATE

On Thursday morning, I change my outfit three times before I leave the house. I want to feel impenetrable. All my clothes seem flimsy, though, ridiculously vulnerable. I can't imagine how I ever allowed myself to enter the battlefield so naked. That's how campus seems now. Like a place of war.

At last, when I'm out of time and have to just decide, I settle on a pair of jeans, boots, a thick cotton sweater, and my father's leather jacket, a World War II bomber. It's way more casual than anything I'd normally wear on a workday, but I want to feel able to move, able to run if I have to.

Is that paranoid?

I just feel so unprotected. It's up to me. Detective Schroeder's squinty questions, Officer Grodynski's restraining order, Officer Huff with his fidgety hands—none of them can help me now. I enter that classroom with full knowledge of everything I'm up against. I know Sam's unhinged. I can feel him coming apart, disintegrating. It's strange. I'm not sure how I know this; I just do. Well, there's the obvious. He did hack my email and break into my house. I'm pretty sure he killed Raul. A bubble of hysteria escapes me as I mentally list these offenses—not so much a laugh as a cross between a snort and a sob. Beyond these glaring warning signs, though, I sense him turning a corner into even edgier territory.

The connection I've never fully wanted to acknowledge is stronger than ever now. It's like a part of me lives inside of him.

When I walk into workshop and see he's not there, I surprise myself with a jolt of disappointment. If I'm honest, though, this is the contradiction that's haunted me ever since I first laid eyes on him. He mesmerizes me. I'm entranced by his smooth, hypnotic voice, his face with its carefully arranged emotions. His slightly wooden affect only makes the occasional flash of real feeling more potent.

He's fascinating.

I realize this as I stare at his empty seat. He fascinates me.

For the briefest second, I regret my unwillingness to surrender completely to his spell. I remind myself how totally crazy this is. He's poison. Running off with him would be a one-way ticket to drama and destruction. There's nothing stable about what I feel for him. I'm embarrassed by the raw, hungry desire he stirs in me. It's obscene. I could never grow old with him; watching him age into salt-and-pepper dapper while I wrinkle and rot like overripe fruit? It's the stuff of nightmares. I will not go gently into that cellulite-ridden night.

"Professor Youngblood?" Jess watches me, her eyes full of glee. I'm reality TV right now; I'm a train wreck. "Is everything okay?"

No! I want to scream. *Everything is not okay. Everything is wrong. My best friend has a parasite attached to her breast, my boss thinks I'm fucking my psychotic student, and the cops are ineffectual!*

"Sure. Everything's fine. Let's get started." I write words on the dry-erase board. *Workshop Today: Kayla, Skylar, Jess, Cody.* I can see my arm gripping the pen, can see the ink, stark black against florescent white, but at the same time, I'm floating above myself, watching it all from the ceiling.

Jess studies the list on the board. "What about Sam?"

"What about him?" I return, too sharply.

A snicker from across the room. I catch Tyler kicking Kayla's foot gently. My vision swims. I'm an animal in the zoo. They're all imagining me fucking Sam, I just know it. God, I'm going to be sick. I can feel the bile rising at the back of my throat. I swallow hard.

Jess flashes an innocent smile. "Isn't his story supposed to get workshopped today?"

"He's not here. If he shows, I'll add his name to the board."

"Is he okay?" She puts on a worried frown. I will destroy this little bitch.

"As far as I know." I hear myself saying words, but they sound foreign, like they're coming from someone else entirely. I'm impressed with how crisp and professional they sound, but they've got nothing to do with me. "Why don't we start with a quick writing exercise? Take ten minutes to compose your own obituary."

Kayla raises her hand, and I nod at her. "Do we write it like we're old or like we died, like, today?"

"Whichever you prefer." I'll never understand why people who allegedly value words cram three "likes" into one sentence.

Skylar groans. Jess checks her phone with a flip of her hair. Mercifully, though, they take out pens or laptops, and before long, the room settles into the quiet, soothing sound of people writing. I have always loved this sound. The gentle click of fingers on keyboards. The scratch of a pen carving its way across the page. It's the subdued excitement of libraries, the claustrophobic coziness of many minds concentrating, burrowing into their private worlds side by side. Kayla scribbles furiously, her dyed-orange hair hanging over her face like a curtain, a soft clicking inside her mouth as she plays with her pierced tongue. Jess sets down her pen and scrolls through her phone again, looking bored. A gust of wind pushes against the skylight, flings a spasm of raindrops against the glass.

That's when Sam walks in. Holding a gun.

SAM

Finding the right gun is like finding the right woman; you know when you've met your match. No amount of research can substitute for the visceral feel of your body melding with hers. I got mine from Motherfucker Number Twelve, a tweaker in Boonville who liked nothing better than to get high as a kite, go out into the hills, and shoot wild pigs. He was a repellant little worm. Vivienne was only with him for about four days—even she could see this guy was trouble—just enough time for me to steal his Glock, which turned out to be the gun of my dreams. It was fate. This little baby has fifteen rounds on tap, an indestructible polymer frame, dual recoil-spring assembly. The streamlined controls and the revolver-like simplicity make it an object of understated elegance. I named her—can you guess? Lolita, of course. *Light of my life, fire of my loins. My sin, my soul.*

With the Glock in my hand, this classroom looks so much smaller than I ever imagined possible. How did I never notice before? It's the perfect space to trap fifteen wannabe writers and one real thing, the ideal hunting ground. Room 313 doesn't look like a place of learning anymore. It doesn't even look like the place where you and I first met. Instead, it's a boxy wooden crate packed with frightened rats. The windowless hovel's only light comes from the skylights overhead. As I take in the circle of shocked expressions around the table, I'm struck again by the malformed *wrongness* of every face except yours. Raggedy Ann with her pierced eyebrows, her studded nose, the tongue piercing that's visible as her jaw hangs slack. Cleavage's lined eyes—now kewpie-doll wide—and shiny, pink lips. Tattoo Man, the vet, who, in spite of his stories about his bravery under fire, stares at me in frozen horror.

Only your face looks right. You're white and luminous, eyes glittering like shards of blue glass. Your face is a poem. You are a study in symmetry, the definition of light and shadow working together for an unimpeachable whole. Everyone else is disposable—defective attempts at human life that should have been aborted long ago. Malformed lumps of tissue, hair, and skin. Tendons and bone and cartilage assembled into wind-up dolls that never worked right anyway. None of them will be missed or mourned. Only you watch me with calm, impenetrable stillness. Your gaze locks with mine; you are as regal and magnificent as Helen of Troy.

Is it strange, at this moment, that I feel a stab of something like hope? Now that nothing can ever happen in a normal way again, now that I've traded in every chance at civilian happiness, my old dream rears up like a sleeper wave from the dusty wasteland of my heart. I can see us standing in the darkened street outside your house. Your hands are out in front of you, palms up. Your face is tilted toward the sky. Your eyes are filled with wonder as you watch snowflakes—big as silver dollars, delicate as lace—floating from the starry heavens.

And now I have to kill you.

Look at this tangle of thorns.

There's a hush in the room, an awkward silence that reeks of fear. Somebody moans, though I don't turn my head to see who it is. Somebody else lets out a strangled sob.

I raise Lolita and point her at the vet. Though he's not showing much sign of heroic action, he's the most likely to make a move, the only one trained to fight, so I'll take him out first. Also, he's the one guy I've seen you bless with a real smile in this room. For that alone, he deserves to die.

I stand with my back to the door, blocking the exit, watching the color drain from their faces, watching their eyes go from bored to electric. Isn't it sad, the way we grasp the beauty of everything too late? We stumble through life like sleepwalkers, fixating on the mundane, resentful of everyday inconveniences. We're slow and stupid, insensitive, unaware. Only in the last seconds of our lives do we realize how much we want to live.

Tattoo Man stares at my Glock, eyes locked on it, mesmerized. He holds his hands up like a child getting ready to catch a ball. His face is rigid, holding back whatever sound threatens to erupt. Some fucking airborne ranger.

"You don't want to do this."

I turn at the sound of your voice. You're standing now, poised at the head of the table. Your white, waxy face still has that look, a mixture of determination and stone cold calm.

"Oh, but I do," I correct you.

The twitchy guy who writes about wizards takes advantage of the distraction and dives under the table. I can hear him whimpering under there. I consider shooting him through the particleboard just to show everyone I can—also, because reading his shitty wizard fiction took up an hour of my life I'll never get back.

"Sam, please." Your eyes do not beg. They command. "This is about you and me. Let them go."

It's noble of you. I'm impressed, I admit. Once again, hope blooms inside me, unfurling petal by petal against my will. I'm reminded of how exquisite you are, how unlike other people. It's crazy that you're volunteering to die, sacrificing yourself to let these bumbling miscreants go on living. They're never going to write anything worth reading. They're never going to make anything beautiful. Their hands are fit only for ass-wiping and masturbating, for diaper-changing and burger-flipping—they're lumpy bags of blood and bone. They're nothing. Yet you, the one with hands so small and delicate, hands that can pluck ideas from the ether and mold them into paragraphs—you're the one willing to take the hit.

You're right, in a way. This is about you and me. It's about your inability to grasp my vision. Your unwillingness to leap into the breach. Why, Kate? Why did you say no to so much beauty?

I'm still staring at you when, from the corner of my eye, movement pulls my attention. It's the vet. He's crouched, ready to tackle me. As I turn, I see the grim determination in his face. Sweat glazes his forehead and forms dark patches under his beefy arms.

For just a second he glances up, and I see the look of naked fear in his face. His run-on sentences make me want to dick-punch him, but in that moment I have to admire his heroic delusions.

He takes another step toward me. I tighten my grip on the trigger.

"I mean it, Sam." You're calm. "I know you have a moral code. None of these kids deserve to die. I'm the only one you have an issue with."

I turn my face to you but keep my gun trained on the vet. There's a vein pulsing in my forehead. It's annoying. I want it to stop. The room has an unreal, flimsy quality. Any second the walls and the ceiling will float away, light as petals.

There's something wrong with all of this. It takes me a second to understand what. With Eva and Raul, it was private. I had my moment with them. I could concentrate. When it was over, I could put it away. Tuck it inside a memory. Take it out when it served me, put it back, like a kid with his favorite baseball card. It was intimate. Personal.

Here there are too many eyes. They're all staring at me. Everywhere I move, they're on me. Maybe you're right. I shouldn't have done it here. I should have gotten you alone, made you listen. I can't talk to you with all these people—all these eyes. I bite the inside of my cheek so hard, I taste blood.

The vet takes another step toward me.

"Don't be a hero, Todd." It's you again, quiet but steely.

He's got his hands out, palms open, like he's approaching a growling dog. He's getting too close.

Fuck him. The bastard. I'm not a dog, and this is not his story.

I shoot over his shoulder. That sends him back. He's reeling, stumbling. He lands in a chair. There's a clean, dark bullet hole in the wall just above him. The Sheetrock's splintered in a spider web of cracks. He doesn't try to get up again. I can see by the look on his face I've made my point.

Several people cry for real then, unable to stifle their sobs.

For a second I think about the photos they'll show on the news when this is over. They'll use the publicity shot from your book jacket, the one with you smirking sideways at the camera like Mona Lisa. They'll have to look far and wide to find a photo of me. I'm invisible. A shadow. Vivienne will probably dig one up for them, sell it to the highest bidder so she can score. It'll be me at fifteen, since after that I learned to leave no trace.

It pains me to think about the narrative the media will weave: lone wolf, obsessed with his professor, history of psychological problems, unstable home life. They'll speculate and fill in the gaps and get it all wrong. They'll make me out to be some Columbine loser, the Millennial reinvention of the Trench Coat Mafia. Somebody will no doubt pontificate about video games, though in my case they'd be better off blaming Nabokov.

Then my manuscript will land in the mailroom at G. P. Putnam. It will float undetected in the slush pile for a few weeks, maybe even a month or two. Some hapless intern will open it, sipping her latte and checking her Facebook and eyeing the editor in the horn-rimmed glasses, a man she aspires to fuck. She'll read the first sentences of my cover letter three times: *By the time you read this, I'll be dead. I will have killed many others as well. This is my story.*

I can see the heated editorial meeting, with marketing and legal weighing in. Some will say they shouldn't glorify my brutality by publishing my work. That doing so will only inspire copycats. They'll speculate that every depressed, unpublished hack in America will dig his shitty manuscript from his sock drawer, stick it in the mail, and go on a shooting spree just to seal the deal. Others will champion my novel's brilliance, pointing out that great literature can't be kept from the world just because the author is nuts. If sanity were a requirement for writers to be published, we'd have precious little left on the shelves.

In the end, the money men will win. They always do. My book will be an international bestseller. Your backlist will soar.

This is the best way. The only way. As you stare at me with icy calm, though, it feels a little empty. I thought it would feel different.

I'm not an exhibitionist. I prefer the shadows, a cool, dark place where I can watch the world, where I can drink in beauty. These past couple of months, watching you—those were some of the happiest moments of my life. I'm a watcher. Always have been. The closest I come to craving the limelight is writing. I need my work out there in the world, need people to read it the way a chef needs his creations to be devoured and savored, but if nobody ever saw my picture or even learned my name, I wouldn't care. It's the work that matters, the words, the characters, the story. That's what I love.

Kayla makes a move for her phone. She's sitting to my right, her pierced face contorted with terror. Her hand darts across the table, her black-painted nails reaching out like demented claws. I aim Lolita at her. She freezes.

"Everybody just stay still," you order.

You're magnificent. I love how commanding you are.

Our eyes lock. I wish all these people would just disappear.

KATE

I can't think. My mind's gone pure white. The blizzard inside me roars. At the same time, a perfect stillness has me in its grip. The eye of the storm. There is blue smoke drifting in the air, and the ringing in my ears is like the emergency broadcast tests they used to do on TV—do they still do them? A block of colored stripes, and then this horrible, piercing sound that makes my teeth hurt. I can hear the roar of my own blood in my ears, and then even that cuts out. I am floating in a pristine, white silence, the silence of snow.

Through it all, from the moment he walks into the room, a part of me hovers overhead, near the ceiling, cool, distant, thinking, *If I survive, this will make one hell of a story.*

Fucking writers.

Suddenly I know exactly what to do. I've never been so filled with purpose. Who would guess I could move with a dancer's grace under fire? I'm not that girl. I'm not brave, not fierce, not heroic. I'm sure as hell not noble. I wouldn't die for these kids— I'd probably shoot them myself if it meant my own survival—but in this moment, doing what needs to be done seems like the most natural thing in the world.

I seize my chair. Wrapping my fingers around the cold metal legs, I heave it overhead. For a heartbeat, it's poised there above me. I'm an ape preparing to beat the alpha male to death. It's weightless; the adrenaline pumping through me turns it into a ridiculous pretend-chair, a featherweight prop. My spindly muscles hold it aloft without effort. I let gravity do its work on the way down. It gains weight and substance then. It becomes real. The hard, plastic seat lands with a satisfying crack against Sam's skull.

He falls. He's on his back. Our eyes meet for a fraction of a second. His expression blends betrayal and surprise. I want to roar, to scream, *Don't ever underestimate me!* Nothing comes out, though. No sound. I'm efficient and lean, all muscle and pounding blood with no use for words.

I stomp hard on his wrist; I hear bones crack, can feel them giving way beneath my boot. He cries out; his fingers lose control in a spasm of pain. His other hand reaches around to grab the weapon, but it drops to the carpet with a heavy thunk.

The despair in his face makes my breath catch in my throat.

SAM

Wizard Boy under the table scampers over and grabs the gun. In his haste, he fumbles it. Still stunned and clumsy from your attack, I struggle with him. Our arms lock, and we grapple like children wrestling. We roll on the floor once, twice. He makes a grunting sound, and I feel a sharp pain in my forehead as his skull collides with mine. His freckly arms have surprising strength. The tendons in his neck pop out. A wild light appears in his green eyes. I can smell the coffee on his breath. Flecks of spittle dot his mouth.

As we fight for control, Lolita goes off. Another deafening crack.

I see the bullet as if in slow motion. It careens toward your heart. Time shudders to a stop. Nothing in the air is breathable. I throw Wizard Boy off and lunge toward you, the pain in my head searing a pale blue arc across my skull. The bullet continues its trajectory, rocketing toward your ivory sweater. Even in this moment, when everything is about to end, I see you in slow motion. I see your hair moving in golden waves around your face. I see the place where your bra strap peeks out from beneath your sweater. I see the fine, delicate beads of perspiration on your forehead, elaborate as lace.

I see your body hunching backward as the bullet makes

contact. Your shoulders shoot forward, and your spine contracts like a modern dancer's.

Breathing deeply, struggling against the gravity pulling at me, I catch you in my arms; I squeeze too tightly. Blood erupts from the wound in your chest. I moan, pawing at it. Blood covers my fingertips.

Your blood.

Because of me.

My bullet did this to you.

I knew this was how it would end, but I didn't anticipate this suffocating wave of regret. All the moments throughout my life when I sat numb and unfeeling have been deposited into a vault; now they're all being released at once. Sadness and longing flood my whole body.

My bloody hand fills me with such revulsion, I want to gnaw it off, like a fox caught in a trap.

KATE

I feel a searing pain in my chest. I look down and make a sound of stupid bewilderment, a tiny exhale of disbelief, like I've spilled my tea.

Blood. Lots of it. I watch it spreading across the cream-colored cotton of my thick, white sweater. It reminds me of a poppy, my favorite flower, the dark red blooming in every direction, blossoming slowly.

I'm in my aunt's garden in Mendocino. The ocean sparkles on the horizon, refracting sunlight into tiny kaleidoscopes. The air's rich with salt and brine. I'm staring at a clump of rich, red poppies. Their blossoms tower and sway. The petals are so shiny, so impossibly red. Behind them, a tapestry of green climbs the leaning lattice fence. A wild tangle of morning glories consumes a cramped garden shed. Gulls circle overhead, calling out their delight. The sight of the poppies consumes me. I put my face closer to one, studying the black nimbus and yellow center.

As I sink to my knees, I can't help thinking how right it is, how poetic, that death should look like my favorite flower, the great opiate, the dark, satin petals unfurling like they have all the time in the world.

SAM

You're bleeding. So much blood, Kate. I've never been bothered by blood before. The smell, like pennies. The color, vivid red, then drying to a rusty brown. I know it makes some people light-headed. In movie theaters, I've seen people recoil from the sight of it, as if even the flickering image of corn syrup and red dye has the power to do them harm. I've never understood that revulsion. To me, blood's another substance, like rain or sap or ink.

Now, though, with you in my arms, your blood covering my face, my arms, my clothes, I get it. Blood equals loss. This sticky, dark substance is the essence of you, the thing that keeps you real. With-out it, I'll never be able to kiss the lily-white curve of your neck. I'll never be able to sink into you, arms braced on either side of your hips, my body pouring into yours, my eyes locked on your face.

"Stay with me, Kate." It's stupid, I see that, my sudden irrevoca-ble regret. I never claimed to be logical. "Please, please, please. Don't fucking die."

Around me, I can hear people crying, sucking in breath. I can hear rain on the skylights, tapping at first but getting faster, more insistent, working up to a good downpour. It pains me to think you will never hear the rain again. Any moment now, the light will go out of your eyes, and whatever sounds reach your ears will not be the ones in this room.

Just as I did that first day, I see you now for what you are: the only person on earth who will ever understand me.

That first day, watching you cross campus. Your boots kicking up explosions of red and yellow leaves. You stopped walking and looked up. So few people ever do that—have you noticed? They keep their gaze locked on the ground or straight ahead. But you stopped that day and stared up into the branches of a slender, silvery birch. You let your head fall back, and you stood still, examining a woodpecker. I sat huddled on a bench nearby, enjoying my first glimpse of you, the real you, not your reproduction on a book jacket. Your throat was white and exposed, swanlike. You watched the woodpecker hammer away, your face full of unguarded fascination.

And then you smiled.

It made me smile. Without even trying.

That's your power, Kate. Your one-of-a-kind potency. You make me feel things. I don't just go through the motions with you, don't just arrange my face into the semblance of human response. I don't have to fake it. With you, everything is real.

"Sam." You whisper my name.

I reach down and brush a strand of hair away from your face. "Don't talk."

"You're fucking crazy," you say. It's not something I appreciate hearing, but there's affection there, maybe even love, so I take it.

"I know."

"You saw . . ." Your voice trails off. Your eyes start to lose focus.

"Don't die, Kate," I repeat, louder this time, a command. "Stay with me."

Someone's out the door now. The Wizard Boy makes a break from under the table, and he's out. Good for him. I don't care. Let him call the cops. I'm not getting out of here alive, and I don't give a shit about anyone else in this room. Nobody except you.

"Let me say this," you wheeze.

A sob fills my chest like a balloon. I purse my lips against it, try to hold it in, but it escapes. It's a desperate gasp in the quiet room. The rain goes on hammering its staccato rhythm against the skylights. My arms tighten around you, trying to keep you with me. I ache all over, but most of all in the place where I think my heart is.

"Go on," I whisper. "I'm listening."

Your blue eyes work hard to stay with me, to hold my gaze. Your hands reach for me, then fall back to your lap, exhausted by the effort. "You saw me. I know you saw me."

There is so much I want to tell you. About the nights I curled into a ball under the blankets with your book and a flashlight. The way I flipped back and forth between your photo on the jacket and the pages, delighting in your words and your enigmatic smile. How I pored over your meager, stingy bio, committing it to memory. I carried your characters and images and metaphors with me like a rosary, pulling the memory of them out and stroking them with the concentration of a saint when the Motherfuckers screamed or Vivienne passed out or the darkness in my head threatened to eclipse everything good and reasonable and true.

But there's no time to say any of it. You're sinking deeper into me now, collapsing against my lap. I try to clutch you to me, but you're limp. Your eyes are almost empty. You're almost gone.

I have never been a screamer, but so much raw, empty despair surges inside me, I throw back my head and let out a sound that is not human.

Thank god I still have the gun. I lift it to my temple. Keeping my eyes on your face, my fingers in your hair, I put my finger on the trigger, and I squeeze.

KATE

It's twilight, and I'm doing one of my favorite things: watching a man watch a woman.

I suppose, after all that's happened, I should be repulsed by anything that reminds me of you. Of what you did. Of your eyes drinking me in. Still, on evenings like this, standing on my balcony in the Village, a gin and tonic in my hand, the cool night air falling like a whisper-soft veil over the streets, it's difficult not to indulge in something like nostalgia.

The man's sitting at a sidewalk café. He's too old to be young and too young to be old—thirty-five, perhaps. In his prime. I would have liked to see you at that age. You would have been handsome with crow's feet. I would have loved to read your writing after it had time to steep a bit, to become, if not seasoned, at least a little salty.

The man's dark-haired and blue-eyed, like you. He's watching a woman waiting tables. She's a dancer. You only have to glance at her to know it. She wears a simple wrap-dress; her mass of dark curls sits piled atop her head in a messy bun. Gathering cups onto her tray and wiping the table with an effortless swipe, her body moves with the bone-deep agility of a woman who spends most of her hours leaping and twirling around a studio. She practically pliés when she delivers a round of mimosas to a table full of old women.

The man's eyes drink her in. He's trying to be subtle, but he's not. He sips his coffee, glances at his paper. Again and again, his gaze returns to her, magnetized. It's not a leer, though it's clear he wants to touch her. The way he studies every line of her body, every curve, every movement, makes it worshipful, not dirty. When she disappears behind a cluster of customers momentarily, he cranes his head slightly, working to keep her in sight, as if losing her even for a moment will prove unbearable.

I know it's crazy, but I miss the way you looked at me. The way you saw me. That wolfish fascination stirring deep behind your eyes. The total concentration, like I was the only woman who ever lifted a teacup, or opened a door, or gazed at a snowflake.

I have a scar like an angry starburst as big as my fist. I can feel it under my left bra strap, an inch below my collarbone. Sometimes, late at night, it itches. It is part of your legacy, yes, but so is this— the memory of you consuming me with your eyes.

It's hard to say if my epilogue will please you. I didn't really know you, after all. There are things I gathered later, after that day in December, things they printed in the papers and online— elaborate biographies I could only read in fits and starts. I didn't get to know you in the real way, though, the right way, didn't spend enough time with you before your death to gauge how you'd respond to the rest of my story.

I wrote a book. *Glass Houses*. Saleswise, it hasn't done as well as *Red-Blooded American Male*. Personally, I think yours needed more editing, but the rush to get it out there before the media frenzy died down was tremendous. School shootings are so common these days; they couldn't count on the fickle public to stay interested. The days of Columbine-level postmortems are over. It's a solid story, with all the deep promise I first saw on that unseasonably warm night in late September when I first read about a nine-year-old girl killing a rabbit. It doesn't have the polish I would have wanted for it. Who knows, though? Maybe exhaustive revision would have drained its raw intensity.

Would it please you to know I moved to the East Village? I teach at Columbia now. I'm still a little stunned they would hire me. Of course, the profile in *Time* didn't hurt, the segment on *60 Minutes*. America loves an underdog. The chair-wielding professor attacking her student-gone-psycho was too juicy a story to resist.

We're so afraid in this country. So frightened. Every morning, as we get ready for work, we consider our fragile bodies—our breakable bones, our tissue-thin organs. We glance at the news and wonder, *Will it be me today?* We ride the subway and eye our fellow passengers, wondering which one is angry enough to snap. What chance do we have against all our homegrown rage? We're furious. Scared. Paralyzed and hypnotized by the bloodshed.

Even though I almost died, my triumph serves as a balm to our wounds. We're dying to believe the unarmed masses stand a chance.

I sip my gin and tonic, still watching my stranger watch his waitress. The city stirs, shaking off the workday, readying itself for night. Traffic rumbles. Taxis honk. A woman in a Yankees jersey leans out of the window across from me and studies the sky. Storm clouds skim the skyscrapers in the distance, but the night will be clear, maybe even balmy. The smell of coffee and singed garlic perfume the air, mingling with the fumes. My watchful café man catches his waitress's eye. She looks away quickly. I can tell she enjoys it, though. The arch of her back, the sway of her hips, give her away. To be seen, to be savored, is a gift.

She won't know how much she yearns for it until it's gone.